COPYRIGHT

The Fairy End
Copyright © 2021 by Ellie Aiden
Cover Art by Ellie Aiden

All rights reserved. Except as permitted by the U.S.
Copyright Act of 1976, no part of this publication may be
Reproduced, distributed, or transmitted in any form or by
any means without the prior written permission of the author.

First Edition: July 2021

The characters and events portrayed in
this book are strictly fictitious.
Any similarities to locations, characters,
events, or persons, living or
dead, is purely coincidental

THE FAIRY END

Aiden

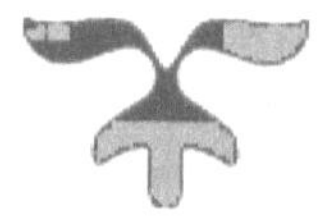

Table of Contents

FIRST WORLD PROBLEMS

Ell

How does this keep happening to me? This will be the third time I've been kidnapped in less than a year. That has to be a record or something, right? I mean, I knew I was awesome, but I didn't know I was this awesome at getting kidnapped. Of course, technically, I'm not kidnapped yet, but in just a matter of inches I will be.

Here I was, just minding my own business, getting ready for mine and Quinn's third date, and this damn Elf showed up in my room out of nowhere. On the outside looking in, some might say I didn't put up much of a fight, but in my defense, it's been a long week. *Hell*, it's been a long year.

Now, I find myself surrounded by a bubble of magic, floating toward my open window. Unfortunately, Quinn is the only one who might find me before it's too late, because I convinced the rest of my boys to give me and Quinn some alone time tonight. They're all down at dinner, and as for Quinn, I really thought he would be here by now.

"I thought this was going to be harder," the Elf mocks me, as I float closer to the open window.

"Same, dude, same," I admit, rolling my eyes.

The bubble, with me in it, bumps into the window frame,

and I once again try to find some crack, some way to break the magic trying to whisk me away. It just doesn't seem to matter what I do though, because as I push and pull nothing changes. I'm stuck, and it's really starting to piss me off.

My body slips out into the night, and looking down, my stomach drops out. I'm way too high up. If I fall from here, I'll definitely end up with broken bones, because we all know my magic isn't good on the fly. And knowing that, I'll just have to ride this out until we get a little closer to the ground, or until my magic decides to help me out. Right now, she's being a real bitch.

As I mentally chastise her, I hear a thud behind me, and twisting, Quinn stands in the doorway of my bedroom. There's a good distance between us now, but I can tell his eyes are wide with fear. He searches the room for, well, I don't know what, but he's definitely searching for something, and then he's sprinting across the room. He makes it to the window just as the Elf slips out, levitating closer to me.

"Ell!" Quinn shouts, looking from me to the ground, the top half of his body leaning clear of the window frame.

"You're too late," my captor wheezes through laughter. He seems to be *real* happy with himself, and he's really getting on my nerves.

My annoyance is pushed to the side when Quinn's tether tickles my belly, and without thinking, I latch on to it. I pull, and instantly my magic gets a boost. The bubble wavers, and I drop five feet, causing me to regret my choices. Scolding mine and Quinn's magic, I try again, but this time, I work to create a barrier between me and the ground, hoping if I fall it will catch me.

When I look back up, I see Quinn soaring through the sky, headed straight for the Elf just above me. The two fairies clash, fists and magic, and they twist in a whirlwind of power. The Elf shouts in pain, but the fight isn't over, and as I try to will myself in their direction, my magic suddenly flares to life. The Elf's bubble surrounding me evaporates before my eyes, and I plummet. Thank God my barrier worked, keeping me floating just a few feet off the ground.

I search the area for some way to help Quinn, because no matter how hard I try my magic won't take me to him, and as I watch, he takes a fist to the nose. I wince, butterflies swimming in my stomach, and I worry he might not be able to beat this guy.

For some reason, my magic holds me back as the two fairies tumble, dropping dangerously fast as two guards rush forward. One is a Sprite, and he immediately takes flight when he realizes what's happening. The other stays on the ground, ensuring that I'm safe even though I made it clear I was.

When I look back to the sky above us, I'm jerked back by my own magic as she thrusts down in the ground, working to find water. Latching on to what I know is an underground aquifer, my magic and I both pull, the water bursting from the ground in a straight line. The spray shoots skyward, slamming into the Elf with a massive force. Unfortunately, he was gripping Quinn around the neck, so my fairy goes flying off with him. I shout his name, instantly feeling like an idiot, because I only managed to make things worse.

I slap my hand against my forehead as more guards rush up, many going to Quinn's aid. The Elf is holding his own against them all, with several others helping from the ground, myself included, and it has me surprised that he's lasted this long.

As soon as that thought flits through my mind though, Quinn and a Sprite, working together, manage to get the upper hand. The Sprite is able to slip iron cuffs on the Elf, and he and Quinn guide him to the ground.

And as fast as my third kidnapping started, it ends.

***

Ell

It wasn't long after the Elf was apprehended that Ari and Nyx showed up. Ari fired two guards within the first ten minutes, and then he tripled the watch near my chambers. To be honest, I agreed with the last decision, but not the first. I didn't interfere though. Ari is the head of my personal guard, and I don't want to tell him how to do his job, at least not tonight. He was mad enough about the whole situation, it didn't need to be made worse by me. Plus, he was already suggesting my date night was over, and I couldn't have that. So, I laid in wait, let him finish his tirade, and then miraculously, convinced him to let Quinn and I continue with our date night.

After Ari and Nyx, followed by Quinn, escorted me back to my room, Quinn and I agreed we both needed a bit to clean ourselves up. He left a few minutes later, heading to his room for a shower, and I proceeded to get re-dressed, despite Ari and Nyx refusing to leave my side.

Seriously, Nyx legit went to the bathroom with me. Not the shower, not me going in there to look in the mirror, *no*, he stood over me while I peed. It got old real quick, so I threw a minor fit, and he and Ari finally left.

And now that I'm dressed for the second time tonight, I'm just waiting on Quinn to get back. He was a lot worse off than me, and he probably needed to see a healer for the gash on his cheek. He said he didn't need to though, and I didn't argue, because I really need this date night with him. He's the last of my five, coming in late to the game, and we need to make up for lost time.

With Quinn being an UnSeelie, my brain tells me we're doomed from the start, but my heart says he's mine, just like the others. Sure it's new, and we're just getting to know one another, but that doesn't change how I feel.

Pulled from my thoughts, a rap at the door startles me, and I call for whoever it is to come in. The door opens, and Quinn steps inside, bowing his head before closing the door back. When he turns to face me, his hands slip into his pockets, and nervously, he rocks back on his heels while giving me a tentative smile.

I return the gesture. "So…" I start, "I planned a picnic."

"You did?" he asks, surprised.

"Yeah, but it's cold now, so…maybe we should do something different?" I lean against the post of my bed, using it to rest my head as I try to think of something else for us to do. "We could sneak down to the kitchens, and steal some dessert?"

"I don't think it's stealing when you're the Queen," he chuckles, rocking back and forth.

I purse my lips. "Take all the fun out of it, why don't ya?"

He winks, a smirk playing on his lips. "Alright, so…how do we sneak in?"

With a conspiratorial grin, I wave him over before slipping my hand in his and giving it a tug. Pulling him across the room, I can't help the grin that's plastered to my face. New love is amazing, and I got to do it five times, which has me feeling pretty lucky.

We make it across the wide space, and since my wardrobe doors are open, I move clothes to the right and left, revealing a small hatch just big enough for us to go through one at a time. I go first, and as soon as I'm all the way in, I feel and hear him crawl in behind me, the hatch shutting with a click.

The tunnel right here is small enough that we have to crawl, so it's slow going for the first few minutes, but when we make it to the first turn, it opens up, both of us able to continue on in a crouch. We head down a small enclosed set of stairs next, coming to another small tunnel, and then we make it to the door that will lead us to the staff hall.

I look at Quinn with a grin like we are really doing something wrong, and opening the door, I check both ways before pulling him along behind me. We sneak down the hall, conscious of our surroundings, so when I hear someone coming, I yank him in a broom closet.

Inside it's dark, and our bodies are close, touching in more than one place. Our breaths intermingle, and as my chest rises and falls, it brushes against his. I know the fairy we were avoiding has already passed, which means we could leave this closet any time we wanted to, and yet, we don't. He's probably waiting for me to suggest that very thing, but to be honest, I'm more focused on our close proximity.

"Do you think they're gone?" he finally whispers, his fingers lightly stroking my arm.

"Yeah," I confirm, breathy.

"Should we go?"

"Yeah?"

He chuckles, and I expect him to open the door and lead me out, but instead, he leans forward, brushing his lips across mine before pulling back. It's not enough to send me over the edge, but it is enough to leave me wanting more. And I do. I want *so* much more.

Another minute passes, and finally, I lead us out, careful to check that we're alone. As we travel down the last hall, I once again find myself wondering if sex is on the table for a third date. I've never been worried about that before, but Quinn and I are doing things differently, trying to take things slow, but slow doesn't really work for me, so I'm praying tonight is our night as I push the door to the main kitchen open.

There's no one here now, so I yank Quinn inside before shutting the door back softly. Together, we cross to the walk-in fridge, and I heave open the massive metal door. Inside, the walls are lined with shelves, and on each one are dozens of desserts of all kinds. This is the dessert fridge, meaning every single thing in here is sweet and yummy. The problem is there are so many I don't even know where to begin.

First world problems.

Quinn, behind me, sucks in a breath, and I turn, seeing his eyes wide, surveying the delectable treats surrounding us. "Shit. This is…insane?"

"But the best kind of insane," I tell him, reaching for a small plate with a mini chocolate bundt cake on it. Chocolate is drizzled over the top, with a tiny raspberry as garnish, but I chunk the fruit to the side because no one needs that kind of negativity in their lives, and not bothering to offer Quinn some, I stuff the whole thing in my mouth. That's right, I just turned a whole cake into a single bite. I'm good at what I do, what can I say.

Quinn laughs at my expense, and then he reaches for his own, taking a small bite as if he's dainty. I roll my eyes because he is a total amateur. I must teach him the ways of the dessert Queen.

When he looks my way, I grab a whole chocolate chip cookie, holding it out for him. He smiles, leaning forward, ready to take another small bite, but I'll have none of that. When he opens his mouth, I cram the whole thing inside. He chokes, and for a second I'm worried I ruined our date by killing him, but he manages to swish it around, swallowing after a few chews. We both chuckle, and then it's a free for all.

We stuff our faces for the next twenty minutes, each of us pointing out things, and trying a little of everything. I'm starting to get full now, but I know I'll want some later, so I rush out of the cold fridge and grab two trays. Quinn helps me pile them both high, and as we step out again, I stop, Quinn bumping into my back, desserts flying.

"What *are* you two doing?" Ari asks, his hands on his hips like a dad.

***

Quinn

We got caught by the group's honorary dad, and as Ell squealed, grabbing me, she took off running, the desserts abandoned on the floor. I knew I would have to come back and clean that up later, because I can't stand the idea of someone else having to clean up my mess, especially in the kitchen, but fleeing as if our lives depended on it was kind of thrilling.

The dessert date really was an amazing idea, and sneaking around was even better. It really made it feel like we were doing something wrong, even though we weren't. Ell always seems to have fun, no matter what's going on. That's what I love about her.

Shit.

Did I just say love?

Shaking my head as I sit on Ell's setae, I'm surprised love is already floating around between the two of us. It isn't like me for sure. I get that we're in the middle of a destiny situation, but still. I'm attracted to her, for sure, and there's no doubt I've been thinking about sex since our date started, but love is a little heavy.

When Ell died, or whatever that was, I felt things for her that I can't even begin to explain, but now that that's over, I was thinking we could just take things slow, really get to know one another. The problem is whenever I'm around her, I just want to kiss her, shortly followed by bending her over and fucking her.

The other night, watching her with her other boyfriends was hot as fuck, and at the time, I really thought I could be satisfied with that, at least for a while. But now, as Ell practically skips across the room, her lavender bathrobe pulled tight, I don't know if I can drag this out much longer.

She plops down next to me, her legs curling underneath her, and an almost awkward silence begins to build. I clear my throat more than once, not sure how this date is going to end. Normally, I would've dropped the fairy off, maybe given her a kiss at the door, but this is different. I have somehow managed to find myself living with said fairy, a fairy that I'm pretty sure is my girlfriend. Although, I'm not sure she's referred to me that way. As her boyfriend, I mean. Sure she's called me hers more than once, but she hasn't assigned a title to us other than that. Alright fine, calling me hers is a pretty big fucking deal. *Whatever.*

"Wanna watch Earth Vision?" she asks, jolting me back to reality.

"Sure."

She grabs the remote, turning the Vision on, and without a thought, she snuggles into my side. I put my arm around her, and before long, I realize I'm stroking her bare skin. Peeking,

I see her robe has slipped past her shoulder, her shimmering skin visible. I'm mesmerized by her, the way she feels. Her skin is so soft it causes me to shiver.

I'm so entranced with the feel of her that I have no idea what we're watching. The voices seem far away, because all I'm focused on is the feel of my fingers against her skin. My gut is driving me to pull the fabric down, just a bit more, but I somehow manage to hold back.

"On third dates," she breaks the silence, twisting slightly to face me, "do people like make out, or is that more of a second base kind of date?"

I choke at her forwardness, but I don't know why I'm surprised. This is who she is, and it's another thing I like about her. Ell does *not* play games. If she wants it, she makes sure everyone knows it. Most fairies, you basically need a degree in forensics to figure out what they want, but not Ell.

Shaking my head, I tell her, "I don't think there's a right answer to that."

"So, then, if we wanted to go to second base, it wouldn't be against the rules?"

"No," I confirm, "it wouldn't be against the rules.

She wiggles, her butt pressing against my hip, and I turn, propping up on my side. We make eye contact, something unspoken passing between us, and before either one of us can back out, she moves to her side, pressing her back against my front. As we spoon, her hips begin to move, rubbing gently against my crotch. The feel of it has me hard quickly, and I let my hand slip from her side to her tummy. Her robe is silk, and it falls loosely around her as I swish it back and forth. My hand stumbles on the belt, and when she arches her back slightly, my fingers work to untie it. The material was barely held up as it was, so as the belt slips loose, her robe falls open and my hand slips inside. When my fingers make contact, I realize she wears nothing underneath. No panties. No bra. *Nothing.* She was prepared for this, which means she knew she was going to push for this before she stepped foot out of her closet. Although, I can't say that I mind.

My thumb rubs a soft circle across her abdomen, and she purrs, making me want her even more. Unfortunately, I now find myself in the age-old debate. North? Or, south? I could go north, and take our time getting to the finale. Or, I could go straight for the kill.

As I debate this, in true Ell fashion, she makes the decision for us. She grips my hand, and without a word, she pushes it south. When she lets go, my hand glides over her mound, and I'm pleased when I realize she's bare. The silky skin feels amazing, and as I descend even further, she moans her enjoyment before spreading her legs just enough to allow my fingers to go where they need to be. I run a digit through her lips, and her juices coat my skin and drip across her thigh. She's more than ready, her pussy slick, and I slide one finger inside her, feeling her out before adding a second. I watch how she reacts to me, and when she groans her pleasure, her hand reaches between us, finding my throbbing dick. Through the material of my jeans, she strokes, and the room fills with our lust as I pump my fingers in and out.

Minutes pass with my eyes closed, reveling in the feel of her. She's getting close. Her leg quivers as she struggles to hold it in place, and her back arches, her robe getting stuck in-between us. Surprisingly, I'm getting close too, which is insane. I still have my pants on. I feel like I'm back in school again. You know, under the bleachers, some fairy dry humping you until you come?

"Quinn," she whispers, turning her neck and kissing me. She pulls her lips away, groaning for me, her pussy clamping down on my fingers. "Oh God," she cries.

I press my forehead to hers as she comes, her hand still stroking me through my jeans, and when she cries out again, I let go. Cum wets my pants, and I'm slightly embarrassed, but Ell doesn't seem to mind. In fact, as she comes down from her high, twisting to face me better, it's pretty clear our night isn't over.

TWO PEAS IN A FREAKING POD

Ell

And we're on lockdown. I knew it was coming, but I hoped I was wrong. This is one of those times I really wish I wasn't always right. What? Oh, come on, you know it's true.

Anyway, when I woke up this morning and went down for breakfast with my boys, I was greeted by eight guards outside my room. Four of them left their post to escort me to breakfast, and as we ate, we were surrounded by no less than twenty fairies, all keeping watch. I don't want to say it's overkill, but I think we all know that's what this is.

At least last night was great. Quinn and I made it to third base. Or, at least, I think getting finger banged is third base. Or is it second? Well, anyway, that's exactly what happened. Twice. We didn't take it any further than that though, and surprisingly, I was completely okay with it. I think when Quinn said we would take things slow he was imagining something a little slower, but for me, it felt like we waited forever to mess around. Honestly, I'm not sure I could've made it much longer.

We engaged in some aggressive foreplay until nearly 3:00 a.m., and then I walked him to the door and we kissed goodbye. It was super sweet. *He's* super sweet. He isn't anything like my other boys. Sure they're all different, each having their own quirks, but there's something even more different about my fifth fairy. I guess his differences could have something to do with him being marked by the Devil, being brought up in a different part of Fay, or the things he's been through in life, but either way, I like it.

And now, as he sits across the table from me, I'm straining so we can play footsy. My shoe is off, only covered by one of my sloth socks, and I run my toe up his leg. I can't reach much further than his thigh though, and I really wish I could.

If I…could just…move…a little further.

I'm slumped in my seat, trying to get where I want to be, and as my foot connects with Quinn's crotch, his dick hard, I realize the room has gone silent. We're all here to bid Helga and Bree farewell, because they are heading out later today to find Helga's friend. While we don't know much, we do know her friend will take the crown of thorns we retrieved on Earth, add a dash of magic, and then somehow turn it into something we can use on King Tobin. But, as I scan the faces around the table, I'm trying to figure out why everyone has stopped talking. Before I started my footsy adventure, there was a constant stream of conversation around the table, but now, crickets.

"What is it that you're doing?" Ari asks, his brow quirked.

"Nothing," I say too quickly, "What are *you* doing?"

"We," he starts in a somewhat mocking tone, "are discussing the fate of Fay. While you are, what, exactly?"

"Playing footsy," Nyx chimes in, smirking.

My foot slips from its warm place, and I attempt to discreetly sit upright. As my back straightens, my eyes land on Quinn, and shockingly, I think he's blushing. His cheekbones are an adorable shade of pink, and his head points downward.

"So I take it you two had a good date last night," Bree suggests, grinning.

"OMG. My dad is in the room, ya damn Pixie."

I'm not embarrassed, but if Quinn wasn't before, he definitely is now. And worse than that, my dad and Ari both shake their heads. Two peas in a freaking pod. Doesn't Earth have a saying about this? Girls marry their fathers? Or wait, no, that's weird. Maybe; girls marry guys *like* their father? Well, I hope that isn't the case here. But as I eye them both, the similarities are almost scary. They both sit the same, eye me the same, and they both sigh at the exact same time. I guess I'll have to address that with Ari later, because I'm not trying to marry my dad.

When Ari clears his throat, ready to get the discussion back on track, he's interrupted by Helga's craggily voice. "We will return in two weeks. You all need to do nothing more than hold down the fort. Or, palace, as it were."

"Are you sure there's nothing more we need to be doing?" Ari asks. "Surely there's something we need to do to ready ourselves for what's to come."

"Didn't I just say don't do anything other than hold down the fort?" Helga clicks her tongue, her head shaking in annoyance.

"Fine," Ari agrees, "We'll hold down the fort and nothing more. But...I still think we should put a call out for more guards. I'd feel a lot more comfortable if the palace was more secure. Last night, an Elf not only made it through the gates of the palace, but into the Queen's private chambers. It's unacceptable."

"I agree," my dad backs Ari up, bobbing his head.

When Helga doesn't dispute it, Ari says, "Good, I'll take that as consent. Calling for more guards won't hurt anything."

With that, Helga rises from her seat, her back hunched as she waddles to me at the head of the table. When she makes it to my side, she tips her head slightly, and tells me, "Try not to get yourself kidnapped or harmed while I'm gone."

I can't tell if she's trying to be funny or not, but I giggle anyway. "I make no promises, but I'll try."

I stand, and she surprises me when she leans in for a hug. Returning the gesture, it lasts longer than I thought it would, and then she's replaced with Bree. We too hug, and I realize I won't see Bree for two weeks. I'm going to miss her.

"Miss you," I tell her, as we pull apart.

"Yeah you will," she smarts off, bumping me with her hip.

Our moment is cut off though, when Helga snaps her fingers. Bree practically jumps to attention, and then the two of them exit the room and the rest of us follow. When we make it out front, bidding them farewell once again, as if we didn't just do this five-minutes ago, my heart aches as if this is the end of an era. I don't know why I feel that way, and I'm really praying this isn't a bad omen.

Stuffing that in the back of my mind, I watch everyone milling about, readying for the trip. They're taking two carriages, so Helga and Bree get in the second one, with two guards inside with them, and a coachman on top. The other carriage has supplies and four guards, also driven by a coachman.

As final preparations are made, I'm feeling glad they have so many guards going with them. We didn't want to take any chances on them running into trouble, and Helga said the two of them having their own contingent of guards wouldn't change anything. I just hope we're sending enough. Their mission is crucial to our success. We need the magic from the thorn to break the protection magic King Tobin has surrounding him. I'm not sure how it will work, but it isn't an option to do this any other way. With one-hundred Dryads protecting him, we don't stand a chance.

As my worry deepens, the carriages take off, and Bree presses her face to the window, flipping me off. Ari shakes his head as I laugh, giving her the double-bird, because I cannot be outdone.

I keep both middle fingers up until the carriages disappear from sight, because my heart hurts like I might not see Bree again. I know that's not true though. Helga said I would help Bree integrate her people, so as long as everything goes according to plan, I'll have my best Pixie friend back in no time. I hope.

***

Ari

The carriages disappeared out of sight, but five-minutes later, as I was directing a few guards on their shift, both carriages reappeared. Helga whistled for me to join her, and then she said she saw something new. She said I did, in fact, need to increase our numbers, build an army for a potential attack. Only, it didn't seem like she was referring to an attack on us, but more *us* attacking the UnSeelie capital. That's the first time that's been brought up. Although, I knew it was probably inevitable. She also told me to keep this mostly between us, until I just couldn't anymore. Whatever that means. I love Helga, but I'll be glad when we no longer rely on a seer to give us our information. It's just too fucking confusing.

Once she disappeared again, I went straight to work. No time could be wasted. Increasing our numbers to a point that we stand a chance at attacking the UnSeelie capital won't be easy. In reality, and under better circumstances, this is something I'd plan out over six months, maybe even a year, but as it is, we don't have that kind of time. So, I need to do a year's worth of work in two weeks. Piece of cake. Not really.

When I barked out orders to the guards, along with Nyx and Blake, I didn't elaborate. I just let them think this was all part of an effort to improve palace security. Based on Helga's words, I'll know when it's okay to fill everyone else in, and until then, this rouse should do the trick. It's not like it's a lie. Well, not a total lie.

It's a necessary lie, I realize, as I pace a line, looking at today's new recruits. In the four hours since Helga left, we've only managed to pull in thirty new fairies. Not near what we need, but pretty damn good for an afternoon of work. If I'm being honest, it was mostly Nyx and Blake. They each spent an hour out in the Keep, talking up the pay and the benefits. I probably don't say this enough, but I was proud of their hard work.

The new recruits in front of me could be better though. I

count five that are somewhere around my age, and the rest are far too old to be starting a new career. The one on the end, with jet black hair, looks too frail for much of anything. But beggars can't be choosers, at least not right now. There's a place for everyone. I just have to find it, and that's what I'm good at.

Nyx stands on my right, jotting down notes as we make our way down the line once again. "What about the one on the end?" he whispers.

"Put him in light training," I tell him, "And then…assuming he makes it through, put him on door duty. But…always with someone good."

"Got it." Nyx's pen moves a mile a minute, and then we're moving on to the next. "The twins?"

"They look big and hearty," I survey the two Ballybogs, "They could be the best two we got today."

"Agreed." Nyx nods his head.

Ballybogs are rare in Fay. When fairies were banned on Earth, the Ballybogs were one of the only types of fairies that chose to ignore the warning. They hid out in a country called Ireland, and for the most part that's where they've stayed. They don't bother the humans much, content with living out their days on boggy land. The few that have found their way back to Fay, tend to keep to themselves, and are extremely shy, sometimes so shy that they can't physically bring themselves to speak to others. On the plus side though, they're always well built, muscles on muscles, and the few I've interacted with are very loyal.

Yeah, these two could be good for us.

After internally nodding my head, we issue out the last of the assignments, and then Nyx and I make our way back inside for the night. It's already near dinner time, and we'll need to shower quickly, because Ell insisted we all have dinner together.

I'm really not looking forward to this though. I plan on breaking the news to Ell that she has to start a training regimen tomorrow, with either me or Nyx, and I know that's not going to go over well.

Dread fills me as I look at my watch, seeing I have twenty-minutes to get showered, changed, and back downstairs. Twenty-minutes to psych myself up for this conversation Ell and I are about to have. This is *not* going to be fun.

***

Ell

"Eeek," I squeal, clapping my hands and bouncing in my seat.

Ari just gave me the best news, and I couldn't be more excited, which is why I can't understand why he looks at me now, stone-faced. His eyes keep jerking back and forth, like he's waiting for a Leprechaun to drop down from the ceiling and steal his watch or something. His lips are parted slightly, as if he wants to say something but doesn't know what.

"What?" I question him.

"You're excited?" he asks, unbelieving.

"Of course I am, ya goob. Why wouldn't I be?"

He closes his eyes, letting out a long, hard sigh. "Just when I think I have you figured out, you go and do some shit like this."

It's just me and my boys at dinner, so there's no reason to be professional, but regardless, I'm not sure what that's supposed to mean. You'd think he would be happy about this.

As for me, I'm ecstatic. This is exactly what I need. After I merged with the magic of Fay, I never really had time to bond with it, which probably explains why she's been a real twat lately. We just need a little bonding experience and time, and that's exactly what this training will give us.

Ari pinches the bridge of his nose, and I still don't get it. He doesn't fill me in though, but Nyx does. "He thought you were going to fight him on this."

"Why on God's green Fay would I do that?" I screech, "This is perfect." And looking to Ari, I add, "So, who's going to do the honors?"

"You're serious?" he asks, and when I nod, he says, "Okay then, well, I guess Nyx and I will take turns. I also think it might be good for you to work some with a few of the elders, and that fairy you befriended a while back."

I know immediately who he's talking about, and I think it's perfect. Rykus stuck around after he helped us take back the palace all those weeks ago, and I think it's been really great for him. It's like his life has purpose once again, and I'm really glad I could give him that. I knew life running a store was not for him when I saw him fight alongside his friends as we stormed through the Keep, and now, the idea of him helping to train me, well, let's just say I'm looking forward to it.

"That's the best idea you've ever had," I tell Ari, bobbing my head emphatically.

Ari snarls, a worried look on his face. "Okay, who the fuck *are* you, and what have you done with Ell?"

EPIC TRAINING MONTAGE

Ell

Yesterday, Ari sent out a letter to what's left of the Summer Court, and the Spring Court as well. I snuck a peek before it was sealed, and in it he asked that they send us a few of their best fighters. He said it was to beef up security at the palace, but I can't help but think it's more than that.

And as I step out on the lawn for day one of my epic training montage, seeing the back lawn is filled with fairies of all shapes and sizes, I know I'm right. Ari knows something that I don't, and while I'm sure there's a reason he hasn't told me, I have zero plans of letting this go.

Random sidebar, I'm legit obsessed with the ID channel on Earth Vision. I know how to kill you and make it look like an accident. Or in this case, investigate what Ari is up to without him knowing what *I'm* up to. Sure I could just come right out and ask, but what would be the fun in that?

Ready to get to it already, I work my way through a hoard of fairies young and old, and I meet up with Ari and Nyx at the center of it all. Ari is, of course, barking out orders, and Nyx is acting as his right-hand-fairy. I spot Blake and Quinn too, and surprisingly, Luke is with them. I'm really hoping our wild night of passion the other night helped break the ice, and as a result, things will be easier with Luke and the group. But, I guess only time will tell.

"You're late," Ari mumbles, stepping away from the group.

"Uh, I had to look the part. Geesh."

And look the part I do. I'm not trying to be shallow or any-thing, but I spent a minute on this outfit. It took Zelda and I forever, but we finally found a pair of nearly skin-tight military style combat pants, and I paired it with a skimpy black tank. The tank is low cut, leaving my girls on display, and I may or may not have sprinkled a little glitter on every inch of my body. After that, I went with a high-pony and combat boots. The fin-ishing touch was the two strips of black paint I added under my eyes. It really set the whole outfit off, even though Zelda thought it was a little over the top.

I'm ready for my close-up. Or training, whatever.

Ari is still rolling his eyes, as he insists, "This is training, not a Project Runway episode."

"Oh my God. Did you just reference Project Runway? I'm so in love with you right now."

He grumbles something under his breath, and then he moves to the platform behind us, climbing up and addressing the whole crowd. "In case you haven't heard, an UnSeelie Elf broke into the palace night before last, and made it all the way to the Queen's chambers. He was caught escaping with her in his possession."

Gasps ring out through the crowd, and that's when a few fairies closest to me notice who I am. Instantly, they bow to their knees, and it causes a ripple effect until everyone is down on their knees with the exception of my boys.

It feels so weird for people to bow to me. Sure I like the perks of being a royal, but bowing always seems a bit pretentious, so I know I have to address it. "Please, we're all in training together. Out here, I'm one of you," I tell those closest to me, ushering them to their feet.

When the handful surrounding me rise, I watch as the rest of the crowd slowly catches on, and before long, I'm back to blending in. Well, as much as one can blend in with the amount of glitter on my person right now. In hindsight, it might've been a bit much, but not the eye-black. I may never take it off. I look *so* badass right now.

Pleased with myself, Ari calls for attention, and once again, all eyes are on him. "I'm sure I speak for all of us when I say an UnSeelie making it to the Queen is unacceptable. We can never allow this to happen again. And that's where all of you come in. Beefing up palace security is the fastest way to ensure our Queen's safety." His eyes drop to mine, and I smile, nodding for him to continue. "And yes, she will be training with us. She is one of the strongest fairies in all of Fay, so I pity the fairy who ends up in the sparring ring with her in eight days."

The what now?

No one said anything about a sparring ring, or me ending up in one. I agreed to train, and nothing more. I guess Ari and I will need to have a talk when he comes down, because this seems like a lot.

Ari talks for another few minutes, and then he introduces team leaders. He's one, of course, along with Nyx and Jack, one of my personal guards. The last leader he announces is Rykus, and that surprises me. He has a lot of experience, but he's one of the oldest fairies here, so I can't believe Ari chose him.

As I contemplate that, Ari hops down off the platform, his first stop, *me*. "Ready to get started?"

"Um, about that sparring ring?"

***

Nyx

It's day two of our crash course guard training. When Ari first told Blake and I to head out and recruit, I believed it really was just to increase security around Ell, but now I'm not so sure, since there's at least two-hundred fairies training with us today. We had about a hundred and fifty yesterday, with another fifty or so showing up this morning, and we just received word the Spring Court is sending another hundred that should be here in three days. This seems like a lot more than just, and I quote, 'beefing up security'.

I questioned Ari on it during our morning jog too, but he brushed it off saying it's better to have too many than not enough. Sure he's right about that, but I can't help but think there's something else going on here.

My line of thinking is only supported by the fact that Ari is pushing Ell way too hard. Yesterday she trained with him, and he was such a dick, when training was over, they got in a huge fight. Ell refused to come back to training unless Ari moved her to a different team leader, and that's how she ended up with me.

I guess part of his behavior could be aftermath of Ell dying. We're all feeling it, this need to protect her more than ever, but I just know there's more to it, and I can't understand why he's keeping it from us.

Mentally shrugging that off, I check out the practicing going on around me. The twins are on my team, and they tag-team Ell. We're currently working on close combat training, and it's an area Ell is lacking in. She acts like she doesn't want to break a nail, which is funny, because I know she doesn't give a shit about that.

Ell barely misses taking a massive fist to her chin, and I stop the group, calling Ell out. "Your Majesty, join me."

She's panting from exertion, and I know she's wishing she worked out more. She fully believes cardio is the devil though, so the chances of that happening are not good. Which means, we're probably going to have to play to her strengths. I'm not letting her leave my group without gaining at least some knowledge of close-quarter fighting though.

Ell saunters up to my side, probably hoping if she looks sexy I'll take it easier on her. No chance in hell. In fact, it might be the opposite. So, I move the two of us to the center of my group, and everyone circles around, waiting to see what I'll do to our Queen.

When I speak, I do so loud enough that everyone can hear. "Yes, we have magic, some more than others." I circle around Ell, eying each fairy as I go. "But, there may be times that magic isn't an option, or you might not have magic as strong as your opponent's. That's when close combat fighting is your best-friend." I square up to Ell. "But we're all different shapes and sizes, so what works for one may not work for all. As you work through these exercises, it's important that you have a basic knowledge for each, but you should be trying to identify the ones that you're best at, the ones that feel the most comfortable. Those will be sweet spots for you."

"Damn," a Sprite says from behind me, "since when did Nyx become such an Ari?"

I turn on him, getting in his face. "This could be life or death, *dude*. Do you want to die? Do you want your Queen to die?" I'm barking now, and I know my face is red with anger.

"No, sir," he changes his attitude, his words nearly a whisper.

"What was that!?!" I shout.

Louder, he answers, "No, sir!"

"Good," I nod my head, turning back to face Ell, "Now, as I was saying, we have to work with what we've got. If you're shorter than your opponent, skinnier, or rounder, or whatever it is, that doesn't matter as long as you know what you're good at." Ell is listening to every word I say, and finally she seems to be taking this seriously. "Your Majesty, you're almost always going to be fighting someone bigger than you. So, what's something you're good at that you can adapt to move a fight in your favor?"

She thinks for a minute, tapping her chin. "High kicks?"

"Good," I praise her, "Which means, a good round-house kick could give you the upper hand if you perfect the skill." I get in a fighting stance, but she still stands relaxed. "Come at me."

She smirks, and I can tell my words turned her on. Maybe not the best time for it, but I'm certainly not surprised by it. This is who she is.

She's still grinning when she shakes her arms out, getting in a loose stance before lunging forward without any real heart, so before she knows what's happening, I sweep my leg out, knocking her flat on her ass. If she were anyone else, everyone around me would be cheering right now, but since it's the Queen, I hear a few gasps, and I'm sure most think I just took things too far.

And it seems Ell would agree with that, because she barks, "What the fuck, Nyx?"

"Your stance was shit, and you came at me like a grandma," I tell her, making sure not to sound as if I'm mocking her. Everything I just said was the truth. One-hundred percent. "If you fight someone like that, you're going to lose. Now, get up and go again."

I don't want to push her too hard. After all, we all saw what happened when Ari made that mistake yesterday, but she also needs to know I'm just as serious about her learning how to properly defend herself.

As she gets back to her feet, she brushes her hands down the front of her fashion cargo-pants, and eyes me with an evil look. I motion for her to try again, and she slits her eyes further. Finally, she jerks forward, and while it is better, it's nothing close to what I know she's capable of. So, this time, *I* lunge forward, sweeping around behind her back and snatching her up in a chokehold, her feet dangling an inch off the ground.

As soon as Ell has time to realize what happened, I set her down gently, backing away in case she decides to turn me into a goat or something. I'm not sure what her obsession is with goats, but she threatens it a lot.

Back on her feet, she growls at me as she steps away, our bodies facing once again. Sweat drips down her forehead, and she swipes a hand through it before scrubbing it off on her pant legs. I can tell she's mad, but this time she doesn't speak on it. Instead, she backs up two feet, and prepares to go again.

This time, she actually gets in a decent stance, her frame firm as she waits for me to come at her. I step to the left, thrusting the palm of my hand out, and she sidesteps. I move right, trying to sweep her off her feet again, but she jumps the action causing me to stumble forward.

Putting space between us, I reset, and she grins, making a come-hither motion. I crack my neck left and then right, and then I'm sprinting. We trade blows, with her taking a hard right-cross to the chin, and me taking a jab to the kidneys. It was a good shot, and I lose focus as I feel pride for her. She takes advantage of it too, pushing me back into the ground, and then she attempts a kick but misses. She's frustrated, the snarl on her face proof, and we trade a few more shots.

The crowd is now chanting, and I realize it's a lot bigger than just our team. As Ell and I circle, I notice Ari and Blake in the group, along with Quinn. Luke is the only one I don't see, but I'm sure he's there. As for the chanting, half are for me, half for the Queen, although the latter is almost drowning out the former. I don't care though. In fact, I'm glad. Ellie Mae needs this. She needs a win.

Ell leans her weight forward, really putting effort into a punch to my side. I grunt, the pain reverberating through me, and I hear Blake let out a, "Whoop."

Taking a deep breath and pushing the pain way down deep, I go for my signature move as she tries to reset, but this time, when I sweep my leg out, ready to knock her on her ass, she catches my leg and spins. She uses her weight to pull me, and the two of us land with a thud, her somehow on top.

As we settle, Ell leans over me, breathing hard, her chest pressing against mine. It's then that I wish all these people weren't here. I don't even care that I just lost and everyone is shouting, "long live the Queen." No, right now, all I can think about is fucking her.

She leans forward, her lips whispering against my ear, "That was hot."

And then she's up, and I'm left with a very obvious hard-on.

***

Ell

I was pissed at first, but in the end, I felt like I actually walked away from training with more than I walked in with. Sure I have a long way to go, and maybe Nyx shouldn't have called me out like that, but he succeeded in more than one thing. The most important being that I now realize I wasn't truly taking this seriously until our little sparring session.

Now, it's game on. I'm going to take this so serious they won't know what hit them. Okay yes, it also has to do with the fact that fighting Nyx was a total turn-on, but that was only part of it. A big part, yes, but not all. Oh, who am I kidding? It was most of it, but still, whatever works.

If all I do for the next two weeks is fight and fuck, then I call that a total win. Of course, the latter won't be easy, because Ari still has me on lockdown. Not as bad as when we were back on Earth, but close. Each day seems to get a little better, but I haven't had near enough sex lately.

And, because I know sex isn't in the cards for me tonight, I'm sneaking down to grab some strawberry ice cream. Sneaking is a stretch since it's my home, but who knows? Ari might tell me no ice cream because it has too much sugar and I could go into a diabetic coma. That's the level he's on lately. It is *not* an exaggeration.

Rolling my eyes at the thought, I slip in the kitchen, finding one of the cooks preparing food for tomorrow. He bows, and I wave him off, asking for a bowl of my favorite. With a nod of his head, he moves quickly, fixing it just how I like, and he even slices a few fresh strawberries for the top. Thanking him, and with spoon and bowl in hand, I leave the kitchen in search of a quiet space to enjoy my bounty. And, I think I know just the place.

I hurry so my ice cream doesn't melt, and moments later,

I'm in the library. I find a cushy chair, curling up with a blanket and settling in. When the first bite slides down my throat, the nostalgia of this room hits me. The library was damaged in the fighting, but for the most part it's been restored, and sadly, the last time I remember being in here I was with my Aunt Bella. While it was after my run-in with Jim on Earth, it was before we truly knew how bad things were going to get, so the memory is a fond one.

I can't tell you how relieved I was when we returned to the palace and found her with Helga and Bree. Unfortunately, things have been so crazy, I haven't truly had time to spend with her. I know I need to rectify that though, because it seems she went on a pretty epic adventure of her own.

I make a mental note to make time for her, and as I take another bite of my ice cream, I'm startled when the door to the library whines open, a blonde Elf peeking his head in. *My* blonde Elf. Nyx.

"Hey, when you said you'd be right back and then you weren't, I got worried."

"I couldn't take any more of the overbearing dad version of Ari," I admit, swallowing my last bite of ice cream and wishing I had more.

Nyx chuckles, "Yeah, I figured. That's why I offered to come find you." He approaches my seat, his body relaxed, albeit tired, and as I search the area, not finding a single guard, I know exactly what could make up for no more ice cream.

"Wanna do it?"

He snorts, but his head bobs in agreement, so I toss my bowl to the side, and in seconds, I'm naked standing in front of him. Sex seems so much dirtier when at any moment someone could walk in and catch you. I like dirty sex.

And it seems Nyx does too, because his eyes scan every inch of me, and I like it. I like the way he looks at me. He's the least experienced of my boys, and so when he looks at me, he does so as if I was the most beautiful fairy in the whole universe.

He pumps his brows twice, whistling his approval. "I like

this look on you."

"What? Naked?" I giggle.

"Yup," he admits, "You should wear this outfit every day."

"That could get awkward, what with me being the Queen and all."

We both laugh as he saunters toward me, and slipping his hand in mine, he tugs me toward the stacks. I've always wanted to do this; fuck in the stacks, and I'm glad it's happening for the first time with Nyx, rather than the whole group.

Despite that, as he presses my back against a shelf full of the classics, I can't process why he still has clothes on. "You gonna get nude or what?" I ask, trying to tug his pants down.

He stops me, my hands gripped in his. "One of us should be dressed. You know, in case someone comes in."

I purse my lips, squinting my eyes. "Fine, but let's get this started. You know I don't like to wait."

He kisses me mid-snort, and I open my mouth and allow his tongue to slip inside. Seconds pass with our mouths dueling, and then Nyx leans back, his lips leaving mine. He brushes them down my throat instead, and the room fills with a heady aroma of lust.

Gripping his shirt in my fists, I yank him closer. "I need your dick in me."

With my words, he thrusts his pelvis forward, pushing me back, hard, books crashing through the other side, and then he swipes his hand across the shelf behind me, removing any remaining books. Satisfied, he lifts me, setting my ass down on the edge. There's a shelf above this one, so I can't sit too far back, but it does give me a little perch so Nyx can take me at the perfect height.

With me in position, he fumbles with his belt, and seconds later his pants drop to the floor. He reaches in his boxers, pulling his dick out of the elastic waistband, and then he strokes down the length three times, his eyes rolling back.

When his eyes open again, connecting with mine, he steps forward. He rubs his hard shaft through my fairy-lips, getting it nice and slick, and then he pushes inside. The tight space spreads for him as he fills me up, and I moan my desire for him.

Nyx pulls back as he pulls out for the first time, his eyes watching me, and I lick my lips. As he watches, my hands that had been gripping the shelf's edge, let go to rove over my body. I run one hand up to my breast, kneading and squeezing, while the other works its way down my stomach. Moving further, my fingers sneak across my mound, and while he watches, his eyes teaming with lust, I find my clit.

"Ellie Mae," he whispers, his dick swelling inside me.

I swirl my finger around and around before dropping even lower. I find his dick, and as he pulls out again, I grip his shaft tightly. He groans uncontrollably, and I fucking love it, knowing I did that to him. It makes me feel powerful.

I revel in the way it feels as his dick passes through my hand and back into my pussy, and on the third pass, he swats my hand away. His eyes slit, and something changes between us. His thrusts become more aggressive, almost like Ari, and he slams into me over and over again. With a growl, he grips my throat, cutting off most of my air, and it makes my head swim, but it also has me climbing the metaphorical hill.

"Fuck me, Nyx. Harder."

He growls deeper, thrusting faster and harder, and I throw my hands out, searching for anything to grab on to. I feel like I can't get enough of him, can't get close enough. I want him to climb inside of me and live there forever, and no, I don't give a shit if that's weird.

"Nyx," I whine in a begging tone, as my body begins to shake.

I'm quivering as the slap of skin on skin echoes through the high-ceiling room, our bodies soaked with sweat. He slides in and out of me easily, and I'm close to coming. When I hit the peak, shattering, my nails dig into his back and he calls my name out into the night. Half the guards had to have heard that, and I don't even care.

Finished, Nyx practically takes a nosedive toward my neck,

and I catch him. We both pant into one another, and I wish we could stay just like this, his dick buried deep inside of me.

As our heart rates slow, I intend to tell him that, but before I can, the party pooper shows up late to the party.

"I should've fucking known."

DOOMS DAY PROTOCOL

Ell

This new killjoy-Ari is *so* not a good time. I want the old Ari back. Sure he was always an ass, kind of, and he prided himself on being professional, but the Ari post-Ell-death is just too much. It's going to come to a head, and he is *not* gonna like me when it does.

He broke up my library-sex with Nyx last night. Sure we'd just finished, but I had plans for at least four more orgasms before we headed back to my room. Ari shut that shit down though, chastising Nyx and I both all the way back. He said, and I quote, in my best, deep Ari-voice, "You let your guard down while the Queen was in your charge. And for what? All for a quick fuck?"

You're damn right, and Nyx and I would do it again in a heartbeat. Of course, we didn't tell him that. It wasn't the time. He was too jacked up, and with one look, Nyx and I agreed to let him rant and let it go. I'm only going to be able to do that for so long though.

At least I'm not training with any of my men today. I'm assigned to Rykus' group, and we're working on pixie dust casting. This is an art form that I have little to no experience in, so I'm hoping to learn a thing or two.

Myself and thirty other fairies sit in a circle with Rykus in the center, after we're each given a small pouch filled with pixie dust. So far, all we've done is listen to Rykus go over a few safety rules. After all, pixie dust can be dangerous to those who don't know how to properly wield it.

Nearly every fairy has pixie dust on them at any given time, but for the most part, we use it for things like portaling and wild, drug-infused nights. Not me of course, on that last one, but you know, *other* fairies.

"All of you should know how to use dust to portal, so I'm not going to waste any time on that today," Rykus tells us, "We're going to focus more on things you might need dust for in the coming weeks. Specifically, in offense and defense in a fight, for interrogation, and advanced glamouring."

A few fairies in our group whisper amongst themselves, especially about the glamouring part. I've been using glamours since I was a young fairy, but I don't recall anyone showing me how to use dust to do it, so I'm interested in learning that part.

"Alright," Rykus starts, standing and dusting off his pants, "first, I may ask questions of you, and when I do the first time, introduce yourself and tell us a bit about yourself, like where you're from." Heads bob around the circle, and Rykus nods, satisfied. "Right then, today we're going to start with interrogation. Does anyone know how pixie dust can be used in an interrogation?"

Several hands go up, and Rykus calls on a young Sprite. Her hair is yellow like a sunflower, and to be honest, she looks way too young to be here. I notice a Spring Court patch on her sleeve, as she introduces herself, "I'm Suri, sir. My family was assigned to the capital, but we're from the Spring Court." Rykus waves his hand, encouraging her to continue. "Pixie dust can be used in an interrogation because of its hallucinogenic effects."

"Very good, Suri," Rykus commends her, and then turning in a circle, he confirms, "She's right. Pixie dust can be used to make a fairy very susceptible to suggestion."

"Like a truth serum," someone calls out.

"That's right," he confirms, "like a truth serum. Now, for

the purposes of our training today, I'll need a volunteer. Any takers?"

This time, not a single hand rises, probably because everyone realizes what this little lesson will mean. Rykus will be using pixie dust on one of us, and then asking us questions. If pixie dust acts as a truth serum, we won't be able to lie. I'm pretty much an open book though, so I decide to take one for the team.

My hand shoots up, and Rykus' head jerks back, surprised that I would be the one to volunteer. Shrugging him off, I grin, standing, knowing he has no choice but to accept me. Moving to the center of the circle so everyone can see me, I turn to Rykus and whisper, "Go easy on me though." He chuckles, and a few fairies in the front row do the same.

Not wasting any time, Rykus pulls a pinch of pixie dust out of his brown leather pouch, placing it in the bottom of an empty goblet. He reaches down, retrieving something from the black duffle bag at his feet, and when he stands, I see it's just a bottle of water. He pours two fingers in the goblet, and then without any additional magic, he hands the cup to me.

"Big swig," he directs.

I down the contents, because what does it matter? And then, I hand the goblet back to him. He places it at our feet, and then addresses the group. "Pixie dust is fairly fast-acting in its raw form like this, so we should start to see its effects in less than five minutes. It's different for everyone though, depending on the fairy's size, age, and even type."

A round fairy in the front raises his hand, and when Rykus acknowledges him, he asks, "Why type? What difference would that make?"

"Well," Rykus starts, "for example, Pixies are almost immune to the hallucinogenic effects of pixie dust. Since pixie dust is harvested from pixie trees, and since Pixies live in those trees, surrounded by the dust most of their lives, they have built up an immunity to it."

Heads bob around our circle, and I start to feel the effects of the dust. My nose is slightly numb, my head swims just a bit, and I have the urge to giggle. I'm able to hold it back though, and after Rykus answers two more questions, he turns back to me.

"How do you feel, Your Majesty?"

"Um," I think out loud, "like I've had four or five glasses of fairy wine?"

"Is that a lot for you?" Rykus asks, his head tilting to the side.

I snort-laugh. "Do you want me to lie to you?" I ask, causing a few fairies to chuckle, and when he shakes his head, I add, "Not really. I'd call this a beginner's buzz."

"Right then," Rykus says, seeming satisfied, "that's right about where we want you to be. So, let's get started. We'll start with something we know the answer to, like, are you the Queen of all Fay? But…I want you to try to lie."

I think that through, and in my head, I imagine saying no, but when my mouth opens, "yes" tumbles out. My eyes widen in surprise, because I really thought I could force the lie. It's kind of scary when you think about it. Someone could slip me some of this stuff, and I could easily disclose top secret information.

I make a mental note to talk to Bree about it when all this is through, while Rykus paces a circle around me, his hands clasped behind his back as he seems to think through what he wants to ask me now. As for me, I'm getting more nervous with every passing second, and I'm sweating buckets. What if he asks me something I'm not supposed to answer? Or worse, what if he asks me something I don't want anyone to know? Like, about me personally?

As I spiral, Rykus taps his chin, and then he approaches a tall Elf, her hair a forest-green color. He ushers her to her feet, and retrieving a pen and slip of paper from his pocket, he hands it to her. Taking the slip, she waits for his direction, her eyes jerking from him to me and back again.

"I want you to write down a number between one and ten.

Then, show it only to Her Majesty," Rykus instructs, "Your Majesty, you'll read it, but no matter what, when I ask you what was on the slip, you cannot tell us. You must say Elf instead."

The Elf and I bob our heads in agreement, and then she's writing. When she's done, she walks to me, discreetly shows me the number, and walks back to her place, the slip of paper folded in her hand. The number was six, and I say it over and over in my mind.

"Do you remember the number?" he asks, and I nod my head. "Okay, tell us what the number was."

I keep my mouth closed, pushing the number to the back of my mind and thinking the word; Elf. I can do this. I'm strong. No one can force me to do anything I don't want to do. I must say the word Elf.

Gritting my teeth, I try to force the word Elf past my lips, and it comes out garbled, but at least I didn't say six. I try again, and still nothing much comes out. Looking to Rykus, I can tell he's surprised.

"Strong fairies can fight it," he tells the group, "That's what Her Majesty is doing now. She's trying to fight the pixie dust. So, when she speaks, she's trying to force the word out that she wants, but the dust is working against her..."

"Six, six, six!" I shout like word vomit, unable to take it another second.

Rykus grins. "Her Majesty put up a good fight."

There's a chorus of agreements around the group, and it's then I notice Ari, a proud grin on his face, standing on the far side of our circle. He nods his head at me, and then he leaves me to the rest of our training.

***

Ari

It's been eight days since we started training, and Ell has done exceptionally well. Well, she's done well with Rykus as her mentor. It was evident on day one that Ell and I didn't need to train together. I know I was being hard on her, but I just want to make sure she's ready for anything.

The good news is I think we still achieved that with Rykus doing the bulk of her lessons. He really is good at this, and I've been thinking this might be a permanent job for him. If not here in the palace, then perhaps at an Academy. I plan to talk to him about it when this is all over, and assuming he makes it through whatever is coming, since he told me last night he wants to be a part of the fight. Of course, he doesn't know what the fight is yet.

I still haven't outright told anyone that Helga told me to build an army. Ell knows something is up, and Nyx has mentioned it twice, but I haven't admitted it to anyone yet. So, if those two know there's more to what we're doing here, then others have caught on too, like Rykus. It doesn't matter though.

Today, I've been working on the Dooms Day Protocol. That's what I'm calling whatever we need this army for. I've created mock scenarios, and assigned each guard a place in each. Rykus, for instance, is assigned to the Queen's guard should an attack occur. The twin Ballybogs have turned out to be just as vicious as I figured, and they too are now on Ell's personal guard. I've assigned others to inventory, air support, and a few other teams, and on paper, I'm ready. In my heart though, I'm not.

I just keep thinking the army isn't needed for an attack on the palace. It just doesn't make sense. Why would King Tobin leave the safety of his palace? He'd be risking himself for no reason. So, to me, it makes the most sense that we'll soon be taking the fight to King Tobin's doorstep. Clearly, we knew that we'd have to go to the UnSeelie capital so we could break the magic the Dryads are protecting him with, but I had assumed that would be a covert mission, and for whatever reason, that seems safer. A massive attack on the UnSeelie could lead to us all being separated, and increase the likelihood of one of us being injured or worse.

It doesn't matter right now though, and it's why I've dove

headfirst into training everyone, including Ell, as much as we can. The more prepared we all are, the less likely something irreversible is to happen.

Our numbers are looking good too, so I feel good about that. In addition to the nearly two-thousand fairies and humans we have left in King Oberon's guard, we managed to raise another six-hundred from our palace guards and other fairies living in or near the capital.

A few days ago, one-hundred fairies showed up from the Spring Court, including their Prince and Princess. Prince Toomey and Princess Alindra are both Selkies, and I was surprised to see they are lethal in their fighting skills. Apparently, and this is a direct quote from Prince Toomey, 'we've been training for this moment since we were five. We're ready to kill some fucking UnSeelie d-bags'. Yeah, they're different, but I'm glad to have them in our ranks.

In addition to that, the Summer court sent forty-three. Unfortunately, after the attack on Brooks, they've been struggling to rebuild. Prince Vlad and the fairies that were left evacuated to his country estate, essentially being forced to move their capital for the time being since the UnSeelie now occupy the Summer palace.

When the Summer Court fairies arrived here a few days ago, they had a message from Prince Vlad. He said if we were under siege at some point, he might be able to send a few more, but he just couldn't part with the rest for more than a few days. I understand, and I don't have any hard feelings toward him. They need to protect their people too, and if they send us all their guards, they leave themselves open to attack.

With all that, our numbers are promising. Considering we know there are still about two-hundred and fifty fairies holed up at the Summer Court, and we know there are bands of King Tobin's guards traipsing all over Fay, attacking towns and villages, we can make a decent guess as to how many guards he has in the UnSeelie capital. Our guess now is somewhere around three-thousand, assuming our intel is accurate. They'll outnumber us just slightly, but if we do attack them, like I think we will, then we'll hopefully have the element of surprise.

The wild card is the fact that they have a seer just like us. If we are following the strict path that Helga's seen, then wouldn't that mean King Tobin's seer would know everything we know? Wouldn't it mean they'll see us coming no matter what we do?

QUEEN BAE

Ell

Okay, I know at first I said I wasn't for it, but I'm so excited for today. In less than fifteen minutes, I'll be entering into my first guard exhibition. Originally, Ari said we would all get in the sparring ring with one another, but two days ago, he decided to make it a whole thing. Like a competition, and you know how competitive I am. But since I'm the Queen and everyone will be watching, I've been actively telling myself to tone it down. It's just so hard because Ari has designed such an awesome event.

There will be four competitions that will take place over the next four days. All four competitions will be going on simultaneously, with some sort of bracket system Ari and Nyx came up with together. The four categories are hand-to-hand combat, aerial combat, magic wielding, and the last is a wild card. The wild card category will be different for everyone. So for example, not everyone shifts naturally, so I would be at a disadvantage in combat-shifting, which means I won't compete in that one, only the fairies who can shift will.

As for my wild card meet, I'll be competing in elemental magic, and I'm so excited. Is it scary that I've been fantasizing about drowning whoever I'm up against? I mean not drown, drown, because you know, we can't kill anyone or we're disqualified, but you know what I mean. Yeah, it's scary, but whatever.

I mentally nod my head as I hear Ari project his voice across the back lawn, calling for everyone to circle up. There are hundreds of us now, and I work my way through the crowd, finding myself a spot toward the center. I end up right next to the Ballybog twins, and I'd be lying if I said I wasn't intimidated by them. The whispers among those competing are that the twins are the ones to beat, and I just hope I don't go up against them at all. Or, at least, not until the very end. If the twins and I make it far in the competition, then there's almost no way I don't fight them at some point.

I pray on that as Ari explains the scoring system, and while everyone else nods their head, I don't because I didn't understand a word he just said. The scoring is complex, and there was something he said about double elimination. It makes no sense to me, so I'm just going to go where they tell me to, and hope I don't need to know that later.

And I should be okay, because behind Ari sits a massive Vision screen, but it won't be playing Earth Vision today. The screen is at least forty-feet by sixty-feet, and it will cycle through everyone's assignments, periodically displaying our ranks and scoring.

Ari points that out, and Nyx clicks a button on the side of the stage, the screen flaring to life. "You'll also get your assignments from your team leaders. The board is more so everyone can see what their competitors are doing, and where you each rank," Ari explains.

I scan the board as it flips through each group within each competition. Finally, I spot my name. I have my wildcard round first, elemental magic, and internally, I sigh, relieved. I've been training using water and earth based magic since I was a toddler-fairy, and so with the new things I've learned in the last few days, this one should be a walk in the park. *Hopefully*.

Not wanting to jinx myself, I mentally make a note to knock on some wood in a minute, and focus back on Ari. "Alright, if you didn't see your name on the board yet, then find your team leaders to wait for your turn," he instructs, before dismissing everyone.

Even though I saw my name, I rush through the throng of fairies, searching out Rykus. I have to throw some elbows, but eventually the crowd thins out, and I spot him near the back steps to the palace. The twins are already at his side, *suck-ups*, and so are a few others, which blows. I was hoping to get some advice from Rykus before my match started, but I don't want to look stupid by asking in front of everyone, so instead, I casually stroll up, trying to keep a nonchalant look on my face.

As I try to blend in, I jerk when I feel someone's hand caress my back, and I'm ready to throw a palm to the face. Ari catches my hand in mid-air, and I instantly relax. He chuckles, and I glare at him, giving him a warning. "Don't sneak up on a fairy like that. I'm on red-alert right now."

He chuckles again. "I can tell." He puts a little space between us, and then he adds, "How are you feeling about your first match? I see you're up against an Earth fairy."

"Been imagining drowning someone all day," I tell him, confident.

He laughs, and so does Nyx, as he walks up, joining us. "Look who's feeling confident," Nyx heckles.

"Just call me Queen Bae," I brag, pursing my lips, my hands going to my hips.

"Well," Ari starts, getting my attention, "remember, don't go for the obvious. You are kind of at a disadvantage, compared to the others. As the Queen, many already know what your strengths and weaknesses are. I don't know the fairy you're up against first, and don't recall seeing him fight the last few days, but he could be expecting you to use water magic."

I take in his words, filing them away, and appreciating the advice. "Got it."

He grins, his hand jerking forward to touch my face, but realizing we're surrounded by dozens of fairies, he pulls back. "Well, good luck."

I thank him, and he and Nyx leave me, heading back to the

platform where they'll oversee the competition and scoring. I watch them go, and as they disappear, Rykus calls for me, pushing his way through a few other team members. He motions for me to follow, and then the two of us head for my first match.

I'm giddy, because I'm about to make this fairy my bitch, but you know, also make friends and learn stuff.

***

Prince Lucas

Things have gotten better in the last few days. Arion and I seem to hate each other a little less, and the others are starting to warm up to me too. Likewise, I'm also warming up to them. I still wish Ell was all mine, but that part of me is pushed down deep. After what happened, us nearly losing her, I'm willing to put up with just about anything to be with her.

That includes the somewhat weird encounters with Arion. I said we're warming up to one another, not that we're friends. *Hell*, I don't know if that title will ever be used in relation to Ari and I, but it's clear we're both putting in some effort. He even included me in this whole training thing, and the competition that started this morning.

Although I will never admit it out loud, this competition is a good idea. Not just for training, but for everyone's spirit, Ell's too. I can tell by looking at her she needed this.

For the last few weeks, it's been full steam ahead, never letting up, and something bad always right around the corner. And, since it's not like we can just leave and attack King Tobin, since we have to wait on Helga, we might as well have a tiny bit of fun while we wait. Not to mention, it's a good teaching tool. Again I say; I'd never give Arion the compliment, but still, this was smart.

I made it a point to watch Ell's matches, and she just keeps winning. In her first match, she used water to nearly drown her opponent, causing her to quickly move up the ranks in the wild-card category. Each match since then, and with each fairy she disposes of, she jogs off the lawn, a smile on her face, her fist pumping in the air. And each time, she says, "Totally made him my bitch." She's a mess sometimes, a hot fucking mess, but in a good way.

Like right now, as she jogs a large circle around her final wild-card opponent. The fairy she's up against is a brute. His head is shaved clean, he looks like he's in his twenties, and his face is marred with scars. He's clearly been through some things.

Looking at him, I can tell he's an Earth fairy, and I noticed that he's watched every single one of Ell's matches. He prepared for this, which means he knows her inside and out. He knows that she favors her left side before lunging, and that's why he sweeps to the right. He knows that she has a slight tick in her eyebrow when she's pulling water from beneath her feet, and because he knows that, he counters, mixing her water with dirt, making a muddy slush at their feet.

He's good, I'll give him that, and I can tell Ell's getting frustrated. She's out of breath as she tries again to pull water, but this time, instead of pulling it from beneath her, I can tell by the look on her face that she's pulling it from above. While she does that though, she uses her wood side to rip roots from the ground, causing her opponent to stumble, his feet wrapped up.

Her opponent grunts as he falls, and I can see it in Ell's eyes, she thinks she's won. She lifts her fists in the air, still pulling water, but knowing she has this in the bag. I'm not so sure though. The Earth fairy still has some fight left in him, and he rolls, using his own earth magic to separate the clinging roots.

If Ell loses this fight, she isn't out of the competition. There are four categories, with a scoring system and some sort of double elimination in the end. I didn't really understand the bracket thing Arion tried to explain, but I wasn't about to admit that. All I know is whoever wins this match, wins this category. If Ell wins, she's one step closer to winning the whole thing, but she still has three other categories to complete. If she loses this one, she'll still move on to the next category.

Someone shouts, and my eyes are instantly searching out Ell. Somehow, in my distraction, Ell has found herself on the ground. Well, not *on* the ground, but more *in* the ground. The Earth fairy has nearly buried her, her head and neck the only thing visible. I knew he had more in him.

The fairy stands over Ell, a menacing look smeared across his face, and if I didn't know he was one of us, I'd almost be worried. Ell looks a little worried too, as the fairy squats down, pushing his magic into the ground and forcing Ell to sink past her chin.

Seeing she has no other choice, Ell realizes her defeat. "I yield."

I can tell it destroys her to say those words, but as soon as they are out, the Earth Fairy releases his magic, the ground turning loose. He reaches his hand out, offering it to her, and seconds later she's topside again.

"Good match," the fairy commends her.

"Good match," Ell repeats, the two shaking hands.

As soon as her back is to him though, her face falls, and as she heads in my direction, she's almost stomping. When she reaches me, I hand her a towel, and she begins sloughing off the caked mud covering every inch of her body. I don't know why she's bothering though, that tiny towel isn't even making a dent.

I lean forward, ready to cheer her up. "I don't think that towel's doing much, but I'd be more than willing to help you clean off, if you get what I'm saying."

Her whole demeanor changes, and she looks up through hooded eyes. "Is that so…" she trails off. I wink, and she steps forward, lazy. Leaning up on her tiptoes, her lips brush my ear, and she whispers seductively, "I want you to clean me with your tongue."

"As you wish, Your Majesty."

"And…because you made a Princess Bride reference, you'll get head when you're done," she toys with me, her tongue dart-ing out and licking across my earlobe.

"And we're done." I grip her hand firmly, and without caring about this stupid fucking competition, I yank her through the crowd.

***

Ari

"Where the hell is Ell?" I ask Nyx and Blake, as we each scan the area. "It's time for her next match. She's already five-minutes late."

"The last time I saw her," Nyx comments, his eyes scanning, "was when she got second place against that Earth fairy."

"Me too," Blake agrees, "but she was pretty dirty from that fight, so maybe she went in to clean up. I'll see if I can find her."

Blake leaves Nyx and I behind, and Nyx and I leave our place, headed to where Ell should be right now. I know she isn't there though, because I was just over there. Her next match is in the aerial combat category, and unfortunately, if she's ten-minutes late, she forfeits.

Worried, I pick up the pace, and as we approach, we spot Quinn off by himself. He begins making his way to us, and after the three of us circle up, I ask if he's seen Ell. He shakes his head no, but then adds, "Come to think of it, I saw her leave her last match with Luke. They went inside, I think."

"Of course they did," I grumble.

Prince Lucas and I might be learning to live with one another, but it still bothers me when she's with him, especially when it's just the two of them. I don't know why that makes it worse, it just does.

Irritated, I turn, ready to storm inside and reprimand her, when I spot Blake pushing his way through the mass of fairies. When the crowd parts, I see Ell practically skipping behind him, and just behind her is the Prince. No one has to tell what they were doing. I can tell by the look on both of their faces.

"You're late," I get on to her, "You almost had to forfeit."

Rolling her eyes and in a low tone, she tells me, "There's always time for sex."

She pushes past me, checking in for her next match, and the rest of us gather up, ready to watch. We blend in with the crowd, and I try to get rid of my bad attitude, focusing on Ell so I can critique her later. It isn't that I want to be mean though. I want her to get better. I want to know without a doubt she can handle anything anyone throws at her. I want to know that her near-death experience is the only one we ever have to go through. At least, until she's old and grey.

Finding a good spot to watch, I notice there's a big crowd for Ell's aerial combat match. Almost everyone who isn't competing in their own match right now is circled up, ready to watch Ell fight. She's their Queen, so I get it. I'm ready to see how she does too.

With a stern face, Rykus signals the beginning of the match, and Ell and her opponent zoom up. They're only allowed to levitate fifty-feet in the air, and must stay at least ten-feet off the ground at all times. That adds to an already difficult skill, a skill that Ell isn't great at.

Even now, as she circles the other competitor, she weaves around, dropping several feet here and there as if she's drunk. Her opponent, a Sprite, laughs at her inadequacies. He throws his head back, his mocking tone only serving to piss her off.

With her cheeks turning red, her feet stretch out behind her as she lurches forward, her fist missing the Sprite by inches. Again he laughs, and with little effort, he thumps Ell in the back of the head as she floats past. He's acting as if this is a game, which pisses me off. This isn't a game. This is to teach them, and to allow them to put what they've already learned to the test. This isn't a fucking joke.

I growl under my breath, wishing I could take a crack at this cocky little shit. "Make a note in his file," I tell Nyx, and he nods, flipping his notepad open, "Remind me later that I don't like this kid."

Someone snorts from behind me, and looking over my shoulder, I see it's Prince Lucas. He nods his head in my direction in a casual manner, like we're friends and I just told a really great joke. I roll my eyes because we are *not* friends. We aren't even acquaintances.

When fairies start shouting though, I let my dislike for the Prince go, turning back to the fight. It's moved a pretty good distance from where it was just moments ago, and now Ell and this Sprite trade blows of magic. Ell takes a fist with an aura of red to the chest, sending her in a tailspin, and I cover up my gasp with a cough.

I'm relieved when she recovers nicely, almost making it look like she meant to soar off spinning. I can tell she's getting madder by the second though, and when her entire body turns purple, I know she's about to finish this fuck off.

With a burst of light, Ell forces her body into a spin as she zooms toward the Sprite. His eyes go wide, and he tries to counter her attack, but her force is too much. She hits him hard, square in the stomach, and her forward momentum causes them to careen across the sky above us. The crowd cheers, because they know their Queen has won, but I don't join in, because another voice has me turning.

I crane my neck, the voice sounding again above the din. "What in the actual Fay is going on here? Are you fairies throwing a party in the middle of a war?"

Helga.

GOING GREY

Ell

And just like that, I'm out of the competition. I *so* wanted to win too. Well, technically, the competition was halted due to Helga's return, but still, I was hoping we had a couple more days so we could finish this out. I was totally gonna win. *What?* I was.

When she put a stop to our fun though, she really gave Ari a talking to, and then she called us all into yet another meeting. Sometimes, I feel like that's all we do anymore. Meet. Meet. Meet. Quickie. Meet. There really needs to be a few more quickies thrown in for good measure. Unfortunately, I know that isn't going to happen any time soon.

Yesterday's meeting was at least a little different from our norm, because I realized Bree wasn't with Helga. When I asked her about it, she said, "I sent her home," and she refused to comment on it further. She even went so far as to swat my hand when I demanded that she elaborate.

On the plus side, she returned with a dagger that this friend of hers imbued with the crown of thorns. She said we need to use the dagger on King Tobin, and if we do, the magic the Dryads are using to protect him will be broken. Apparently, they won't be able to use protection magic on him for as much as a year, because the thorn's magic will actually stay in him for an extended period of time. I was surprised by that. Actually, it's kind of scary knowing there's magic out there like that.

After that, though, Helga wouldn't elaborate much more. I wasn't sure if it was because she didn't know what we needed to do yet, or if she just wasn't supposed to tell us. She hasn't given us any further instruction since then either, and we don't even know when we're supposed to leave. When she didn't tell us to leave right away, I kind of thought we might have time to finish out the competition, but she nixed that pretty quick.

I haven't even seen her today, and we just finished lunch. Ari said he figured she needed to rest, given she just returned from a perilous journey. And yes, he used the word perilous. He is such an adult sometimes.

I eye him across my sitting room while all five of my boys engage in casual conversation. Ari looks tired and worn, but with a quick glance, they all do. I'm sure I look the same. I still haven't put on any weight, and when I showered this morning, I couldn't help but notice I'm even skinnier than I was just a few weeks ago. On top of that, there were bags under my eyes too. I'm way too young for that shit. We need to do what needs to be done before I waste away to nothing. I swear if I start going grey, I quit.

"What are you thinking about?" Blake asks, nudging me.

"Going grey," I tell him, point blank.

He looks confused, but I just shrug and turn, hearing my chamber doors opening. When the door is open fully, Helga steps in, escorted by a guard, and once I nod that it's fine for her to enter, he leaves us, the doors shutting back quickly.

Helga joins our group, taking a seat on the loveseat, her back hunched. "You'll leave tomorrow," she blurts with zero preamble, "You'll head to the UnSeelie capital, and hide out until an opportunity presents itself." She yawns, and leans back in her seat.

"What if an opportunity doesn't present itself?" Ari asks my exact thoughts. "What if the next sacrifice happens before we manage to get to him?"

Sighing heavily, she says, "Don't worry about the next sacrifice. At this point, we only need to worry about the fourth."

"The fourth?" I squeak, "A fairy is going to die, and we shouldn't be worried about stopping it?"

"Many have and will die in order for you to succeed, Ell," she lowers her tone, a hint of understanding in her voice, "This is a fact that you must learn to live with. Being Queen is not easy, and yet, you must do it."

That was more elaborate than I'm used to from her, but it still didn't truly answer my question. I understand what she's trying to say though, but I don't have to like it. Many have already died in our quest, and many more will. I just wish we could stop King Tobin now, not after thousands of my people have died. It seems so wasteful.

Seeming as frustrated as I am, Ari huffs, "So who then? Who goes with us?"

"The six of you," she answers, before stretching her back.

"You've gotta be kidding me?" Ari barks, "You want the six of us to infiltrate the UnSeelie capital, get close to the King, and stab him with absolutely zero backup?"

Helga looks to Quinn, annoyed. "Was I unclear? I felt like I was pretty clear."

Quinn doesn't respond, probably not wanting to get in the fight brewing between Helga and Ari. Ari is right to be concerned though. This is an impossible task. Just getting into the city unseen will be dangerous, but hiding out until we happen to stumble upon King Tobin, that's insane. In fact, I don't think it can be done.

I open my mouth to comment, but Helga snaps at me, "Don't do it. Don't you dare do it. Close your mouth, girly."

My head jerks back in surprise at her tone. I can't tell if she's joking. It sounds like something I would say to be funny, but based on the look secured to her face, I think she's being serious.

"You can't say what you were about to say," Helga adds firmly.

Now I'm not even sure what I was about to say. I think I was going to call this an impossible task, but I can't be sure. It doesn't matter though, because if she says I can't say it, then it probably means she's seen a version of the future where I do, and things don't go well.

But, since I can't even remember what I *was* going to say, I seal my lips, unwilling to screw anything up. Leaning back, I eye Helga, and based on the look in her eyes, she seems happy with my choice.

Too much time passes in eerie silence though, and I think it's because everyone is scared to say the wrong thing. Everyone's shoulders are nearly to their ears, and the whole group is on edge, myself included. Helga is just about the only one that seems relaxed.

After another minute though, Ari asks, "Is there anything else at all that you can tell us?"

Helga thinks, rubbing her chin. "It must be Ell…"

"What does that mean?" Ari asks when Helga's sentence goes unfinished.

"She must be the one to break the magic," Helga adds with a humph.

Opening my mouth, I wait a few seconds before speaking, making sure she doesn't stop me. "So…I'm the one that will stab him with the dagger."

Her head nods once, confirming my thought, and I'm really glad Ari asked her for more details. If he hadn't, would she have not told us that part? That seems like a pretty important part of the plan. I would imagine that in the moment, one of my boys would want to be the one, thinking they were keeping me out of harm's way, and if that happened, then our whole mission would be a failure.

Despite this extra tidbit though, I don't feel good about this. My brain tells me we're walking into an impossible task, blind. My heart tells me something really, really bad is going to happen, and my stomach tells me it's time for dinner. Or dessert. *Whatever.*

***

Ell

With the help of Helga and a few other fairies, we loaded a platform first thing this morning, headed for the UnSeelie capital. Helga said it was okay for us to take the platform to a certain point, but after that, we would need to go the rest of the way on foot.

The fairies that helped us load this morning are riding with us on the transport. Ari asked the twin Ballybogs to go with us for security, plus two Elves I don't know. I recognize one from training, but I don't recall his name. It doesn't matter though, because they won't even be with us the whole time. The two Elves are cloaking our platform anytime we find ourselves over a populated area, but it takes a lot of magic, and may potentially wear them out, so they can't do it the whole time. We just have to hope the wrong person doesn't spot us on this trip.

The trek on the platform won't take long though. By tomorrow morning, we'll be at our drop-off location, and from there, our guides will leave us. As long as we can make it unseen up to that point, the rest of the trip will only take us two days. Of course, that part of the trip won't be the hard part. The hard part will be walking right into the UnSeelie capital like we own the place. We have a plan for that, but our plans don't always work, and this one is sketchy at best.

As of now, we're about halfway through with day one, our platform soaring along with the clouds, the wind whipping my hair. My boys and I are all seated together, while the twins keep an eye below us, and both Elves take turns steering us along.

"Anyone who's strong enough and looking will be able to break our glamour," Nyx worries, lines forming on his forehead, "This doesn't seem like a good plan."

"I know," Ari agrees, "but I'm not sure what other choice we have."

"Listen," Quinn butts in, "the UnSeelie capital isn't like the Seelie one. UnSeelie are all about having fun, engaging in debauchery. Most of the fairies living there will be high or drunk the biggest part of the time. What we really need to worry about are the guards. They'll be stationed throughout the city. Probably more so now, with everything that's going on."

Ari considers that, scratching his chin. "Will they have a heavy force on the outskirts of the city? Could we stay further out? At least while we work on a plan."

"The last time I was there, the answer to that would be yes, but there's no telling what's going on there now. I think we just need to wait and see what the outskirts look like when we get there," Quinn tells him.

I've been relatively quiet up to this point, mulling everything over, but now I have questions of my own, and my first one is for Quinn. "How close are you with your boss? The one that owns the tavern you and Tika worked at." A plan is forming, and when he doesn't answer right away, not understanding why I want to know, I elaborate, "I'm just saying, would he turn you into the guards? Didn't you say there were apartments above the tavern? Could you convince your boss to let you hide out there?"

"I mean…" Quinn starts, thinking it through, "he knows I was forced into the guards, and out of all of my friends, he probably hates the King the most. So, if anyone would let us, it would be him. But…" he pauses, working it all out, "we need to come up with a backstory. One to explain who you five are. If he knows you're Seelie, he won't be okay with that. He's progressive, but not that progressive."

"We can do that," Ari chimes in, "Does he know your whole family? What if we're cousins or something?"

"He doesn't," Quinn confirms, "but that's a lot of cousins." He chuckles, and then adds, "Let's say Ell is my cousin, and you four are her boyfriends and leave it at that. The closer to the truth we stay, the easier it will be."

"Good thinking," Ari agrees, "So it's settled. We'll see what things look like on the outskirts of the city, and glamoured, if we can make it through safely, we'll head to this tavern."

Heads around the circle bob as one of the Elf guards approaches us. "We have a problem."

***

Ell

Okay, the problem wasn't as bad as I thought, but still. I'm so tired of trucking right along, and then; bam! Shit is constantly hitting the fan in my life, and I'm completely over it. Just once I want things to go smoothly, and not hear a single person say, 'Houston, we have a problem'.

At least this time was a mini problem and not a colossal problem. One of the cities on our path was swarming with Un-Seelie guards. Even where we were, about twenty miles out, the guards had camps set up. The Elves' magic had worked though, keeping us hidden, but it was still scary passing over so many. If they had spotted us, there's no way we would've come out of the fight alive. There were just too many of them.

The Elves kept us hidden until we were well past the city, but because of the scare, we decided to go a little further tonight than we had originally planned. The extra miles, and the scare earlier has my nerves on red-alert, and it's truly worn me out, so I'm just ready to get some sleep.

We landed less than five-minutes ago, and Nyx, Blake, and I are huddled together against a massive oak tree. Ari said we couldn't have a fire, and while it irritated me, I knew he was right to make the decision. It's cold here though, which means we probably won't get much sleep. The main reason we stopped wasn't for us though, it was for the Elves. They can only keep at it for so long, which means they need the night to recharge their metaphorical battery. We need them at top performance, so if that means we have to sit here in the cold, then so be it.

The Elves are kicked back not far from me, their hands behind their head, and I can tell from the slow rise and fall of their chests they're already asleep. That's good too. The faster they recharge, the faster we can head out. Ari said we wouldn't even wait until morning. As soon as the Elves feel like they're good to go, we'll head out again.

While they sleep and I snuggle, Ari and the twins are on first watch. They're spread out around our makeshift camp, keeping an eye on our surroundings. I doubt we will run into anyone this far out, but I'd rather be safe than sorry.

As I continue to rest, the sky above us is cloudy, casting us in total darkness, making our stay here even more eerie. I'm not one to be afraid of the dark, but with everything going on, when the wind howls above us, I flinch, clutching Blake's bicep. He pulls me tighter in response, and Nyx moves with me on my other side.

"We're fine," Blake assures me, "They're keeping watch. Plus, Quinn and Lucas aren't asleep either. Get some rest."

His words are comforting, but that isn't what has my attention, because Blake just referred to Luke as Lucas. I think that might be the first time. All of them still call him the Prince or Prince Lucas. Well, except for Quinn, that is. But he wasn't here for the whole cheating debacle, so it's different for him.

I relax slightly with the thought. They're starting to move on and forgive. I haven't wanted to push them, but I *was* starting to get frustrated with how long it was taking. I know I need to be patient though, especially in light of everything, but as we all know, patience isn't my forte. It's just that I know in my heart these boys are going to best friend so hard when this is all through, and I want to get to it already. I want to get to the point where they all get matching tattoos or some shit. *OMG.* Matching tattoos. *Yup,* we are totally doing it.

JEDI MIND TRICK THINGY

Ell

We parted ways with our traveling companions this morning, and now we're on foot. If all goes smoothly, we should be in the capital in two days. We haven't decided if we want to push through and arrive late tomorrow night, or wait, pulling into the city the next morning. Ari said we could play it by ear. I'm for getting where we're going and fast, but that's how I think about all things, so I'm just going to let the group decide.

So far though, the six of us have walked quietly for most of the day, sticking to wooded areas as much as possible. For the first leg of our walk, we won't come across any towns or villages, but no matter what we do, tomorrow we'll have to pass through or near at least a couple. Quinn seems confident it won't be a big deal, but I can't help but worry.

"Let's take a five-minute break," Ari calls from the front of the group, pulling me out of my thoughts.

We all slow, and once we circle up, we each take turns getting a swig from one of the canteens. Once I've had my fill, I check out our surroundings. The woods here look the same as the woods we've been walking through all damn day. Trees, trees, and more trees. Oh, and there's a bush, which is basically just a short tree, so like I said; trees.

Annoyed, I circle around a grouping of, yup, you guessed it, trees, and I notice Nyx is following me. Turning on him, I ask, "Can I help you, sir?"

"I'm on Ell duty," he chuckles, trying to act like he's kidding, but I know better. "Don't mind me. Just keep doing what you're doing," he encourages, waving his hand in my direction.

I huff, refusing to comment and start a fight, because I know it was Ari that insisted on this measure. It's so annoying though. I don't need a babysitter, but it isn't worth arguing over. I'm just going to take Nyx's advice, and keep doing what I'm doing.

Shrugging it off, I continue on in the direction I was headed, and after a few minutes, I come to an enormous tree that sticks out from the rest. It might be one of the largest trees I've ever seen, with dozens of branches jutting off from the main trunk, and leaves as big around as my head. It reminds me of something though, but I can't quite put my finger on it.

As I circle around, trying to figure out why it seems so familiar, something niggles in the back of my brain. It's like my mind is trying to tell me something, but I'm just not getting it. It's probably nothing anyway. It most likely looks familiar because we've been surrounded by nothing but trees all day. So, brushing it off, I spin, facing Nyx.

"Looks like the pixie tree," Nyx comments.

And with his words, I realize that's why it looked familiar. It does look like the tree we lived under, the one that Bree calls home. I know this isn't the same one though, even though I wish it was. I miss my friend, and I wish she was with us right now. At the very least, she could provide some much needed comic relief from Ari's stoicism.

My heart sinks a little knowing I may not see Bree for a very long time, but I tamp down on that as Nyx and I work our way around the beast of a tree. When we finally make it to the other side though, we both freeze. We aren't the only one's frozen in our steps though. A Pixie, her hair a bright-orange, stands stock-still, her jaw dropped and her eyes wide with terror. I know why too, even though I shouldn't. She isn't her normal size. In fact, as she tries to slowly back away, she's taller than me.

"We mean you no harm," I assure her, my hands out in a soothing gesture, "I promise."

She isn't convinced though, and she continues to back away from us. She readies her magic, and if I don't fix this fast, I'll have to fight one of my dearest friend's people. I don't want to do that, so I try to think of what I can say to stop this.

And then it hits me. "You have a hive mind. Your Queen knows me. In fact, we're best friends."

She still backs away, but I can tell my words give her pause. "I don't know what you're talking about. What Queen?"

Oh, right. We aren't supposed to know about that either.

"Listen, we know about your Queen, just like we know you have the ability to grow full-sized. You're a Pixie. Don't you think we'd be more surprised by your current size if this was news to us?"

She seems to think that over, but she doesn't back down. "I don't know any Queens, and you're trespassing in Pixie territory. You know we have a hive mind, which means you know I can call thousands of Pixies out of that tree. You and your friend won't stand a chance." Her tone is confident, and her back is now straight, almost ready for the fight.

"Well it isn't just them," Ari chimes in, walking up with Luke, Blake, and Quinn right behind him.

"But," I jump in, my hands still out, "we don't want to fight you, or your hive. I know Bree personally. I'm telling you, use your little Jedi mind trick thingy. You'll see I'm telling the truth."

I force my hand across Ari's chest, begging him with my eyes to back off. He nods, and our group takes a collective step back, trying to look less intimidating. I don't know if it worked, but she hasn't started fighting us yet, and a horde of Pixies hasn't shown up, so I think we might be okay.

Putting a few more feet between us, the orange-haired Pixie's eyes go somewhat vacant as we stand as still as possible.

No one says a word, the Pixie included, until finally she looks at me thoughtfully. Her head tilts left and then right, and then she's nodding.

"This isn't a safe place for you," she tells us, suddenly on our side. "Is it just the six of you?"

"Yes," I confirm, bobbing my head and feeling relieved that we avoided an unnecessary fight.

"Alright, well Bree says we should help you, so stand still."

Come again.

***

Blake

Damn it. I hate getting shrunk. Honestly, it's the worst thing I've gone through since being in Fay. Half the time those little assholes don't even give you a warning first, and this time was no different.

Within seconds, our group of six was no bigger than my hand, and once again my head was too big. Well, bigger than everyone else's anyway. I used to think Bree did that shit on purpose because I'm a human, but now I'm not so sure.

After making us little though, the Pixie guided us into her home, and I found myself reeling. In all the time we stayed with Bree, not once did she take us inside. We stayed outside, or in our temporary home, but never did she invite us in. I never thought that was weird. Really, I was glad, because it meant not having to get little. But now, I'm kind of pissed, because this place is fucking awesome. It is, in fact, a fully functioning city. The center is hollowed out, and their homes are burrowed into the walls of the tree. The first little home we passed not only had balconies overlooking everything below, but it also had a slide next to the front door, and when I followed it, it ended in a tiny little pool of water. They have fucking pools. It was and is insane, and my mind is forever blown.

I'm still not over it hours later as we sit down to an impressive feast surrounded by dozens of tiny Pixies. This clan has their own leader, and he sits at the head of the table, eying us thoughtfully. His stare makes me uncomfortable though, so I dart my eyes across the impressive spread in front of us.

There's definitely fairy meat on the table, but there's also pig, along with every fruit and vegetable you can think of. We each have a tiny goblet too, filled to overflowing with fairy wine, and while I've been nursing mine, Ell's already finished three glasses.

Speaking of Ell, she's already stuffing her face, and I can't help but laugh at her expense. She grins over her corn-on-the-cob, and I wink, but then I look away from her. I don't even know where to start, but when I take too long, Ell starts piling food on my plate. She hands me my own piece of corn when she's satisfied, and finally, I start eating.

The rest of the guys are immersed in their food too, as the leader clears his throat. "I'm Elron," he introduces himself, his tone formal.

"Hi," Ell greets, waving, "I'm Ell."

Elron tries to suppress a grin, but it's no use, because she's just too fucking adorable. "You should know, King Tobin has increased security throughout the city. It won't be easy to get in unseen," he tells us.

"How did you know…Oh, right, hive mind," Ell comes to the conclusion on her own. "So…then what do we do? How do we get in?"

"Where were you planning on hiding out?" he asks her, but it's Quinn who answers, "A tavern near the city center. I know the owner." He holds his wrist up, showing off his UnSeelie mark.

Gasps sound around the room, and everyone but Elron goes on the defense. With everyone freaking out, I notice none of the Pixies have marks. I assumed this far into UnSeelie territory they were either UnSeelie or at least supporters, but given their reaction, I'm betting I was wrong.

"Calm down," Elron orders, "He is one of hers, and *she* is protected by Queen Bree."

I never thought I'd say this, but I'm grateful for Ell and Bree's friendship. It's probably the only reason we aren't dead right now, or at least fighting for our lives. Pixies might be assholes, but it's pretty clear they're also loyal as hell. Well, loyal to *their* Queen anyway. And their Queen is loyal to mine, which has worked out in our favor more than once.

Most everyone has settled down now, with only a few remaining anxious, but with little thought, Elron brushes their fears off and continues, "As you can see, there is no love for the UnSeelie here. King Tobin cares only for himself, and not for his people. We claim neither Seelie, *nor* UnSeelie."

That's interesting. I wonder how they live so close and manage to stay out from under the King and his supporters.

"Moving on," Elron says, motioning for someone to bring him more fairy wine, "You won't be able to make it to the city center in one go, at least not safely. I would suggest spending a day or two on the city's edge, get your bearings, and gradually work your way to where you want to be." He taps his chin thoughtfully, and then looking at Quinn, he asks, "Are you familiar with The Grotto?"

"You mean the drug den?" Quinn's head jerks back.

Elron nods. "The very one. You'll be able to get rooms there easily, and no one would think to look for the Seelie Queen there. Not to mention, anyone staying there will be too high to notice her or break her glamour."

"That's not a bad idea," Quinn agrees, as Ari asks, "But will that be safe for Ell, for all of us?"

"Safer than what you were planning," Elron answers, almost mocking Ari.

His tone didn't go unnoticed either, and Ari's jaws ticks as he forces himself to keep quiet. I'm just hoping Ell can do the same. Her nose has turned red, and her eyes are slit nearly closed. She eyes the Pixie leader, and I can feel the hostility rolling off of her in waves.

Before she can go off though, Elron adds, "We'll put you up

for the night, and then you can head out tomorrow morning." And with that, he rises from his seat, and so does everyone else, except for us, that is.

We're the only ones left now, and I see the moment Ell realizes what that means. All the food is still out, and it's all ours.

"Mine, all mine," she cackles.

****

Ell

Elron was like most Pixies, a real bitch, but he did put us up for the night and give us some pretty decent intel. Well, at least, I think he did. I guess we won't know if it was good until we make it to the capital tomorrow morning. But regardless, we had a warm, dry place to sleep, and our bellies were full. We even had enough privacy so I could get in some much needed coitus.

Did you know coitus is a word that means sex? I didn't. It was news to me when Blake said it jokingly last night. And now, it's my new favorite word, and I can't stop using it.

"Coitus…coitus…coitus," I sing, humming in-between the words.

Nyx and Luke chuckle, but Ari just rolls his eyes, as he groans, "You know, I really wish you wouldn't have taught her that word."

"Sorry," Blake apologizes, sheepishly.

"I'm not. It's the best word ever," I hum, positive I'm right, and then turning to Blake, I add, "Teach me some more sexy words, oh wise one."

Blake snorts, shaking his head. "Well, there's…"

"No!" Ari and Luke shout at the same time. "Don't do it," Ari begs, "Please, I can't take it."

"God, you suck," I tell him, sticking my tongue out for good measure, "This trip sucks, and you suck. You suck all the fun out of everything."

"I'll let you suck something," Nyx quips, his eyebrows pumping.

"I *would*...but Ari is too busy sucking on his own." I purse my lips in Ari's direction, raising one brow for emphasis.

With his face set in stone, he raises his right hand and flips me the bird. My jaw drops because I don't think he's ever done that before. He doesn't even do it right. It's like his pinkie thinks it should be out too, like he's fancy.

I try to hold it back, but I can't. I keel over, a howl of laughter forcing its way out of my mouth. Blake and Nyx are also laughing, and when my hiccups start, Quinn lets go too. Everyone is struggling to breathe now, more than one of us keeled over, and Ari does *not* seem amused.

Not wanting to piss him off too badly, I try to stand upright, but I can't get it together. I do, however, catch Luke smirking, trying to push back his own laughter.

"*What*?" Ari insists, annoyed.

"You..." I struggle to form words, "You don't...your pinkie was out...I. Can't. Breathe."

"Hey guys," Nyx draws our attention, raising his pinkie in the air, "I'm *fancy*. My name is *Arion*."

Tears pour down my face, and I hear Luke lose it, unable to hold it back any longer. When we hear him snort, Blake has to use the trunk of a nearby tree for support, and I fall into him, unable to stand on my own two feet. It's only made worse when Nyx starts prancing around in a circle, his pinkie high while his other hand rests on his hip. He bounces his hips back and forth, with his nose held high.

"*Whatever*," Ari grumbles, "You guys suck." He turns his back on us, setting off in the direction we were originally heading, and refusing to look back.

"Oh...Ari, come on," I call at his back, "It was a joke."

We're all still laughing, and when he flips us off again over his shoulder, my hiccups return, and I can't stop the snort that tumbles out. I don't know what it is about snort-laughs, but they're funny as shit, and it only makes us laugh harder.

After way too long, each of us try to move forward, following Ari, but every time we make it two feet, Nyx or I one holds our pinkie out, and we all lose it again.

"God," I swear, "that might've been the best thing that's ever happened."

"At least in the top ten," Nyx chuckles.

"You guys are assholes." Ari shouts from up ahead, "Let's go!"

Nyx catches my eye and mouths, 'let's go' in a mocking way, his head bobbing back and forth, and I lean into him, his arm going around my shoulder, as I whisper, "Like I said, sucks the fun out of everything."

ELL DRANK THE KOOL-AID

Ell

Not five-minutes ago, we crested a hill, and at the bottom was the capital. It stretches on as far as I can see, surprising me. I never imagined it would be this nice, or to be honest, this big. I mean, it isn't as big as the Seelie capital, but it's damn sure bigger than I expected.

To the right, are buildings that stretch high in the sky, their tops scraping the clouds. To the left, home after home. And in the center, far from where we are now, I can just make out the turrets of the UnSeelie palace. As far away as it is now, and as big as it seems, I can tell it rivals my own home.

"Damn," Nyx muses, "this is nicer than I thought it would be."

"Yeah," Quinn agrees with him, "but wait until you get down in there. It's kind of like a Monet." Everyone but Blake and I look confused, and he adds, "He was a human. He painted these paintings that were beautiful from far away, but when you get close up, you can see all the imperfections."

Everyone seems surprised by his explanation, myself included, so when Quinn looks at me, almost sheepishly, I grin, turned on by this little smarty pants. I know full well who Monet is. Don't judge, but I'm kind of an art connoisseur. So, knowing one of my boys is into art too, that's exciting.

I brush past him, my hip bumping his. "You. Me. Sex Trivial Pursuit."

"Huh?"

"You'll see," I flirt, winking.

Sex Trivial Pursuit isn't a real thing. I just made it up, but it's gonna be so awesome. I can't wait.

"Circle up," Ari orders, cutting off my excitement.

With his order, everyone moves to his side, and we squat down in a perfect circle on the top of the hill, the city at my back as Ari grunts and leans over to pick up a stick. He hands it to Quinn, expecting him to draw us a map, I guess, and when Quinn starts, making a big circle for the palace, my guess turns out to be true. When he finishes the circle though, he moves on to drawing a big X. The X represents where we are now, in comparison to where we need to be.

After that, he draws a few more buildings in the dirt, and then he says, "The Grotto...it's *here*. We can come down this side...*here*...and stay in this residential area until we get...*here*." He draws a small triangle in the dirt, and then thinking out loud, he adds, "Or...if we run into any trouble through *here*, which is possible, we can circle back through this area over-...*here*. It's a shopping district."

"Okay, looks like a decent plan," Ari commends him, slapping him on the back before looking behind us, and asking, "Should we wait until dark?"

"No," Quinn insists, confident, "I think it will look more suspicious if we're sneaking around at night. Ell can glamour herself, and honestly, she can probably glamour all of you too."

"No way," I dispute, "I've never done that. Why can't they glamour themselves?"

"Well," he explains, "your magic is stronger than any of ours. It might take a lot out of you, but your magic will be the hardest to break. I don't see any point in glamouring myself, given we want people to see my mark, but *they* need to be glamoured, and their magic might not be strong enough." He nods to each of my boys. "It's just a thought. But...I think you can do it, and it will be the safest thing."

Hesitant, I look at Ari, and he nods. *Ugh.* "Fine," I give in, "I'll at least try."

Quinn grins. "With everyone glamoured, we walk right in the city like we're supposed to be there, and then we head straight for The Grotto. Once there, I can start asking around and checking out the city, see how much security has been increased. Then, once we know the safest route, we'll head for the tavern. It's pretty close to the palace. In fact, King Tobin came in there once. That's how I ended up forced into the guard."

As Quinn finishes, Ari scans the group, and asks, "Thoughts?"

I look at Blake, and he shrugs. "Hey, I'm just along for the ride."

A few chuckle at that, and Luke weighs in, "Sounds decent, at least with the information we have. We just need to be ready to be flexible if something happens."

"Agreed." Nyx inclines his head.

"Right then," Ari finishes up, and looks at me, "You're up, Ellie."

Fear builds in my chest because I know this all rests on me. We all know my magic is totally unreliable. She has a mind of her own to say the least. So, what if she decides halfway to this drug den that she doesn't want to play anymore and disappears, the boy's glamours right along with her? That's a lot of pressure.

"I..." I stutter, unsure if I can handle the responsibility.

"Ellie," Ari coos, "it is or it isn't. If it doesn't work, we'll improvise." He squeezes my hand, and a tiny amount of stress washes away.

Feeling slightly better, I look around the circle, seeing the supportive faces of my boys, and I suck in a deep breath. Pushing it back out, I slap my hands on my knees, mentally preparing myself to kill it.

"Here goes nothing..."

***

Ari

Things never go smoothly with Ell's magic, or Ell in general, but it definitely could've been worse. It took her a few tries, and the magic dropped the second we stepped foot in the city, but before anyone saw she was able to get it back.

Each of us were glamoured, including the glaring Seelie marks on our wrists. Quinn is the only exception, and it was *his* mark that got us past the front door of the Grotto, easily. In fact, no one even questioned it when he got us two rooms upstairs.

Both of our rooms sit in the far northern corner of the nearly derelict building, and as we worked our way through the drug den downstairs, I've never held Ell so tight. I also couldn't help but notice she looked like a child in a candy store, looking at everything and everyone with wide eyes, as if she was learning as we hurried to the stairs and up.

We got two rooms so it didn't look suspicious, but we have no intention of using the second. We're all crowded up in the corner room, and Ell is resting after her excessive magic use. The rest of us are too nervous to sleep, myself included. This is by far the most dangerous thing we've ever done. We literally walked into the lion's den, with no real way out if shit hits the fan. We are cut off from any help, and if we're caught, I can't even imagine what the King would do to Ell.

"We'll have to go downstairs some," Quinn comments, pulling me out of my thoughts, "If we don't they could get suspicious."

"So what..." I trail off, and then figuring out what he's suggesting, I add, "So you're saying we need to go down and blend in...it's a fucking drug den. You're suggesting we take the Queen of all..."

"I know what I'm suggesting," Quinn interrupts. "I can go

down by myself, maybe that would work, but the more we blend in, the less likely anyone takes notice of us, including the fairy sober staff."

I can't believe it when he chuckles at his own word play. "This is insane," I worry, looking at Ell, curled in a ball on the bed with her hands clutched to her chest.

"I know," Quinn agrees, "but this is my home. You don't have to listen to me, but I'm telling you, I know what I'm talking about. We got rooms at a drug den. If we weren't wanting to use and drink, party, then as far as everyone here is concerned, we're either hiding out or…"

"Or what?" Blake asks when Quinn doesn't finish his sentence.

"We're either hiding out or here to use, and if we aren't then they're going to wonder why we didn't get a room at a local motel or tavern, especially the staff. They *will* take notice."

"Shit," I curse, running my hand through my hair and realizing I need a shower. "Okay, but we all go down together, and no one uses. We can have a few drinks, maybe a fairy bomb or two, but nothing more than that. We can't risk letting our guard down, even for a second."

"Agreed," the Prince says, bobbing his head.

"We'll need to watch Ell like a hawk," Nyx insists, and Blake nods.

"There won't be any guards down there, unless maybe they're off duty," Quinn tells us.

"That's not what I meant," Nyx explains, "Give Ell two seconds down there, and she'll be in trouble. We need to keep any hard drugs far away from her."

"Ohhh," Quinn hums in understanding.

"Definitely," Blake agrees, eying her.

"Do they serve food?" I ask Quinn, and when he says, "Yes," I add, "We'll go down for dinner then, maybe an early dinner. Eat, have a couple drinks, be seen. Then we'll head back up, and you," I point to Quinn, "can hang out and see what you can find out."

"Got it," he confirms.

"Alright," I peek at Ell, still sleeping, "we'll wake her in a bit, but…someone always has eyes on her. Period."

We all nod in agreement, but my head jerks toward Ell when she says, "You guys know I can hear you, right?"

***

Ell

"If you're a good girl…I'll personally reward you later," Ari tells me, his hand sliding discreetly across my ass as we descend the steps to the first floor of The Grotto.

"Promise?" I sigh, leaning back against him.

His mouth flies past my ear. "Promise."

Hearing the guys earlier, talking about me like I wasn't there, I had planned to show out tonight, but with Ari's promise, I'm thinking I might try to behave. Oh, I'll have a little fun, but not enough to lose my reward. I can be discreet. Probably.

We make it downstairs, our whole group following Quinn as he leads us to a corner booth. He slips the waitress a few coins, and she nods, allowing us to have the spot. Since he had to pay for the table, I assume it must be a desirable one, which is odd, considering this whole place looks like a shit-hole.

I let it go though, and we all crowd in, me in the middle, just as the waitress returns with a handful of menus. She hands them out as she asks for our drink orders, and holding back, I only order one glass of fairy wine. Each of the guys except for Ari order wine too, and I guess he's the DD for the night. AKA, designated dad.

After the waitress leaves, I check out the menu. It's just a single slip of paper, the front covered in handwritten script, the back blank. The options are pretty simple and straight to the point. They have pheasant, pig, a couple sides, and something called the chef's surprise.

My eyes widen in excitement because I know what I'm

ordering, but before I can even mention it, Quinn thrusts his hand out. "No. Not the special. Don't anyone order the special," he barks, firm.

Damn it.

Fine. Pheasant it is.

The waitress returns a short while later with our drinks, and we place our order, but before she even leaves the table, I've downed my wine and asked for another. She nods her head, turning and leaving to place our order.

Once she disappears, Ari gives me a look from the end of the booth, and I shrug. "High tolerance," I tell him, having to yell over the blaring music and shouts of the patrons.

I don't wait for him to respond either, instead I crane my neck so I can check out the room. It's dark in here, almost too dark, and I can barely see past our table. On the far side of the room though, there's a bar lit up with a single spotlight. The bartender stands behind the counter and spins a bottle in his hand, tossing it in the air and catching it behind his back. I squeal, wishing I was closer.

My eyes leave him when he finishes his little show, and I check out the rest of the customers. There are dozens of fairies in here, and they all look a little worse for wear, some more than others. The booth in the opposite corner from ours is filled with eight fairies. Some kiss, while others play what looks like a drinking game, but instead of drinks, they use various drugs laid out in front of them, displayed in glass containers. A green orb of dim light floats above the center of their table, and I wonder why we don't have one.

Nyx bumps my shoulder. "Don't get any ideas."

"Har. Har." I roll my eyes his way.

"What are you, a pirate now?" he jokes.

"I said har, not argh," I bite back. "You know what? Forget it."

He chuckles, and Blake, on my other side, does too.

Ignoring them, I eye our waitress as she gets slapped on the ass trying to carry trays with our food perched precariously on top. I jerk to my feet, but I'm blocked in by the table and my boys. I'm ready to defend her, but Nyx grabs me, pulling me back. I try to pull away, but the waitress turns to the offender, giving him a wink and mouthing, 'later'.

I'm confused by her reaction, and Quinn leans across the table. "If they work here, there's a reason. Nothing will happen to her that she doesn't want." He jerks his head to the wall across from us, and I notice two beefy Trolls standing with their chests covered in too tight, black t-shirts, their arms crossed tight against their chests. Their faces are set in a scowl, and they scan the waitresses as they flit about. "Security," Quinn explains, "It isn't total mayhem here like you'd expect."

As he leans back, our waitress drops off our food, along with my wine, and when she walks away, she goes straight to the fairy that smacked her ass, making it obvious Quinn was right. So with that resolved, I reclaim my seat and we eat our food in silence.

As I cram a bite in my mouth, the boys all keep their eyes on our surroundings. I can tell they're paranoid, and rightfully so, but my magic is cooperating, which means the glamours disguising them right now are good. I'm not saying we're safe, I'm just saying the more out of place we act, the more fairies will take notice.

Luckily, the rest of our meal passes in nervous silence, with no drama, but as I finish the last bite of food, Nyx swats my hand away. *What*? I didn't say it was *my* last bite of food. And now, I'm eyeing the roll on Blake's plate. Seeing me, he chuckles, and as I devour the squishy goodness, the music is turned up and several fairies cheer.

A large group of patrons gather together in the middle of the room, and they sway back and forth. As they do, a waitress walks past them with a tray, and they each down something in a rainbow colored glass. Once they swallow, a puff of pink escapes their lips, and I'm instantly begging. "Gimme. Please."

"Not that," Quinn insists. "How about a fairy bomb?"

"Ugh," I throw my hands in the air, "I guess if that's my only option."

Quinn shakes his head and leaves our booth, fighting his way through the hazy room and pushing up to the bar. He orders, and a minute later, he returns with a small tray. He hands everyone but Ari a fairy bomb, and using the sticks Quinn provides, we all down the gelatinous blob. Almost instantly, my head swims, and the room spins. This is just what I needed. Now, to blend in.

Pushing Nyx and realizing Ari won't move out of his way, I wait until everyone is distracted, and I duck under the table, crawling out and away as fast as I can. I disappear in the crowd, my high ramping up with the thumbing base. Everyone around me sways, and I close my eyes, throwing my head back.

I'm just getting into it when hands slide across my hips, pulling me back. I smile, working my ass back and forth and leaning back against Quinn. I turn over my shoulder slowly, looking at him seductively as he moves our bodies in rhythm with the beat, and my eyes roll back as the crowd closes in on us. We're surrounded now, and the temperature increases, both from the mess of bodies and the lust building between Quinn and I. This is my idea of fun, so I just hope Ari doesn't put an end to it.

The song ends and a faster one begins, but Quinn and I continue with our slow, sensual dance. As we grind, a waitress walks by with one of those rainbow glasses, and before Quinn can stop me, I snatch it, downing the contents. Flavors explode on my tongue, seeping into the roof of my mouth as Quinn curses behind me.

I roll my body across his, turning to face him. "Don't be an Ari. I don't need an Ari right now."

His response is a bruising kiss against my lips, and when he pulls back, a second body slides in at my back. Luke presses his cheek to mine, and the three of us sway in unison, totally oblivious to anything going on around us.

Another song begins, and the floor grows even more crowded. I don't mind though, and I turn back, kissing Luke. When I pull away, I steal a kiss from Quinn too. This goes on for long enough that I lose track of time. They continue to trade me back and forth, and it gets so confusing, I suddenly find myself kissing both of them at the same time. Both of their tongues toy with mine, even grazing across one another, and desire fills me. My body tingles, and all I can think about is getting back to the room, but when I try to pull them away, they both yank me back.

Quinn leans in, his face close to mine. "Not yet, Ell."

I want to pout, but I hold it back, willing to enjoy them here, like this, a little longer, but as Luke grinds his crotch against my ass, and my pussy clenches, I want him in me right now.

They press in closer, and with all these bodies and as high as everyone is, I doubt anyone is paying any attention to us. Clearly that's what Quinn and Luke are thinking too, because when I turn back to Quinn, my head falling back on Luke's shoulder, Quinn slips his hand down inside my jeans. Wiggling, he sneaks his fingers inside my panties, and then he's inside me, thrusting in and out.

I'm so engrossed in the feel of it, I don't notice a third fairy join us. When I breathe in though, I know it isn't one of mine, and my eyes jerk open. My eyes connect with an Elf just as my body begins to shake. I'm so close to that peak, but before my boys can do anything about it, the stranger grips my mouth, forcing it open and cramming a pink liquid inside.

And that, ladies and gentlemen, is how Ell drank the Kool-Aide. *Fuck.*

The liquid burns all the way down, and that's how you know it's going to be bad. It wasn't necessary though. I knew it was bad without the burn or the fact that it was a strange fairy doing it.

Why would someone do that anyway? I get that everyone is high and clearly stupid, but damn.

Madder than me, Luke pushes me into Quinn, his arm going around me and securing me to his chest. Luke grips the fairy's collar, slamming him against the wall, the glass mirror above his head shattering. He takes two swings, his fist connecting with the fairy's nose both times, and it's then that I realize Quinn's hand is still in my pants.

Maybe I'm a sociopath, or a masochist, or whatever, but watching Luke beat the shit out of that fairy while Quinn's fingers are inside me, well, let's just say, I may or may not be grinding against his hand right now, seeking release.

I'm almost there when two security guards rush up, pulling Luke and the other fairy apart. I watch, my body vibrating, and a new high comes over me, a new high in the form of a very aggressive orgasm.

As my release comes to an end, I'm surprised when the guards don't kick Luke out, or the other fairy for that matter, and when Luke turns back, he searches me out, his eyes dropping down to my pelvis, moving. He storms, mad, toward me, his lips slamming into mine, hard. His dick grinds against my side, and with me being so jacked up, his movements manage to push me over the cliff a second time.

The high continues for way too long, and I realize this isn't the orgasm. This is whatever that damn fairy shoved down my throat. I'm not about to let a good high go to waste though, so I rub my hand across my breasts. It feels fucking amazing, but before I can remove my top, Luke lifts me, carrying me away from Quinn and upstairs, my other boys, minus Quinn, right behind us.

NURSING A SERIOUS HANGOVER

Ell

"What were you thinking!?!" Ari shouts way too loud, the morning after my fun-filled night.

"Dude," I whisper, rubbing my head, "I'm nursing a serious hangover right now, so I'm gonna need you to not."

He growls in frustration, stomping across the room, and I can tell by the look on his face that he's preparing an epic rant.

Can a fairy just get a sec? Clearly not, because he's now going off, and I have no clue what he's saying. It sounds like gibberish at this point, and I'm not sure if it's because he's irate or a result of my hangover.

I grumble, falling back into Blake's arms, burrowing in and pulling the blanket back up. I'm allowed to have one fun night. Damn it. Am I right? Yeah, I am. I've been through a lot, and we needed to blend in. I did that. Sure, I probably did it a little *too* well, but dang, that last part wasn't even my fault.

"Ell," Ari calls for my attention, "are you even listening?"

"Do you want me to lie to you?" I ask from under the covers.

He growls, and I hear him chunk something across the room. I know he's been waiting all night to get onto me for what happened, because I was way too fucked up when we got back to the room, and I passed out within minutes. There might have been some heavy petting, but that also might have been a dream. I'll have to ask later, when Ari isn't chastising me for all my life choices.

The door to our room opens and closes, putting an end to Ari's tirade. I sneak a peek, and finding Quinn just coming in,

I wiggle so I can get a better look. He plops down in the wood-backed chair, kicking his shoes off and looking exhausted.

With a sigh, he asks, "Do you want the good news or the bad news first?"

"Shit," Ari swears, as Nyx answers, "Good."

"This side of the city hasn't seen much of an increase in security from what I could tell. I spoke to a few fairies last night, and that seemed to be the general consensus. Plus, I pretty much confirmed it when I went out this morning."

"Wait," I stop him, "Is this the first time you've been back?"

He nods his head, and then Ari insists he give us the bad news. "Well…" He leans forward, resting his elbows on his knees and scrubbing a hand down his face. "King Tobin tripled the guards in and around the palace. That includes the block where the tavern is. So…I don't know if that's a viable option for us now."

"Why increase security that much? Unless…" Ari trails off.

"He's expecting us," I guess.

Quinn agrees, "Yeah, that's what I'm thinking. We know he has a seer, so it isn't out of the question that he already knows we're here. Or, at least, he knows we're coming at some point." He pauses, a new look coming over his face. "Now…do you want the *really* bad news?"

"What the hell?" Ari curses. "It gets worse?"

"Ell's face is plastered all over the capital." Quinn sinks back in his seat, exhausted.

"But she's glamoured," Blake offers, his arms cinching tighter around me, "They aren't seeing the real her."

"True," Quinn nods, "but it means they know she, specifically, is here or coming, and it means they're looking for her. Any guards with enough power will be watching for glamours. If Ell stumbles across the wrong guard, well, that's it."

Curses ring out around the room, and I sit up, my head pounding, which forces me to lean back again, just pushing the covers down. Luke and Nyx are whispering to one another, Ari, of course, paces, and Quinn stares at me as I pull Blake's arm tighter to my chest

This isn't good, but I think the boys are overacting, at least a little. "Listen," I call for their attention, "there isn't anything we can do about it now. We have to be here. It's not like we can leave. We just need to be smarter about things from this point forward." I try sitting up again, and this time it doesn't feel like my head is going to explode. "It's pretty cold here, right? So...I can wear a cloak. The Elves, especially, wear them all the time, so it won't stand out. With the five of you around me, we can just blend in with the crowd and head for the tavern. The faster we get there, the faster we can hunker down while we work out the rest of our plan."

"It's too risky," Ari insists adamantly.

Frustrated, I throw my hands in the air, dropping them back down with a huff. "What then, Ari? We can't stay *here*. It's too far away from the palace. There is no way we'll just accidentally run into King Tobin this far out. Eventually we have to make our way to the palace. What does it matter if it's now or later? Plus..." I pause, thinking through my thoughts as Ari continues to shake his head, "They've got a seer, and we pretty much know they know I'm coming. The longer we take to make our move, the more likely they are to know I'm here." I sigh. "Our only advantage right now is that they might not know I'm already here, Ari."

Quinn points at me. "Actually, she might be right about that." Ari looks at him, motioning for him to go on. "Sure there are wanted posters up all over the city, but if they thought she was already here, *knew* she was already here, they would be scouring every inch of this city."

Ari seems to really think that through, as Nyx agrees, "That's a good point."

"Shit," Ari mumbles under his breath, worry evident on his face. His cheeks, sprayed with freckles, are a deep shade of crimson, and tiny beads of sweat are breaking out on his forehead. I'm not sure I've ever seen him this worried, but finally, he grumbles, "fine" and the rest of the group agrees.

"Okay," Quinn says, "I'll go purchase everyone a cloak from the shop on the corner."

"We brought cloaks though," Nyx reminds him.

"Yeah, but Ell's...and probably Lucas' too are far too fine a fabric for average fairies in the UnSeelie capital. We need to blend in. And those two, at the very least, are gonna stick out like a sore thumb." Without waiting on anyone to respond or give him permission, Quinn stands, and with a single backward glance once he reaches the door, he leaves us.

***

Blake

All of us were on edge after finding out Ell's face is plastered all over the city, but Ell was right, there isn't a damn thing we can do about it. Knowing that, I agreed with the decision to not waste another second this far out, and instead head straight for the tavern. It made sense that the longer we waited the hotter things were going to get here. If the guards start doing mandatory searches, we're screwed, especially at The Grotto. At least Quinn is friends with the tavern owner, so if we can make it there before things get too crazy, maybe we'll have help staying hidden.

Quinn wasn't gone long this morning, purchasing all of us new cloaks, and after a bit more discussion when he returned, we headed out after clearing our tab at the front desk. We haven't run into any trouble so far, but it's clear what Quinn said is true, the closer we get to the palace, the more guards we see.

Ell remains close at my side, and we each keep our heads down, trudging ahead, each block bringing us closer to safety. Well, at least, safer than we are out here, exposed.

As we continue on, Quinn leads the charge, since he knows the area best, and since he's the only one with a real UnSeelie mark on his wrist. Ell has us all glamoured still, despite the cloaks, but if someone stops us, I'm not sure she'll be able to maintain her hold on the magic. Not to mention that Quinn is supposed to be dead or a prisoner of war, so if anyone that knows that sees him, we're screwed anyway.

As I worry about that, Quinn walks a few feet in front of Ell, Nyx, and I, and behind me I know Ari and Lucas are following along. When Quinn turns right, we all do the same, but when my eyes cast up for a brief second, my heart stutters. Everywhere I look, guards surround us. They aren't paying any attention to us, thank God, but there are too many to count. They line both sides of the cobblestone street, and they come in all shapes and sizes. Some are clearly on duty, while others laugh and joke as if they're just hanging out.

With my head down, I watch as two massive Trolls push and bully a Leprechaun who's just trying to go about his business. They won't let him though, and as we pass, one of the Troll's knocks him on his ass. More than one fairy laughs at the spectacle, while we try to hurry along

Finally, we turn another corner. Unfortunately, this block isn't any better. In fact, it might be worse. I have no clue how far we are from the tavern, but if we don't get there fast, we might not make it at all.

I'm relieved when Quinn cuts down an alley next. Where we are now, the herd of guards has thinned out quite a bit. The alley stretches on for as far as I can see, and despite it being the middle of the day, the tall buildings on either side of us cast the alley in darkness, so Quinn slows us for safety purposes.

As we move, I grip my shirt with my free hand, pulling it up to cover my nose, because the area around us smells like shit. *Literally*. Ell gags, and someone else does too, although I'm not sure who.

It takes a good ten minutes, but I can finally see a turn up ahead, and it looks like it's a main street. I don't see a single fairy passing the opening though, and I'm not sure if that's a good thing or not. It doesn't really matter though, and as we near the mouth of the alley, Quinn slows, allowing us to catch up.

"This is one of the main streets. Turning right, this street would take us straight to the palace gates," Quinn explains, wiping sweat from his brow, "The most guards will be on this street, but we have to turn right so we can get to the tavern."

"How far?" Ari asks, eying the opening.

"Two blocks," Quinn answers, "and then we'll take a left and go three more. It'll be on the right."

"So we're almost there," Ell muses, almost to herself, as if she's psyching herself up.

Quinn reaches out, touching her face gently. "Almost there."

With that, there's nothing else to discuss, so Quinn turns back, inching the last few feet. I still worry that we haven't seen anyone yet, but maybe it's just that someone is watching out for us today. Maybe God is watching out for us. After all, Ell *is* marked by God. Of all days, I hope he favors her today.

We're just about to step past the opening of the alley when a shout sounds from behind us. "Hey!" Quinn jerks back, as another calls, "Who goes there?"

We all turn as one, and as we do, I whisper, "Keep your head down, Ell." I see her nod as we come face to face with two guards.

"I said who goes there?" the round one with a buzz cut asks.

Quinn shoulders past me, speaking up for the group. "Headed to work, and taking my cousins with me tonight."

"Where do you work?" the guard interrogates, eying each of us more than a little suspiciously.

"King's Crest."

That's the first time I've heard him use the pub's name, and now I'm more worried than before. The King's Crest? Kind of sounds like a place a lot of higher ups might frequent, or at least, their guards. I trust Quinn, but you just never know about people, and I've learned, especially in the last few months, you can't trust anyone one-hundred percent.

I'm trying not to look worried when the skinny guard, with what appears to be a baton clutched tight in his grip, circles our group, as the other one grills Quinn, "Why are they with you? What, you can't go to work by your *wittle* self? *Awww*, poor baby." He laughs, throwing back his head, but his friend doesn't join him. No, he's too busy gawking at Ell.

The skinny one thrusts his baton out, and I'm instantly ready to defend Ell, but instead of hitting her, he knocks the hood of her cloak back, revealing her whole face. It isn't her face he'll see though, assuming her glamour holds up. The way she explained the magic to me before we left The Grotto, is we'll be able to see each other clearly, but anyone else will see what she wants them to see. With Ell, there's no telling what she looks like to them. I wouldn't put it past her to look like an old hunchback, with sores, puss, and all.

The guard doesn't flinch back though, but he does notice my reaction to him, and Ari's. Ari is probably the tensest out of all of us, and it didn't go unnoticed by me that this whole time he's been inching himself closer to Ell. If I noticed, then the guards noticed. Not good.

"Who are *you*?" the skinny one barks, demanding an answer from Ell.

"My name is Calla," she introduces herself, her voice low. Although, I doubt what I hear from her lips is the same as what the guards hear.

The guard opens his mouth to speak, but his counterpart beats him to it. "Yeah well, you lot are awfully suspicious. What are you doing back here, anyway? Why not take the main road? Where are you coming from?"

I assume his intense line of questioning might throw Quinn off his game, especially since we didn't talk about a backstory like that, but when he speaks, he sounds confident and sure of himself. "Honestly, my cousins came in from out of town, and we might have had a little too much fun last night at The Grotto. We slept most of the day away, and then I had to go to work, so I figured they could just go with me. Have a few drinks, ya know?"

Both guards grumble under their breath, and while it seems

like a legit story, their faces say they aren't convinced, and it's confirmed when the round one says, "Yeah well, she'll need to drop her magic. We're looking for someone, and I can feel her glamour from here."

As soon as the words are out of his mouth, Quinn and Ari are both moving. They didn't even look at one another, they just seemed to know the time for playing it cool had ended. As for me, I grab Ell, pulling her to the side, and Nyx and I both shield her with our bodies as Quinn and Ari tackle the two guards. Lucas moves to the mouth of the alley, placing his hands out in front of him, and I can just make out a few mumbling words coming from his direction while the others fight. When he quiets, a glimmering film seeps across the alley exit, and I know he's shielding us.

"Stay with her," Nyx orders, slapping me on the arm so my attention is pulled back to Ell.

He leaves us, jumping into the fray, and Ell and I both gasp when he's almost immediately thrown back with a burst of magic. Quinn and Ari are holding their own though, and Ell bullies her way past me to get to Nyx. I snatch her back, throwing her over my shoulder and refusing to let her go. She kicks and yells, demanding to be put down, but this is my one job, and I'm not fucking failing.

"Damn it, Blake, so help me..." she trails off, as we both see Ari finish off the skinny guard, and now there's only the round one left. If they can just take him out, we can quickly walk away like none of this ever happened. "Come on, Ari!" she shouts. "You gonna let a Troll get the best of you!?!"

That girl knows exactly how to get under Ari's skin. Honestly, sometimes I don't even know how they're compatible. They bicker like siblings, almost. Of course, that doesn't explain their fucking. When I see them do that, it's the only way I see them working out. When they are together like that, all the hostility is redirected.

Hearing Ell's taunting, Ari growls, gripping the Troll's wrist and twisting. I hear a pop, and the Troll howls a godawful sound. I hope whatever Lucas did blocks all sound too, otherwise we're screwed.

The pain from a broken wrist must've been bad, because the Troll pretty much gives up. He's subdued, on his stomach, breathing heavily against the stone street, and now a silent communication passes between Quinn and Ari. I know the conclusion they're coming to. They can't leave him here, not alive anyway. If he goes back to the palace and tells anyone important about this, they might put two and two together, figuring out that Ell is inside the city. We can't let that happen, which means we have to do whatever it takes.

As Ari holds the Troll still, his knee pressed into the beast's back, Quinn holds out his hands, ready to issue a killing blow.

"Stop!" Ell shouts, still slung over my shoulder, "Stop!"

Now that the danger is more or less over, I set her down, straightening her cloak after her feet hit the ground. She pulls away from me quickly, and crosses to Quinn. Putting her hand on his arm, she begs him with her eyes before turning to Ari and doing the same.

"We can't leave him, E…" Ari stops just short of using her real name, but I don't think the Troll noticed anyway. "They'll be looking for us." His explanation is just vague enough as to not tip the Troll off, but enough so Ell gets it.

"I know that, but wipe his mind instead, please," she begs, "He's just doing his job. He doesn't have to die. You've wiped minds before. You can do this."

Ari seems to consider this as he looks to Quinn, and Quinn shrugs, but before they can agree, Lucas calls, "Guys, we need to move this along. Now!"

PUPPY PILE

Ell

I'm feeling pretty good about myself today. I totally saved a fairy's life, and he wasn't even one of the good guys. I saved that Troll's life, and I didn't even have to. While Ari wasn't happy about it, he did give in to my begging, wiping the Troll's mind instead of killing him like his friend. The other one couldn't be helped, because he was already dead by the time things calmed down to a more manageable level, and while I do feel bad about that, I'm just glad I was able to save one out of the two. Fifty percent isn't half bad, if I do say so myself.

Anyway, after that, Quinn rushed us toward the pub, and we hurried inside, his boss' jaw dropping at the sight of his former employee. It didn't take much convincing on Quinn's part to get his boss to let us stay in one of the apartments upstairs though, and given we were all exhausted from our trek across the city and the encounter with the guards, we headed straight up, everyone feeling the need for a nap.

It's only been a few hours since then, and while I did sleep for a bit, now I lie here staring at the water-stained ceiling. The room we're in is what Quinn called an efficiency apartment. Everything is crammed into one room, but the bed is fairly large, and sits in the far corner next to a small kitchen table. On the other side of the table is a kitchen with nothing more than a fridge, a one-sided sink, and a small stretch of counter, with two cabinets above and below. On the edge of the kitchen, just past the fridge, is the only door in the room, with the exception of the door leading into the hall, and behind that door is the smallest bathroom I've ever seen. It has a toilet, a pedestal sink, and a standing shower, barely covered by a dirty, off-white curtain. The space is barely big enough for one person, which means there'll be no sex in that room while we wait to *off* the King.

Before we fell asleep, Quinn said he would go later and grab a few groceries, stock the fridge so we didn't have to go out, because the more we stayed out of sight, the better. His boss knows we're up here, of course, and while Quinn gave him a fake story on our identity, he didn't strike me as the type that would give us away. I think we're safe here, for now.

I try to convince myself of that as my boys and I cuddle in a puppy pile, with the exception of Ari. Not long after we all piled in, he said he couldn't get comfortable and grabbed the extra blanket at the foot of the bed. He's in the floor now, all alone.

I check each of the boys around me, and seeing their chests rising slowly, I know they're all still asleep, so I carefully wiggle myself loose. Nyx grips me around the waist, and Blake has hold of my arm, so it isn't easy, but after five-minutes of finagling, I finally manage to break free.

Climbing in the floor, Ari's eyes remain closed as I approach, but when I reach his side, he lays his arm out, welcoming me into his side. "Can't sleep?" he asks.

It isn't that I can't, more that I don't want to right now because something has been nagging at me. Ari and I made up, he forgave me and said he couldn't live without me, but while our relationship has always been aggressive, and yes, that's one of the things I love about him, I can't help but feel it's even more aggressive now. He and I are much more likely to jump down the other one's throat, and I just worry if we really are okay, so I ask, "Are we okay?"

His head jerks to the side, surprised by my question. "You

mean because I didn't want to sleep in the puppy pile?"

"No," I giggle, "I mean in general."

"Why would you ask that?" He sounds worried. "Do *you* think we aren't okay?"

I grumble under my breath, "Why can't you ever just answer the damn question?"

"Well, I mean, what the hell?"

"See," I point, jerking sideways so I can see him better, "that's what I mean. We almost can't even have a conversation lately."

The annoyance and anger leaves his eyes, and he deflates, pulling my body flush against his. "I'm just worried. That's all. And while I know we've always fought, I think maybe my worries are making it worse. And…I'm sorry if I've made you feel like things aren't okay."

"I'm not trying to make you feel bad," I tell him, nuzzling my nose against his neck, "I just wanted to make sure it wasn't still the whole Luke thing, or even Quinn."

"No," he assures me, "it isn't. I promise."

Ari turns on his side, snuggling me close and stealing a kiss. "We aren't drifting apart. We aren't really even fighting. This is what we do. But I love you more than anything in the universe. You need to know that."

"I do," I tell him, grazing my lips across his, "I do…and…I love you too."

I hear a snort as I pull back, and then Nyx mocks, "Awww, you two love each other."

"Isn't that precious," Luke gets in on the fun.

"Fuck you guys," Ari curses, chunking his blanket at the bed.

They all lose it, laughing uncontrollably, and while Ari's irritated, my heart fills to overflowing.

***

Quinn

I left the pub about an hour ago, headed to the corner market down the street. I told everyone else I was just going to get groceries and I'd be right back, but I really had something else in mind. I didn't tell them because I didn't want to worry them. I already think some of the guys are questioning my loyalty, and this would make it even worse. Blake even commented on me taking Ell to a pub called the King's Crest, and I get it. I assured them the King had only ever been there once, but I saw the look in Blake's eyes.

They'll question me when I get back too. I'll be showing up with just a handful of groceries, but I'll have been gone for nearly three hours, and that's assuming I don't run into any trouble.

Turning the last corner, I come up on the backside of the palace walls. I took the long way, that's why it took a little over an hour, but it was the safest way. And as I saunter along, I try to act casual as I approach a small wooden building, after all, I'm UnSeelie, there's no reason I can't be here. Unless, of course, anyone that knows I was a guard sees me.

Climbing onto the porch, I rap twice on the pockmarked door in front of me, and hear a groan from the other side. Boots clomp on wood, and then the door swings open, the hinges squeaking an awful sound. When my eyes adjust, I see the irritated scowl of one of my best childhood friends.

I haven't seen Thrill since we were in school, and yes, in case you were wondering, Thrill is a nickname. And for good reason.

"Thrill?" I greet, almost like a question.

My friend, the fattest Elf I've ever known, squints his eyes, glaring at me as if he has no clue who I am. I can't imagine I've changed that much though, but as I glance past him and see dozens of empty glass bottles, I know it isn't me that's changed.

"It's Quinn, from school, remember?"

"Quinn," he repeats under his breath, acting as if he plans to slam the door in my face. I can't imagine why though. We didn't end our friendship on bad terms. We just haven't seen each other in years.

As he continues to slowly, and dramatically shut the door, I step back, ready to bolt, just in case. When I make it two steps away from the door though, Thrill lets out a maniacal laugh, throwing his head back with the force. His greasy, long black hair sticks to his face as he leans forward, grabbing me roughly by the collar and yanking me inside. He slaps my back, laughing again.

"Holy shit, Quinn. Long time no see. Where ya been?" He pulls me to a worn couch, with more holes than fabric, and forces me to sit.

"I've been around, man. What about you?" I ask, both of us sitting as he offers me a partial bottle of fairy wine. I decline, shaking my head. "No thanks, man. Gotta work tonight," I lie.

He shrugs, finishing off the bottle's contents. "Yeah, I've been around too." He sets the bottle down, leaning back with his arm resting on the back of the couch between us. "What brings ya over after all this time?"

"Listen," I start, feeling guilty because clearly my friend has seen better days, "I know it's shitty that we haven't seen each other in years, and even more shitty for me to show up after all that time needing a favor."

"Eh," he sloughs my words off, shrugging, "What are friends for? Am I right?"

"Right," I agree, slapping him on the shoulder. "So listen, you're close to the palace, and I know you see and hear things."

"Fuck the King," Thrill barks out of nowhere.

I'm not surprised by his outburst. Thrill has hated the King since we were young. I remembered that, and it's why I chose to come to him instead of someone else. He was adopted when he was a baby, and while he has no idea who his biological parents are, his adoptive dads were pretty amazing. They gave him a good life growing up, at least from what I could tell. Both of his dads served in the King's guard, but since we weren't really at war during that time, they each had decent daytime shifts at the palace. It was good work from what I can remember, but all that changed when we were in mid-school. Someone close to the King accused one of Thrill's dads of theft, and the King didn't even think twice about it. He sentenced him to die, but before he could see it out, Thrill's other dad attacked the King. They were both beheaded.

I remember that like it was yesterday, because we were on a field trip, our whole class together when one of the instructors pulled Thrill aside and told him. I was close enough that I heard the whole thing, and I saw his face slump. He was beyond devastated, and rightfully so.

From that day forward, he was a totally different person. And from the looks of his tiny home, things have only gotten worse since then.

"I'm glad you still feel that way about the King," I tell him, "because that's why I'm here."

"If it involves that piece of shit, I'm in," he growls, slamming his hand down on the back of the couch, dust pluming up from the fabric and causing me to cough.

I clear my throat. "The King has my sister, forcibly, and…my girlfriend's best friend."

With my words, Thrill charges to his feet, chunking glass bottles across the room. "That mother-fucker. Let's go." He storms to the door, reaching for the handle, but I stop him.

"Whoa, buddy," I call him back to me. "This is more complicated than that. And…" I chuckle, "it's not like the two of us would be successful in storming the palace on our own."

His face is set in an enraged scowl, but he does return to the couch. "Fine. What then?"

"I'm here with my friends, but, technically, I'm supposed to be a Seelie POW," I explain.

"No shit?" His eyes widen in surprise, and he laughs, almost proudly.

"Yeah, so, I can't be seen by any of the guards stationed at the palace for sure, and honestly, I need to avoid the guards all together. Which means, I need someone else to gather information for me."

Thrill leans up, rubbing his hands together. "I'm listening."

"I need you to be my guy, Thrill," I psych him up, "We have a way to get to the King, to stop him and his bullshit tyrannous reign, but we have to get close to him, and we don't know how to do that without going in the palace." I pause for dramatic effect. "Obviously we can't do that. It's just too risky."

"What way?" he asks, almost excited.

"Huh?"

"You said you had a way to stop him. What way?" he asks again.

"Oh," I bob my head, "Yeah, don't be pissed, but I can't tell you that part." He opens his mouth, but I stop him, "And before you ask, I can't tell you why I can't tell you either."

He seems to think about that, and then his head is nodding in agreement, a grin splitting his face. "Doesn't matter. I'm in."

"So you'll do it?" I'm a little surprised.

"Fuck yeah!" He laughs, slapping me on the back a little too hard, and causing me to wince. "Where you staying, man? I can gather some intel and holler at you in a week or two."

"Yeah, see, we don't have that much time. I was thinking a day, two tops," I tell him sheepishly.

He doesn't respond right away. Instead, he pulls a rubber band from his wrist, using it to secure his messy hair in a man-bun. "Well then, I guess I have my work cut out for me."

I let out an inaudible sigh of relief, and I let him usher me to the door. "I'm staying at the King's Crest. You know the owner, right?" And seeing him nod, I add, "Just ask for him. No one else can know I'm staying there though, so be discreet."

He opens the door. "I got your back, Quinn."

I step outside, and realize the sun is nearly set. It'll be dark before I can get back, but before I leave, I need to say one more thing, so I turn back around, seeing Thrill still standing in the doorway, but unlike when I first got here, there seems to be life back in his eyes. Before, they just seemed, I don't know, dead?

"Thrill, I…" I scramble for what to say, not wanting to make this weird but knowing I need to say it, "Listen, I'm a shit friend. I should have kept up with you after school. I didn't, and I just want you to know that I'm sorry."

An almost sad smile splits his lips, and he nods. "Thanks, man."

There's no need to drag it out any longer, so I step away from the hut and hurry away. I took too long here as it is. I need to get groceries and make it back before Ell flips the fuck out.

***

Ell

"What the fuck, Quinn!?!" I screech, throwing my arms around his neck. "I was worried fucking sick. Where have you been? We thought the guards got you."

He squeezes me tight, pulling away before I'm ready. "I know. I'm sorry. I had something I had to take care of."

Nyx takes one of the sacks filled with groceries from Quinn's hand, while Luke grabs the other. Blake eyes Quinn, suspicious, and Ari is engaging in his normal worried pacing. They all watch Quinn as he unties his boots, kicking them off and flopping down on the bed.

"Well..." I demand impatiently.

"I went and saw a friend of mine, and I asked for his help," he rushes, like he hopes he can just gloss over this whole thing. He should know me better. That isn't in my nature.

"You what?" Ari barks, and again, I can't help but notice Blake's look.

"It's okay," he assures us, "He's one of my best friends. We can trust him."

"He's an UnSeelie," Nyx growls, not even realizing the implication of his words.

"*I'm* an UnSeelie."

Nyx tips his head, almost looking guilty. "You know what I mean."

"No," Quinn tells him, firm, "I don't. You guys are operating under some sort of outdated notion. And I get it, I was too, just with the Seelie. But I'm telling you, not all UnSeelie are bad.

Honestly, most of them are just trying to survive."

"I know," I support him, as I join him on the bed and rest my head on his shoulder. "He didn't mean it like that. And I agree with you. They aren't all bad. You are proof of that." I cozy up to his side, and he slips his arm around me, as I add, "So...tell us. Was he able to help?"

"Well, of course he didn't have any information for me today, but I knew he wouldn't. But...he hates the King. Loathes him, in fact. He'll do anything to help you kill him."

"What the fuck, man?" Blake guffaws. "You told him about Ell?"

"No," Quinn insists, and I'm totally over Blake's attitude. "I didn't. I told him my girlfriend, and a few of my friends had a way to rid the UnSeelie of King Tobin once and for all. I never mentioned Ell. But, even if I had, I'm telling you, we can trust him."

"I'm not even sure we can trust you," Blake argues.

"Blake," I scold, but he doesn't back down.

"No, I'm serious. I've had a weird feeling since we got here, and it centers around you." Blake points a finger at Quinn, and then he scans the rest of us. "I mean think about it. We're staying at a pub called the King's Crest, close to the palace. How do we know this isn't a trap he's in on?"

"Blake," I stop him, leaving Quinn and placing my hands on the big guy's chest, "What's with you? It's Quinn. He's one of us. Helga said so. And, even if she hadn't, I can feel it. I know you can too."

Blake looks down at me, and his features soften just a touch. "I don't know what it is...I...I don't know. Something isn't right."

"I kind of feel it too," Nyx agrees from the kitchen counter.

I look at Ari, and he nods, and when I search out Luke, he agrees, "Yeah, I don't know what it is, but I feel something off too. Except...my feeling isn't associated with Quinn, necessarily. It's..." he pauses, looking unsure, "it's associated with you, Ell."

"What?" I squeak, wide-eyed.

"It started this morning," Luke explains, "and it feels like a betrayal. I just brushed it off, but every hour that passes the feeling gets stronger."

"Like I'm going to betray you?" I ask. "I would never do that. I love you all too much."

"I know," he sighs, rubbing his eyes, "But it's just a feeling. Maybe it's nothing."

"Maybe we're just tired," Nyx offers in.

"Maybe…" But I can't help but think it's more than that.

UNCHARTED TERRITORY

Ell

Yesterday, the dynamic in our group changed. Everyone is wary of everyone. It started with Blake, Nyx, and Ari feeling like Quinn can't be trusted, and then Luke revealed that he's been having this feeling that I was going to betray them. First off, I would never, but then, later, when we were all piled up ready for bed, no one wanted the others to touch them. Even Nyx, who normally sleeps on top of me, scooted down to the foot of the bed, curling up in a ball. Ari and Luke both slept on the floor, leaving Blake, Quinn, Nyx, and I the bed, but they still kept their distance from me, and each other.

Then this morning it was worse. Nyx and Ari got in a fight over a slice of bread, and while it was only words, the whole thing was weird. Around lunch, Blake accused Quinn of stealing his socks, making me laugh, but pretty quickly it was clear he wasn't joking. That argument had resulted in fists being thrown, until I found Blake's socks shoved under the covers.

Then, not long ago, we all had sandwiches for dinner, and not one word was said. In fact, we all sat on opposite sides of the room. I tried to sit with Ari at first, but he got up and walked away from me, saying he was just tired. Too tired to cuddle? What kind of paradox have I found myself in?

After we finished our meal, Quinn said he needed to go

downstairs and try to get some intel. Fairies talk when they drink, so the fact that we're staying over a pub was a plus. But then, Blake said he didn't trust Quinn to go alone, and the rest had quickly agreed.

So now, since I can't risk being seen, glamour or not, I'm alone in our tiny apartment, while those five ass-hats are probably drinking it up, living the good life. Yeah, probably not, but still. Honestly, they'll probably get kicked out any minute for fighting each other.

My head throbs with worry as I sit with my back against the wall, waiting for them to come back up. I just can't understand what's going on. Luke and Ari fighting is nothing, but the rest of them? This is uncharted territory. Sure they bicker and sometimes disagree, but this is different.

I hear footsteps in the hall, and my body tenses. The knob turns, and just to be safe, I prepare a little magic. It's dark in here, since I had the lights out hoping it would help my throbbing headache, but I'd recognize Ari's mop of flaming-red hair anywhere, so I drop the magic, allowing it to settle.

"What are you doing back?" I ask, standing from my seat and crossing the room.

"I came to check on you," he answers, and while he does shut the door, he doesn't move any closer to me.

"Oh really? Well, you didn't seem to give a shit about me earlier." I cross my arms, my feelings hurt.

"I know," he agrees, shaking his head, "but it passed. It's... something is definitely wrong."

"What do you mean?" I soften my features, wanting to go to him but holding back.

"I don't know. Earlier," he explains, "when you wanted to sit with me, it was like something was pushing me away from you, like I couldn't stand to be near you."

Now my feelings are really hurt. "Tell me how you really feel, *Arion*."

His head tilts to the side, and he finally crosses the room, coming to a stop with no more than a foot between us. "Don't do that. Not the full name game," he tries to joke, but I'm just not feeling it, and seeing I'm not into it, he lets his smile drop, as he explains, "Anyway, when I was downstairs, it was like that feeling went away, and all I wanted to do was be near you again. Plus, those assholes are all bickering down there. They'll never get any decent intel in their current state."

I try not to laugh, but I can't help it. "What *is* going on?" I worry.

"I don't know. Something."

Ari steps forward, his hand tilting my chin up so he can steal a kiss. When he's done, he leans back slightly, licking his tongue across my bottom lip, and sending a shiver down my spine. His hands drop to my hips, and I gasp when he spins me around, pushing me toward the small kitchen counter. My body is pressed into the surface by his, and my stomach begins to ache, but in a good way. The best way.

Ari sweeps my hair to the side, lining my neck with his kisses, and I need him to fuck me right now. I tell him that, and he groans against the back of my head, grinding his dick against my ass.

"Too many clothes," I mumble.

With my words, Ari reaches around and unbuttons my pants before ripping them down my legs, leaving them exposed to the cool room. A chill courses through me, and I shiver as I feel Ari's hands heat up, beating back the chilly air with his magic and making me moan.

With no foreplay, Ari uses his magic to burn away the thin fabric of my lavender panties, and then gripping my hair, he thrusts into me, deep. He pulls my head back with the next stroke, and I groan, probably too loud, but I don't care. It seems like I haven't been fucked like this in years. Yes, I realize I lost my virginity less than a year ago, but who's counting? Not me for damn sure. King Tobin's bullshit plan has really thrown a kink in my own plan; eleven orgasms a day. Or was it twelve? Doesn't matter.

"Ellie," Ari groans," bend over and grab my balls."

Did he? What the? Oh my. I think I just came.

I don't argue though, because that was fucking hot, and bending over at the waist, I grip his balls in one hand, and squeeze. The pressure causes him to moan my name for all to hear, and this time, I really do come, his thighs, slapping my ass, dragging it out.

Seconds later, he comes too, breathing heavy against my neck. We stay bent at the waist, both of us gripping the counter for support. Sweat pours off both our bodies as we pant out our bliss, and I wanna go again.

***

Ell

All the boys came back last night at various times, with Quinn staying gone the longest, but once again, no one wanted to be around the others, even Ari. It was like once everyone was back in the room, even *he* didn't want to have anything to do with the group. I can't say I was much different though. Sure I was sated from the hot counter-sex, but I didn't have much of a desire for anyone the rest of the night.

Which is exactly how I realized there is definitely some bullshit happening. Me? Not wanting sex? Yeah, something is severely wrong. A. I'm a Nymph. B. I'm me. C. I'm a Nymph. And yes, I felt like the first one needed to be said again, and thus the reason for C.

Anyway, I don't know what's happening, but it's definitely something. I tried to tell Ari what I was feeling this morning, but he was so put out with me that he didn't want to listen. Sure he's always put out with me, but this time I didn't even do anything. He was so irritated, he left the room, followed by Nyx and Blake. After they left, Quinn and Luke listened to me worry for a few minutes, but then they too left the room.

I'm really tired of being up here by myself. I want to go downstairs and cuss all of them out for being assholes, except deep down, I know this isn't their fault. No, this is someone else's fault. But who's?

The door to our room opens with a whine, and all five of my boys walk in, followed by a fairy I don't know. He's tall, and he's definitely an Elf, but he doesn't look like your average Elf. His hair is long, like an Elf's, but it's black, which is weird. He's also the widest Elf I've ever seen. I don't want to say fat, because I'm not mean like that, but yeah, there isn't really another way to describe him. I don't think I've ever seen an overweight Elf. At least, not on this level.

"Ell," Quinn greets, "this is Thrill, my friend I was telling you about."

Quinn steps to the side, and Thrill now has a clear view of me for the first time. Almost immediately, his eyes go wide, and his jaw drops. He looks to Quinn, and then back to me twice before finally stuttering out words, "I...she...it's..."

Quinn turns to Thrill. "I'm trusting you more than I've ever trusted anyone in my life, Thrill."

"She's the Seelie Queen," Thrill finally gets out.

"Yes," Ari jumps in, "and that doesn't leave this room. It won't be good for you if it does."

I can tell Thrill doesn't like Ari's tone, because he tenses, slitting his eyes, but before he can say anything, Quinn steps between the two of them. "He's right, Thrill. It can't leave this room no matter what. I'm trusting you here."

Thrill relaxes just a bit, taking a step back as a grin rolls across his face. "You're dating the Seelie Queen." It isn't said like a question, more of an acknowledgement. "You 'ole, sly dog." He chuckles, slapping Quinn on the back and pulling him in for a bro-hug. Pushing him away, he steps closer to me, and everyone in the room steps closer to me too, ready to defend me if need be, but that isn't the vibe I'm getting here. He throws his arms around me, and Ari lurches forward, stopping short when I wave him off. It's just a hug. *Damn.*

When Thrill pulls back, he says proudly, "Any friend of Quinn's is a friend of mine. Even if you *are* a Seelie." He laughs at his own joke, and I give him a grin.

With introductions settled, Thrill puts a few feet of distance between us, and everyone relaxes. He props himself against the door, kicking one foot up on the cracked wood, and shoving his hands in his pockets, he waits for the rest of us to get comfortable.

I hop on the small counter, with Nyx resting against my knees, and the rest take up various positions around the room. I stroke my fingers through Nyx's long locks as Thrill fills us in on why he's here. "So, I thought it would take a bit longer, but I think I have a way for you to get close to you know who."

"I'm listening," Quinn encourages him to go on.

"So, this morning, an announcement was made. The King will be leading a parade through the city in two days." Thrill reaches back, tightening his ponytail.

"Why?" Ari asks, as that very question sweeps through my mind.

"It's a celebration," Thrill mocks, rolling his eyes for effect, "A celebration of the defeat of the Seelie."

"What the hell?" I curse, pushing Nyx forward and hopping down from my seat. "They didn't defeat us. If anything, *we* defeated them. *We* took back the Seelie palace. *They* called for the retreat."

Thrill shrugs. "Yeah, well, that's not what he's telling the UnSeelie. He says that was all part of his plan, and in less than a week, the Seelie will fall and he'll be King of all Fay."

"Shit," Nyx mumbles before asking, "You think his seer knows something that we don't?"

"Could be," Ari muses, once again taking up an aggressive pace around the room, "Or…it could be that he's trying to boost morale in his guard. And, the part about the battle at the Seelie palace…well, that could just be him trying to save face."

"True," Luke agrees, as he leans back against the wall on the far side of the room, "but I'd say we better assume that isn't the case, and that he knows something we don't. Which means, this parade is our only shot."

I reach for Nyx again, wanting comfort, but he pulls away from me, moving to the bed and sitting next to Blake on the end. What the hell, man? We're back to this again? When they came in the room, they all seemed a bit better. Nyx even came to stand with me, letting me play with his hair, but now it's as if they all hate me again.

As I grumble in irritation, Ari stops in the center of the room. "Okay, then we go after him at the parade, but before then, we're going to need to do some serious recon." And turning to Thrill, he adds, "We're also going to need more information; where the parade starts, where it ends, and what the route is."

Thrill agrees, as Quinn chimes in, "You said he was leading the parade, so I assume that means he'll be on the first float. But…he'll be well guarded. He might be a piece of shit, but he isn't dumb."

"So then how do we get close enough to him so Ell can do her thing?" Blake asks the room.

"That's what we need to figure out," Ari responds, squatting down with his back tense. "Thrill, if you can gather as much info as possible, we can use that to figure out the best course of action."

"On it," Thrill barks, and turning to me, he bows, legit bows, "Your Majesty." He smirks, and then opens the door to leave after shaking Quinn's hand aggressively.

After the door closes, I want to address how everyone's been acting, because I know we can't let this fester any longer. "I think we need to talk about what's been going on."

"What are you talking about?" Blake asks, a little too aggressive, especially for him.

I point at him, quickly. "That. That's what I'm talking about. Your tone, the way you asked that, it was totally off. You guys are all acting off, and I want to know why."

"I don't know what you're talking about," Ari grumbles, which is weird, because even *he* said something was going on before.

"We're probably just stressed," Quinn offers, "This is a lot to deal with, Ell."

"I get that, but…"

"No," Ari insists, irritation dripping from the word. "Just let it go. We don't have time to deal with your feelings." And with that, he storms across the room, slamming the bathroom door and leaving me in shock.

I hear the shower turn on as a weird look comes over Nyx's face. He opens his mouth more than once to speak, but it isn't until my eyes start watering that he does. "That was…" Nyx pauses, unable to figure out how to respond, "That wasn't normal, right? I've seen him mad at you, but I've never seen anything like that. Well, not over nothing anyway."

Nyx joins me by the fridge, and wrapping his arms around me, he rests his chin on my head. I suck back the tears, and try to tamp down on my hurt feelings. Deep down, I know that wasn't Ari, but it doesn't make it hurt any less. Something else is at play here though, I just need to figure out what.

DICK FIGHT

Nyx

Blake and I are on recon duty today. We've walked every possible route the parade might take, listened in as fairies talked about the King, and plotted out what we think will be our best bet. Of course, all of that could change if Thrill comes back with new information, but Blake and I are confident in the decisions we've made.

If the parade leaves the front gates of the palace, or returns through the front gate, then they almost have to pass down Center Street. Center Street just happens to be the narrowest road in the whole city, which means if the streets are lined with citizens watching the spectacle, then there's a good chance we could sneak our way on the float using the crowd as coverage. The street isn't even wide enough for two carriages to pass side by side, so I think we've found our best option.

I feel confident as Blake and I step through the apartment door, locking it behind us. Inside, the whole gang is here, including Thrill. I wasn't expecting him, but that's okay. This is actually a good thing. With him here, we can go through what Blake and I are thinking, and make sure Thrill agrees.

"Any luck?" Ell asks, leaning up and giving me a quick kiss. I want to take it further, but that will have to wait. I just hope I'm still in the mood later because my moods have been all over the place lately.

"Yeah," I tell her, giving her ass a soft tap, "We're thinking Center Street is narrow enough that we can use the crowd as cover and sneak on the King's float." I look at Thrill, and try to gage his reaction.

His head bobs, and he scratches his chin. "That could work. Viewing of the parade is mandatory, which means thousands of fairies will be lining the streets to see it pass. Center Street will be packed. It could definitely make it easier to get closer to the float."

"That's what we're thinking," Blake agrees.

"Thrill was just telling us that the parade will head out of the front gates of the palace at 4:00 p.m. And...that based on the schedule and route, it should return to the gates at a little after five," Ari explains.

"So, will they go down Center Street on the way out or on the way back?" Prince Lucas asks, rocking back on his heels.

"The parade route shows them using it on the way back," Thrill answers.

"That's good," Ari nods, "That means a couple of us can follow the parade as it leaves the gates headed out into the city, while the rest can already be on Center Street, and have plenty of time to get in position."

"So what..." Ell speaks up, "am I supposed to glamour myself to look like a guard or something?"

"Actually," Ari starts, "you might be onto something."

"I was kidding." Ell's eyes are wide as she pulls her knees to her chest.

"No, I'm serious. If you are strong enough to hold our glamour for days, even when we aren't near you, then surely you could make us look like guards. If you glamour yourself and maybe...Quinn to look like guards, the rest of us could keep the easier glamour, and you should be good. You two could basically walk right on the float."

"There's just one problem," Quinn tells him, "Any guards on the King's float will be very close to the King. He'll know all their faces. He's going to recognize someone new."

"We could concoct some sort of emergency," Ell muses, almost to herself, "Create a diversion, chaos."

"That could work." Quinn nods.

"That's the dumbest idea I've ever heard," the Prince spits, "You're going to get us all fucking killed."

"What the hell?" Blake barks, his chest puffing out.

"Yeah, what the hell, man?" I repeat.

Luke's irritated scowl washes away, and he stutters, "I…shit…I don't know where that came from. Ell, I'm…"

"It's fine," she brushes it off, but I can tell her feelings are hurt, and while she might be willing to let it go, everything inside me is telling me not to.

So, unable to stop myself, I storm the room, and bow up to the Prince. "What the fuck is your problem? You can't talk to her like that. She's still your fucking Queen."

Before the Prince can respond, I hear Thrill ask, "What's happening right now?"

No one responds to his question as the Prince backs up, putting his hands out and trying to calm me, but rage is building in my chest, and one-hundred percent of it is directed at this dirt-bag, so before I can stop myself, I swing, my fist connecting with the Prince's cheek. A sickly crunch sounds, and then he's stumbling back into Blake. Blake pushes him back in my direction, and I push him back the other way. Now the three of us are in a shoving match, and all of a sudden, I don't know why.

It's like everything is whisked away, and I step out of the line of the Prince's stumbling. I fumble on an apology, but even if I was in the wrong, I can't bring myself to say it. Instead, I seek Ell out and find her pressed against the wall, her jaw slack. She looks devastated, and I hate it, because I know we're the cause.

"Ellie Mae…" I try, but she shakes her head, and before I can go to her, Ari speaks up, "I don't know what the hell just happened, but we don't have time for this shit. The parade is tomorrow, and we have a lot to work out."

"That's my cue," Thrill tries to joke, but when he sees no

one is in the mood, he sees himself out, the door closing with a crack.

***

Ell

The silence right now is deafening. Even though I know there is someone or something causing these mood swings, it still hurts, it still feels like maybe we're drifting apart. And just when I finally felt like we were all starting to get to a good place, the universe has to go and screw it up.

It hasn't been long since Thrill left, and since then no one has really moved or said a word. I can't take it anymore though, because it's clear no one else plans on talking about it, so finally, I ask, "Am I the only one that sees there is something wrong? It isn't that we're tired or stressed out, something is wrong with us."

"Well that's just rude," Quinn quips, rolling his eyes.

"Damn it," I curse, "No it wasn't. I'm telling the truth. I think someone did something to us. This isn't how we treat one another."

"No one is treating anyone like anything, Ell," Ari insists, leaning his back against the counter and giving me a look that demands I let this go.

"Then why are you calling me Ell?"

"Because you're getting on my damn nerves," he growls.

"Fuck off," Luke barks, ready to charge Ari, but Blake thrusts him back.

This is out of hand. The only time things seem normal is when I'm with only one or two of them, but the second we're all together it's like there's a wedge between us. Plus, if this was just Ari and Luke fighting, it wouldn't be weird, but they're also being asses to me, and each other in general.

Hold the phone.

"Get out!" I shout over the arguing that just popped off.

Everyone stops, turning to me in shock, but I point to the door, unwilling to back down until I test this theory.

Luke is the first to follow my order, and he stomps past the group, slamming the door behind him. Nyx and Blake take off next, followed by Quinn, and that just leaves Ari. That's good. He's the one I wanted to test things with. After all, he's our second in command. *What*? I'm first in command and everyone knows it. Don't take this away from me.

When Ari finally gives in and starts marching toward the door, I stop him, "Wait." He turns, finding me approaching his back quickly, so I beg, "Stay with me."

His face is set in a harsh scowl though, and his hand is still on the door. "I'm not in the mood."

Well, *shit*. I really thought that was going to work. Everyone else is gone, and when that happened the other night, Ari and I got kinky. I wanna get kinky again, damn it, so reaching my hand up, I let my fingers graze down his arm. He still looks pissed though, but I don't think I'm wrong when I say his eyes are starting to waiver. Despite that, he still hasn't moved, and he isn't giving in. I guess I'll just have to take this up a notch.

I sway my hips, trying to look sexy as I pull my shirt over my head, chunking it at his face. When he whips it off, throwing it over me, the scowl looks worse, so I unbutton my pants and shimmy them down my hips. I let them pool around my feet, but I don't take my eyes off my Fire Fairy.

"Ari, please…" I'm begging, but I'll do anything to test my theory, even though it doesn't seem to be working.

I reach for the button on his jeans next, popping it open, and he grabs my wrist, roughly. He stops me with a growl, but the growl is filled with more than just anger and hatred. Now it's filled with desire, as he grips my neck, spinning me and slamming me against the door, pressing his front to my back.

"I'm going to fuck you until you scream, Your Majesty."

"Well that settles it," I decide, pushing him off and getting dressed again.

Let it be known, this is a first for me. Putting my clothes

back on before I get an orgasm is not something I do lightly. There are bigger things at play though, and now, I at least proved what I was thinking.

"What is going on?" Ari asks, confused.

"There's some kind of magic on us," I explain, dropping my top over my head.

"And does that magic prevent me from fucking you?" He tries to reach for me, but I pull away, because I still need to test my theory on at least one more of my boys. You know, just to be sure.

"Well, technically, the answer to your question is yes." I open the bedroom door, finding Blake sitting in the corner at the end of the hall. I didn't know he was going to be there, but that does make things easier, so I call for him, "Blake, I need you."

In a flash, he's up, hurrying down the hall. I step back to allow him in, and when he first steps inside, he looks at Ari with loathing, but then I push Ari back, and on my tiptoes, I slam my lips into Blake's. He tenses just slightly, and then I feel him let go.

Pulling back, I grin. "You don't hate me anymore."

"I could never hate you, Ell." He brushes his nose against mine.

"Well ya did a few minutes ago," I argue, pushing him playfully.

"Hate is a strong word," he says, "but yeah, I guess I did. Why?"

"Magic," Ari and I say at the same time.

He and I look at one another thoughtfully, and then he asks, "But who's? And...why?"

"I don't know," I admit, shrugging, "But get the rest of the boys back in here. We need to figure this out."

***

Ell

It took Ari thirty-minutes to track down Nyx, Luke, and Quinn, and while they've only been back for maybe five minutes, they're already at each other's throats. Even Blake and Ari who now know something is amiss are fighting.

All five of them stand in a 'I'm bigger than you' circle, and I know punches are going to be thrown at any second, so while they're distracted, I eye them, pulling a little magic out and trying to be discreet. I don't want them to know what I'm about to do, because like everything else, it'll just start a fight.

Once my magic is ready, and I've told it what I want, I push it forward, out into the room. It washes over my boys naturally, so much so they don't even notice. Of course, that's probably because they are now actively engaged in a dick-fight. Okay, not literally, but like, they are dicks and they are fighting, kind of thing. Not like a sword fight with their dicks. You know what, never mind.

Back on track, I swish my magic this way and that, asking it to find the thing that's out of place. Because to be clear, there is definitely something out of place. Someone has put a hex on us, or something, and I should be able to find it. Unfortunately, every minute that passes with my magic failing, that gets less and less likely.

I try harder, using more magic and begging internally. While I work, the guys are still fighting, although they've taken it down a notch, as my magic moves through every inch of them, but time and time again it comes up empty. I do this so long, I don't notice at first that everyone is staring at me. The bad part; they look pissed.

"Are you using magic on us?" Ari asks, irritated.

"Yeah," I huff, throwing my hands up, "so what if I am?"

"You can't just use magic on us without permission," Ari scolds me, frowning.

"Hey, don't get salty with me, mister. I'll do whatever I damn well please." I stomp to the door, opening and storming out into the hall. I don't look back as I slam the door, the frame shaking with the force. When I get to the end of the corridor and turn though, I stop at the top of the stairs.

What am I doing? That's *my* room. Why am *I* the one leaving? It's not like I have anywhere to go. If they want to be dicks, *they* can leave. Wait. *Shit.* I don't leave like that. I stay and fight. Fighting is half the fun. Fighting leads to mad-sex.

Knowing that, I march back, slipping in the room after peeking in and seeing everyone still staring at the door. They seemed to have calmed down in my absence, and that's good, so as I walk in the room, I place my hands out, hoping they'll listen.

"There is something making us fight," I explain, trying to sound calm but being able to hear the fear in my voice, "I have this feeling that if we don't figure it out soon, our plan tomorrow is going to fail miserably."

"How do you know that?" Ari asks, only slightly hostile.

"Damn it, put your listening ears on," I scold, "I said it was a feeling." Again I realize I'm angry for no good reason, and I take a deep breath, letting it out slowly. "I'm sorry, that was uncalled for. But it's exactly my point. We're all being unreasonable. *All* of us."

"Speak for yourself," Nyx smarts off.

"Stop that," I reprimand, wagging my finger at him. "My magic didn't find anything, but I'm telling you I know it to be true. Someone has put some kind of magic on us. They're trying to break up the band."

"The band?" Quinn questions, his forehead wrinkled.

"Yeah, she says shit like that sometimes," Blake grumbles, "Just ignore her. I do."

"Whoa," I stop him, putting my hands out, "slow your role."

I don't know how to make them see this though, and if this continues, we'll all descend into a massive argument again. Plus, my magic didn't find anything, so then where is it? Could it be on me?

Ari rubs his head as if he's trying to remove a foreign object, his head shaking. "Break up the band...break up the...break up..." His head shoots up, and his eyes are bulging. "Shit. Someone is trying to break us up."

"Um, duh. Where were you when I said that five-seconds ago?" Now I'm just annoyed, but for really real this time, and not just because someone hexed us.

"No," he barks, "I heard you. That's what I'm saying. Helga said we had to be together," he makes air quotes around the word together, "like, together, together. If we're fighting and even one of us leaves, then we fail. We deviated from the right path."

"You're right," I agree, "but I scanned you for foreign magic, and I didn't find anything."

"Did you scan yourself?" he asks, stepping forward but not touching me, his hands out as if I have the plague.

"Is that a real thing?" I'm serious when I ask the question, because I'm not even sure how that would work.

Knowing that, Ari and I both look at Nyx at the same time, and he rolls his eyes, put out. "Whatever. I guess I have to fucking do everything."

I snort, because, *whatever*.

Nyx reaches me, placing one hand on my head and the other on my heart. He closes his eyes, concentrating, and it doesn't take long for me to feel something stirring. I recognize it though. It isn't the bad magic, it's Nyx's.

Nyx stays like that for quite some time, until suddenly he stumbles back, looking terrified. "Um...there's something inside you."

I don't know how to respond to that, so it's a good thing Ari speaks up. "What do you mean there's something inside her? Like someone else's magic? Or, like a thing?"

"Like...a thing. Or...or, I don't know." Fear laces his words as he stumbles back, bumping into the wall.

"O...M...G...like an Alien? Do I have an alien baby in me? Oh God, or is it like a parasite? Dear God, it's a parasite, isn't it?" I shake my head. "I always knew that's how I'd go."

Blake almost laughs. "You always knew it would be a parasite that killed you? You are so random sometimes." He didn't say it in a mean way, but regardless, I don't have time for it.

"Go back to the first part," Nyx redirects me, his eyes still bugged out.

"Fuck! It's an alien!" I'm freaking the fuck out, man. "Somebody get it out of me."

"No...but..." Nyx can't seem to make his mouth work, and he's clutching his middle. "The...fuck! The baby part!" He spits those words out as fast as he can, like uttering it was terrifying.

Everyone in the room freezes at his words, but I'm just gonna gloss right over that because it's not possible. Fairies choose when they get pregnant. When a girl fairy loves a boy fairy very much...okay, I'll skip ahead. Female fairies choose when to release their egg, allowing the boy sperm to do its job. I would never, so I know it can't be true. Well, I say never, but I mean, like, give me ten years.

I hear Blake mumble, "a baby," as Luke stumbles, the back of his legs hitting the bed frame. Blake mumbles the word baby three more times, and finally, Ari snaps, "Get ahold of yourself, man. She can't be pregnant. It isn't possible."

"Unless she was trying to trap us," Luke muses out loud.

"Fuck you," I bark, "I might be willing to do a lot of questionable things, but that isn't one of them."

"Maybe it was an accident then," Nyx offers, "Maybe you were drunk and just thought it, not realizing what you were doing."

"Don't be ridiculous," I brush off his suggestion, as a thin line of sweat breaks out on my upper lip, brought on by the serious ball of nerves running through me right now.

"Nyx has to be wrong then," Ari insists, confident.

"I know what I saw, *dick*." Nyx leaves the wall, squaring his shoulders with Ari's. "This is probably your fault. You said you wanted Ell to get pregnant. You said you wanted little Ell and Aris running all over the palace."

"I was drunk when I said that," Ari nearly shrieks.

Nyx pushes Ari, and Ari pushes Nyx right back. As for me? This whole time I've been low-key backing it on up, all the way to the door, because I'm about to bounce. I don't know where I'm going, or what I'm going to do, but shit just got real. Also, remind me to come back to Nyx's comment on little Ells running around. Another time though, because I'm out.

I'm almost to the door when Ari shouts, "Stop her!"

Quinn lunges for me, but I manage to sidestep. Unfortunately, I sidestep into the waiting arms of Blake. His massive arms snake around me, squeezing, and I know that unless I'm willing to use magic, I'm not going to be able to get away from him. And, I am *not* using magic on my teddy bear, so I guess my getaway plan failed miserably.

As I settle, I realize Ari and Nyx have stopped fighting, and Ari looks like his head might explode. "Maybe…maybe it's the baby's magic?" Ari muses, worry lines breaking out on his forehead.

"That's the dumbest fucking thing you've ever said," Luke barks, ready to start another fight.

Ari ignores him, and I can tell by the look on his face it was one of the hardest things he's ever had to do. And with a sigh, he looks back at me with a pleading look as he scrubs his hand down his face. "I'm being serious. The baby could be really strong. What if he…or, I guess, *she*…I don't know, but what if the baby's magic is jacking with us. Maybe not on purpose, obviously, but still."

Quinn has been especially quiet, so I'm surprised when he says, "I've never heard of something like that, but I think I know someone I could ask."

The room goes quiet again, with everyone still staring at Quinn, and then finally, Ari barks, "Well, what are you waiting for? Go!"

A TOTAL TWILIGHT MOMENT

Ari

Quinn's been gone for nearly two hours, and Ell's been in the bathroom for nearly that long. I know I heard her crying at one point, but none of us have gone in to check on her. Honestly, I don't even know why.

Within five-minutes of Quinn leaving, I felt all the hostility drain from my body. The rest of us discussed it, and we think that regardless of whether the baby is the cause, it definitely only happens when we're all together. Or, at least, it's only really bad when we're all together.

Despite that problem, I'm trying really hard not to think about the fact that Nyx felt a baby inside Ell. I can't even process that ball of chaos right now. It's just too much. I don't know how it's possible either. But no matter how or why, while we're wasting time on all this, time is running out. In less than twenty-four hours we need to be in position around the city. We haven't even finalized our plan. We needed to go out and walk the route, make sure we didn't find any issues that might affect what we think will work, but instead of doing that, we're sitting here, waiting on Quinn to find out if a baby inside Ell could be using magic on us.

As I pace, something breaks in the bathroom, like glass shattering, and all of us jerk toward the door. I get there first, and with a pause, I rap lightly. Ell doesn't respond though, but I can hear her moving around in there.

"Ell," I call softly. Again, silence, so I try once more. "Ellie?"

"I'm okay," she insists, her voice shaky, "I dropped my glass of water."

"Ellie, come out." I don't order it, instead it's more of a plea.

"I…can't."

I press my forehead to the wood, trying the handle and finding it locked. I knew it would be, but I had to try. When I hear her sniffle though, I've had enough.

I beat my fist on the door twice. "No, this is ridiculous. Come out. Right now!"

"You aren't the boss of me." Her voice is muffled through the door.

"Nyx," I call over my shoulder.

Nyx steps up beside me, and placing his hand on the knob, he easily unlocks it, so before Ell can lock it back, we both push inside quickly, leaving the door open for the others who are now standing near the doorframe.

When my eyes land on Ell, my heart sinks. Her hair is a mess. It's soaked to her face, either from crying or sweating, and most of it has fallen out of her messy braid. She looks like crap, with her eyes puffy and swollen, and snot running out of her nose. She rakes her hand across her upper lip, wiping the liquid away before depositing it on a towel hanging from the rack.

"Ellie," I coo, reaching for her, but she pulls back, pressing her ass to the sink.

"I'm fine," she hiccups, "Really. I just have a cold or something."

Nyx snort-laughs as the two of us box her in. Luke and Blake are now in the bathroom too, and the space doesn't really allow for it. We're crammed in like sardines, each of us touching more than one person.

"You don't have a cold, and you aren't fine," I tell her, rubbing my hands up and down her arms, "Talk to us."

"No," she growls, adamant, but when I start to step back, she rushes, "You think I tricked you into marrying me or something by getting pregnant you hate each other you hate me King Tobin is gonna open a new realm because you all are gonna leave me I'm gonna be an old spinster with a child out of wedlock," she rushes, not stopping for a breath in between all of the reasons she isn't okay right now. "And…there's a baby in me." She wails, tears and snot mixing together.

"Oh God," Nyx swears. "Is this pregnancy hormones? Oh God, this is pregnancy hormones."

I slip my arm around Ell's waist, giving Nyx a 'you're not helping' look. "Ellie, none of us are leaving you." I give each of the guys a look, and they all voice their agreement. "And as for the baby, well, we don't even know for sure."

"I do," she whispers, causing my stomach to flip, "I knew it the minute he said it. I just didn't want to admit it out loud."

"Admit what out loud?" Luke asks. "If you planned to get pregnant on purpose, you can tell us."

She gasps. "Stop saying that. I would never do that." Her tone leaves no room for argument. "I just mean that when he said it, I knew in my heart it was true." She cries again, tears leaving tracks down her already wet cheeks. "This is a total Twilight moment," she wails.

"A what now?" Luke asks, looking to Nyx to see if he knows, but he just shakes his head.

"A Twilight moment," she barks, annoyed, "She gets pregnant, but the baby is weird and like a part vampire or something, and it sucks her dry. From the inside."

"You think that's what the baby is doing?" I ask, happy when she lets me stroke her hair.

"Well, not exactly, but I'm being dramatic here. Just let me have it."

I snort, grinning. "You can have whatever you want, Ellie."

She looks at me out of the corner of her eye, suspicion written all over her face. Then she looks to each of the others, eyeballing us. "Wait, why are you guys being so nice to me? And why aren't you fighting?"

"Yeah, about that," I start, "we think we've figured out that whatever is happening, only happens when we're all together." She crinkles her nose, and I continue, "Think about it. When you got me alone, within a few minutes of everyone leaving, all my hostility had gone away. I just wanted to fuck you, which is normal, and not something I was feeling with everyone else around. The others have noticed the same thing."

Ell's shoulders slump. "Why doesn't she want us to be together?"

"She?" Blake and Luke question at the same time.

Her eyes go wide, as she stumbles to explain, "I...I mean...I think so."

All four of us wear matching grins now, and Ell seems shocked by it. Nyx and I are already touching her, and now Blake and Luke step forward. They each grab one of her hands, and still, none of us can stop smiling. I don't even know why. Would we have felt the same if she had said he?

"It's a girl..." Nyx muses, trailing off.

"Oh God, it's a girl," Blake swears, eyes wide, "Two Ells."

"We are *so* screwed," Luke worries, and yet, he's still grinning.

"Screw you guys," Ell scolds, trying to yank away from us, "I'm taking my toys and going home."

"You aren't going anywhere," I tell her, yanking her back.

My mouth drops to her neck, and I breathe her in, peppering kisses on every inch of skin I can reach. She's still tense though, but not for long if I have anything to say about it.

I drop my hand to her belly, but then, under the circumstances, I think better of it, and move it around to her ass. I can feel the others moving closer too, touching her, and I carefully guide us out of the tiny space and into our room. We each rub up against her, and every second that passes, she puts up less of a fight.

I'm just about to remove her shirt when I hear footsteps in the hall, and I pull back, listening closer. When Quinn steps in the room, my heart sinks because I know this will have to wait.

"God dang it," Ell swears, throwing her hands in the air, "What's a fairy got to do to get an orgasm around here?"

***

Ell

So help me, the next person that interrupts my orgasm is getting turned into something not nice, something irreversible. This is just getting ridiculous. It's like the universe is out to get me. Or, at least, out to ruin my sex life.

All the boys have moved away from me now except Ari, and I grumble under my breath about goats as everyone waits for Quinn to give us the news. I'm really hoping it's good news too, because if it is, I might get lucky.

"Alright," Quinn starts, "let me lead with; it's not the baby. Well, assuming we are one-hundred percent sure there *is* a baby?" He looks around the room, and everyone nods, except for me. "Okay," he shakes his head in disbelief, "Okay, it's a baby then. Wow."

"Focus," I insist, snapping my fingers.

"Right, I went to see the loony lady on Icker Street," he tells us with a straight face.

"The what now…" Because this has to be a joke.

"I know, I know." Quinn shrugs. "She's like two-hundred years old, and she lives on Icker Street. Everyone calls her the loony lady on Icker Street because she tells people she isn't a fairy…but a witch."

"Witches aren't real," Nyx chimes in, pursing his lips.

"And that," Quinn says, "is why they call her loony. Anyway, I don't know if she's a witch, or just a batshit crazy fairy, but regardless, she said it would be impossible for the baby to use any magic that would harm us, especially you." He nods toward me.

"And what makes you believe her?" Ari asks. "I mean, you said she's loony, so why would you trust that she knows what she's talking about?"

"I can't answer that," Quinn admits, his shoulders slumping, "But I believed it with everything in me. She even pulled out an old tome, and showed me this passage talking about it. It had to be two-thousand years old, and it was talking about the baby's magic being one with the mother's, and in some cases, the father's too."

"Well, it isn't definite, but it does make me feel slightly better," Ari remarks, scratching his chin.

"There's more," Quinn tells him, but before he can go on, Luke barks, "Who fucking cares. This is ridiculous. I'm out of here."

"Shit," Ari curses, as I say, "It's happening again. Blake, stop him."

Blake rushes to the door, blocking Luke's exit, and I tell Quinn to hurry.

"She made a potion of some sort." Quinn reaches into his pocket, and pulls out a small vile. "She said you and you alone had to drink this. She said the magic would've been cast on you, that it was a repulsion magic, and from you it would cast out on the five around you." He pauses, shaking his head. "The thing is, I didn't tell her there were five of us."

Holy crap. Are witches real?

Well, whether they are or not, I'm about to drink the shit out of this potion, because I can already see Quinn's eyes changing as he thrusts the vile in my direction. Ari is shaking his head too, huffing like he's just dying to start a fight.

"Whatever, she's probably full of shit anyway," Quinn grumbles, flippant.

I snatch the vile, pulling the tiny cork out and holding the glass up to the light. The liquid inside looks thick, and it's a dark-brown color. It doesn't look appetizing at all, or safe, for that matter.

"What if..." I think out loud, "What if it isn't safe for the baby? What if this is a trick and she works for King Tobin?"

"Just drink it already," Blake barks, clearly having slipped back under this horrible repulsion magic.

They are no use to me like this. None of them are able to think clearly, logically. I have to make the decision myself. I have to do what *I* think is best. So, what do I think is best? If I don't drink it, then they are going to leave me and all of our plans will fail. Helga was very clear; they have to be with me. We have to be together. But, if this 'witch' is working for Tobin, then this potion could kill our baby. I don't know if I could live with myself, and that's saying a lot, because before today, I had zero desire to have children any time in the near future.

This is too much pressure.

I look at each of them, wishing they could give me advice right now. Quinn seemed sure of it, at least until the magic got him again, but the others didn't really weigh in, and I really wish they could have, because this is a decision for all of us to make. I at least need one more person's opinion. Just one. That's all I'm asking for.

"Drink it," Luke growls, and while that wasn't what I meant, I'm taking it as a sign from the universe.

I throw my head back, pouring the brown substance in my mouth. I gag when it hits my tongue, because it tastes like ass, literally. I'm not being funny either. It tastes like a dirty butt-hole smells.

Thinking about dirty butthole only makes it worse, so I gag one more time, but then I'm finally able to get it down. I feel it burning as it slides down my esophagus, and it hurts almost enough to be alarming, but then it settles, and now my stomach almost feels cool.

My hand goes to my belly, rubbing, and my stomach rumbles like I'm hungry, but I know I'm not. I hiccup, and I growl, hoping that's the only damn one.

"Fuck this," Luke growls, "I'm out."

This time, Blake doesn't stop him. In fact, he joins him. Once they're out, the door slams behind them, and it's just Ari, Nyx, and Quinn left in here with me as I wait.

Quinn didn't say how long it would take, but I imagined it

being quick. I was clearly wrong, evidenced by two of my boy-friends leaving.

"Well…" Quinn barks at me, demanding I tell him what's going on. More evidence it hasn't worked yet, and I don't know what to tell him. Ari looks impatient too, but I just shrug, unable to speak words.

"Well this is just fucking great," Ari growls, pissed, "It didn't even fucking work. How much did you pay for that shit? That fucking witch cheated you. You need to demand your money…" Ari stops his tirade, his body still. He doesn't move for a long time, and part of me worries he's stuck like that. Finally, though, he spins, facing me and Quinn. "I…"

The door bursts open so hard it breaks off the hinges, hanging at an odd angle, as Blake barrels through the door. He sweeps me up, spinning me in a circle, breathing heavy against my ear. Luke is next to appear, and each time I face him in mine and Blake's spinning, I can see that he's grinning.

When Blake sets me down, I see nothing but love in his eyes, and when he speaks, his voice is filled with awe, "We're having a baby."

SHOWER-GASM

Blake

I always knew I wanted children someday, especially once I met Ell, but I never imagined it would be this soon. At first, I figured Ell and I couldn't have children together. The whole human-fairy situation, and yet, I still wished for her to have children with the others so I could be a bonus dad. But then, when we met the Celestials, and they said humans and fairies could have babies just fine, I let myself hope. Sure I was hoping for something way down the road, but I fully believe we are all on God's time. His will be done. And that's exactly what this is. It has to be. Ell made it very clear she wasn't responsible, and I believe her.

Unfortunately, all of the excitement over it will have to wait. Whoever put repulsion magic on Ell did it for a reason. We still don't know who, why, or when, but right now it doesn't matter. Because of it, we wasted too much time bickering, and then, trying to break the magic. All of that time needed to be spent on our plan, a plan that has a lot of holes, if you ask me.

I'm letting that go for now though, because Quinn and I are working our way down Center Street, side by side. Nyx walks ahead of us on the other side of the street, and as we move, we're looking for any issues. A number of things could go wrong this afternoon, so anything we can spot now will just decrease the likelihood of something stupid and avoidable screwing things up.

Last night, after the witch potion fixed us, we all slept in a pile on the bed, wrapped around each other, and as Quinn and I sidestep a Leprechaun, I'm realizing that might have been our last night together. We didn't even have sex. I think we just all wanted to be near her so much that sex wasn't even a thought. Of course, it could have something to do with the fact that Ell is carrying a baby inside her. I have no idea how that works. Luke's dick is by far the biggest, I'm man enough to admit that, so what if he, I don't know, hits the baby with it?

Yeah, we're probably on a sex-timeout for a while.

"Look alive," Quinn whispers.

Up ahead, two guards work their way through a small group of fairies. They eye every person they pass, but they don't seem to be stopping anyone, so as long as Ell's glamour on us holds, we should be good.

When they pass by us with nothing more than a once over, I let out a sigh of relief, and Quinn does the same as we make it to the corner of Center and the King's Circle. The circle is a massive stone area with four different streets emptying out into it. In the center of the circle stands an area with lush, green grass, and in the center of *that* is a massive, one-hundred-foot-tall statue.

I lean in to Quinn. "I assume that's King Tobin."

"Yup." He rolls his eyes. "Grade A douchebag."

I chuckle under my breath, because yeah, only a douche would have a statue like this right in front of his home. I saw a few statues back in the Seelie capital of Ell's uncle, but nothing like this. This is monstrous. And, if I was to guess, unlike Ell's uncle, I'd say King Tobin probably commissioned this piece himself.

Shaking my head, Quinn guides us around the statue, and now we're going the way we just came from on Center. When we make it a couple blocks, Quinn keeps his eyes forward, as he tells me, "The next two blocks are the narrowest because of these vendors."

"Wouldn't these vendors have to move for the parade?" I ask in a low whisper.

"Not typically, and I checked," he says, certain, "Early this morning, I talked to the grocer..." He points across the street, "and he said they are staying open. They'll be selling candy, popcorn, and drinks."

Quinn slows, and we stop at one of the vendors, buying us each a goblet of fairy wine. He hands one of the two to me, as he chuckles, "Here, I think we could use a drink." And when we walk away from the owner, he adds, "It'll help us blend in."

I look around, and he's right. Nearly every fairy within sight is carrying bottles or goblets. They all look drunk too, but that seems to be a pretty common occurrence here. I mean, who can blame them? They're ruled over by a dictator, after all.

I take two swigs, and try to relax. "I think you're right about these two blocks, especially if those vendors really are set up later."

Quinn nods, and I spot Nyx again. He jerks his head, motioning for us to turn at the next block, so we follow, staying about a truck's length behind him. I don't have the city totally mapped out in my mind yet, but I know we're headed back to the pub. Luke and Ari stayed behind with Ell, and they're waiting for us to return with news. Once we do, we'll only have a couple hours until there's no turning back.

***

Ell

I'm starting to get nervous. Like, ridiculously nervous. My head is swimming, and I can feel a panic attack coming on. I can't afford to have a bad one, not today, so for the last thirty minutes, I've been doing everything in my power to keep it at bay. Luke hasn't seen one of the bad ones, and Ari's been so busy pacing that he hasn't noticed, so I continue to keep it from them.

"They should've been back by now," Ari worries, looking at the repaired door.

"That's just what I was thinking," Luke agrees, "Maybe I should go look for them."

"No," Ari and I say at the same time. "No," I repeat. "Then you'll just be missing too. Let's just give it a bit."

Luke agrees and settles back in, while I mentally coach myself on my breathing.

You can breathe just fine, Ell. You've got this. In and Out. In and Out.

"Ellie?" Ari stops, his eyes casting up and down my body, and when I don't respond, too busy breathing, he asks, "Are you okay? Are you…"

"I'm good," I breathe, "I'm just…I'm okay."

Ari rushes to my side before moving me to the bed. His hand rests on my lower back, but he doesn't say anything, not yet. He's letting me try to handle it on my own, and Luke not knowing is probably for the best.

"It's alright," Ari insists, "She's alright." I'm pretty sure his words were more to convince himself than anyone else, but I still listen to them, using them to talk myself down off the ledge.

Luke sits down on my other side now, resting his head against mine, totally unaware of what I'm dealing with. "This stress isn't good for the baby. Tell yourself that. Your instincts will kick in and protect the baby." I pull back, and Ari and I are both looking at him with wide eyes. "What?" He shrugs. "I used to get them when I was younger. I convinced myself that I was damaging my body every time I had one, so I just figured that if you could convince yourself the panic was hurting her, then maybe it would work for you."

"How did you even know?" I ask in disbelief.

"I mean, it's been written all over your face for the last two hours. I was just trying to let you work through it yourself."

Luke picks my braid up, rolling it in his fingers, and it's then that I realize my chest doesn't feel quite as heavy. Actually, I'm breathing fairly normal now.

"Distraction works too," Luke chuckles.

I move, kissing him without warning, and when I pull back, he winks, as I ask, "You know, sometimes, magic makes us say things we wouldn't normally say but that deep down we were thinking…"

"No, Ell," he insists, shaking his head adamantly, "I do *not* think you got knocked up on purpose. You have a million other things to worry about right now, and that is *not* one of them."

"Promise?"

He kisses me, and the answer is clear. When he pulls back, I look at Ari, and he too shakes his head. "None of us think that, Ellie. None of us. We love you, and I, of all fairies, know you would never do that."

"Then how?" I ask, because I just can't understand it. There is no logical explanation for how this happened.

"I don't know," Ari sighs, "but I do know that everything happens for a reason, and…I know that someday we'll find out the why and the how. But right now, it doesn't matter."

"I'm walking into a battle with a baby inside me though." It's the one thing that's been heaviest on my mind. What if?

Ari opens his mouth to comment, but he doesn't get the chance, because we both hear the other boys in the hall. Seconds later, the door opens and they step in, and no one looks injured or dying, so that's one less worry off my plate.

"We've got a spot," Quinn leads, and we all gather up.

***

Luke

When Quinn and the others showed back up, they said they'd mapped out a good spot. Ell and Quinn will start at the far end of Center Street, following alongside the parade as it heads back to the palace. When they are about four blocks from the King's

Circle, they'll need to be directly behind the float. That's when the rest of us will create a massive diversion. We're hoping that with a big enough explosion on the parade route, the King and his closest guards won't question two newbies hopping up on the float to protect the King. The more the merrier, right? Well, that's our hope.

It's all on Ell from there though. Quinn will be with her, which is good, given he's the only one of us that's actually an UnSeelie, but I'm really wishing I could be with her too. I suggested that very thing, twice, but I was shut down, and I know in my gut it was the right decision.

It will take Blake, Ari, Nyx and I to pull off this diversion. Plus, even after the explosion, we have to manage to get away before getting caught. That won't be easy. If even one of us is arrested, well, that won't be good.

As of now, we have two hours left to kill before we have to leave the pub and make our way into position. It's noon now, and we plan to leave at two. Even if the streets are crowded and it takes us a while, that should put us all where we need to be with at least an hour to spare. The problem is, sitting here is killing me.

"I need a bath," Ell muses, smelling her under arm.

"You'll have to settle for a shower," Ari tells her, motioning to the bathroom, "We should all clean up, actually. It will help pass the time, and who knows what will happen after today." Ell's eyes go wide, fearful, and Ari apologizes, "Sorry, I shouldn't have said it like that."

Changing the subject fast, Quinn tells us, "The hot water will run out quick in this place."

Ell's whole attitude changes in a blink. "Then maybe someone should join me. You know, to conserve water." But she pumps her brows, so we all know what she really means.

"Ell," Ari chastises, as she moves to the bathroom door.

"Luke will do," she rushes, gripping me by the arm and yanking me in the bathroom. She locks the door quickly, giggling, as Ari beats on the door.

"Ell!"

"Hey, you had your chance," she hollers through the door, giggles bubbling out of her mouth as she adds a bit of magic to the door lock. She spins, her back pressed against the wall, and she rakes her gaze up and down my body, one brow quirked. "Wanna fool around?"

"He's gonna kill us both," I warn, snaking my arm around her body.

"That's half the fun."

With another giggle, she pushes me away, and moves to the shower, stripping her clothes off before turning on the water. It takes quite a while for it to get hot, but when it does, steam fills the small space.

I begin removing my clothes as she disappears behind the curtain, and I can hear Ari cussing on the other side of the door. That kind of makes this better. I don't loathe him anymore, but I don't mind fucking with him either.

Stripping off the last of my clothing, I join Ell in the smallest shower I've ever been in. It makes me think it was built for something more along the lines of a Gnome. In fact, the showerhead is so low, even Ell has to duck to get under it, and as she does, I pull the curtain shut and watch, hard, as she soaks her body, the water raining down on her perky tits. I want to put one in my mouth, and so I do, without permission. She moans, rubbing the back of my head and pressing me closer, while my tongue circles her nipple and my hands sneak down her stomach.

It's when I feel her stomach that I pause though, hesitant. Should we be doing this? This feels different. Ell is carrying a baby. We don't know who's it is, but we know she's in there, so what if we hurt her? I would never forgive myself.

Knowing that, I pull back, and a scowl slips across her face. "Why aren't you giving me an orgasm right now?" I look down at her belly, and she curses, "Son of a bitch. Not you too. Listen," she growls, pointing from my dick to her stomach, "we can all agree your dick is massive, but it will not reach her, Luke. She won't feel it and it won't hurt her. In fact, I happen to know that sex, orgasms specifically, they're good for her, *and* me."

"How do you know that though?"

"I saw it on Earth Vision. TLC, I think," she muses. "So listen, if you don't want to do this, fine, you can shower and get out. But I'm having an orgasm today, so it can either be you or someone else. This could be my last day in Fay. I'm not taking any chances."

"Don't say that," I stop her, stepping forward again, "This won't be your last day." I drop my lips to hers, kissing her. "And also, how dare you suggest someone else give you a shower-gasm."

"Ha," she laughs, "Shower-gasm; I'm totally stealing it."

We kiss again, and I'm feeling much more at ease, even though I'm not sure what she said is true. In fact, I'm so not sure about it, that I've already made the decision not to fuck her until I can confirm it. From an actual medical professional. Of course, that doesn't mean I can't make her scream.

As the water sluices down on us, my hand moves south again. I avoid her belly, because it's just too weird, and find her bare mound. I cup her, squeezing, and with my other hand, I play with her nipple. She writhes against me as I force her to step wider, and when she does, I run my fingers across her swollen lips. I want to be inside her so bad, but I hold back, slipping a finger inside instead.

"Luke," she groans, "fuck me, please."

"No."

"Luke," she growls this time, but again, I tell her, "No."

Even though I have no intentions of giving in to her demands, I do want her to enjoy this, so I increase the speed of my pumping, letting my thumb bump her clit each time I pull out, and despite me telling her no, she calls out, her body vibrating against me. Her legs go weak, and I catch her, one arm around her waist, pulling her tight. She reaches down, her hand gripping my cock, and I kiss her roughly. She bites my bottom lip, and I growl.

"Come on my hand," I order, adding another finger, stretching her walls.

Her strokes on my cock become erratic as she nears her release, and when she comes, she screams my name. That's right, *Arion*, she screamed *my* name.

WHAT A TOOL

Ari

We left the pub nearly an hour ago in groups. Nyx and I left first, circling around to the western most point of the parade route, and then Luke and Blake left next. They headed north so they could take a roundabout way to the same area as Nyx and I, but not be seen with us and end up on the opposite side of the block.

Quinn and Ell left last, with a plan of heading for the King's circle. We agreed, they would follow alongside the parade from the beginning. That way, if they saw another opportunity that they thought might be better, they could take it. Otherwise, they'll just keep following until they get nearly back to the Circle on Center.

Once the King's float hits the area we've picked out, that's when the rest of us will create the diversion. We're hoping it will cause total chaos, and that fairies will flood the street, running toward the King's float, because the more fairies that stampede that direction, the easier it will be for Ell to get close to the King.

I've run the plan over and over in my mind dozens of times. I'll run it one time and think; 'hey, this is a pretty good plan'. I'll run it the next, and think; 'what are we, idiots?' Yeah, so, every five minutes or so I'll have a mental breakdown, and then the next five minutes my chest is puffed out and I'm proud of the work we've done. Today's been a total rollercoaster ride, to say the least.

I try to push my worry to the back of my mind as Nyx approaches, two goblets of fairy wine in hand. We stand on the corner of Center and Orc, and Nyx thought the wine would help us blend in. He's right, because every fairy within eyesight is either drinking or drunk. We have quite a bit of time to waste too. The parade is set to start in ten minutes, and that's assuming they begin on time. After that, we'll have about an hour to waste until the front of the parade passes us. Again, assuming it goes off as planned.

"Stop stressing," Nyx mumbles over the rim of his goblet.

"Is it that obvious?" I chuckle nervously, before taking a small sip.

"Your forehead is covered in so many wrinkles right now I can't even count them all," he tells me.

"I just don't know if we're doing the right thing," I admit, "What if..."

When I trail off, Nyx insists, "It's the right thing, or we wouldn't have come up with it. I believe that."

"I wish I shared your confidence," I admit, taking another sip.

When I tip my goblet back again, the crowd pushes us nearly half a block before we're able to stop ourselves. We stumble through a group of Cons, finding a spot against the wall, as I worry out loud, "I don't like that we're not with her. That's the part I'm worried about the most."

"I know."

Before we can discuss it further though, two guards start clearing the street, and when I check the time, I realize the parade should be starting.

As soon as that thought runs through my mind, speakers on every corner crackle to life, and an upbeat tune blares through the streets. Several fairies dance a jig, but when they stumble out in the street, they're pushed back by guards.

"There's a lot more guards than I was expecting," I whisper, counting and getting to twenty within seconds.

"Yeah, I count twenty on this block alone, and there's two in the alley behind us." Nyx drops his empty goblet, and casually he leans down to pick it up. As he rises, he casts his eyes down the alley on our left. "Make that three, and two that I can see out on the street at the end."

Honestly, that's double what we were expecting. Everything we heard, and everything Quinn said, suggested there would be somewhere between five and ten guards per block. This is more than double the high-end even, and that doesn't bode well for us. What if there are too many guards for us to create the diversion Ell and Quinn need? Not to mention, the parade isn't even near here right now, and we know there are dozens of guards walking alongside the floats. That means there will be even more when it's time for us to do our part.

As much as all that worries me, in the back of my mind I'm thinking of a far more likely scenario than us not being able to create the diversion. What if we can't get away afterward? This is a lot of guards for us to be able to slip away from. Someone is sure to see us, even with so many fairies lining the streets.

With a deep breath, I notice a vendor pushing his cart a little too close to me, and he bumps into my shin causing me to gasp in pain before stumbling into Nyx. I rub the muscle, glancing up and seeing a fairy I recognize; Thrill. I wasn't expecting him. We never discussed him being here or helping with the diversion. Quinn said he didn't even want to ask that of him. He didn't want to put his friend in any more danger, and I don't blame him. He's already helped enough. Without him, we'd know next to nothing about the parade, the route, among other things.

"Fairy wine?" he grumbles, hunched over, his cloak slipping across one eye.

Nyx tosses him two coins, and Thrill hands over the full goblets as we set the two empty ones down in the bin. No words are exchanged, and he's just about to move the cart away from us when an Ogre, dressed in a guard uniform, approaches.

"Where's your permit?" the guard barks, his hands resting on his duty belt.

Shit. This isn't good. No, the guard doesn't know we're with Thrill, but if he makes a scene now it could screw up everything. I just don't understand why he's even here. This wasn't part of the plan.

Despite my worries, I'm surprised when Thrill pulls out a slip of paper from inside his cloak. Hostile, the guard snatches it away, scanning the wording before thrusting it back. He grumbles, "You know it's supposed to be displayed on your cart. Don't let it happen again."

"Yes, sir," Thrill croaks, but the guard has already turned his back, and is moving away and out into the crowd. Once he's out of ear shot, Thrill starts to push his cart away, and as he passes, he says, "Forty-five minutes", and then he nods across the street.

Nyx and I don't look right away. We wait until Thrill has moved a few feet down the street, and then we glance across to a small storefront. Just in front of the glass doors, my eyes land on Blake and Lucas. They both nod, and I let out a sigh, realizing we're all in position now, and we only have forty-five minutes left.

***

Ell

The parade started about ten-minutes ago, and Quinn and I have been casually going with the flow, our hands linked together. Every once in a while, we'll slow to look at wares being peddled on the side of the street, or buy some piece of candy or a drink, and then we'll continue on. It helps us blend in as we do our best to stay about four floats back from the King, six at the most. We don't want to be too close, until it's almost time.

When the parade started, we were standing beneath King

Tobin's statue in the center of the King's circle. The gates opened, and about twenty guards walked out in formation first. Next was the King's float, and while I tried to act casual, I nearly broke my neck trying to get a look.

As they moved, the King sat on a massive throne toward the front of the float itself. The trailer, carrying him, was lined in dozens of white and black roses, and standing around the King were eight beautiful fairies. I didn't get a look at all of them, but it was obvious they were there to make the King look desirable. Behind the throne though, there were two lines of four guards, for a total of eight on the float, and then six walked on each side. Behind them and before the next float were another eight guards.

As we catch up once again, I can't help but think of how well guarded he is right now. Is this all for show, for effect, or does he know something is going to happen and he planned for it? I don't know, but either way, this is more than we were expecting.

On top of that, there are more guards lining the streets than we thought there would be too. Nearly double, in fact. It's too late to back out now though, so I just have to pray our plan works.

I'm sweating bullets as Quinn tugs my hand and we hurry past one of the cross streets. We've caught up to the third float in the procession, and when I look up ahead, I see the King stand from his throne for the first time. He steps forward, and he waves his hand like a freaking beauty queen. *What a tool.* His adoring fans are eating it up though. Fairies scream their heads off when he chunks a few roses out in the crowd, and two girls fight over a black one, forcing guards to rush up, bringing it to an abrupt and violent end when one of them gets knocked over the head with a baton. I watch in horror as she slumps to the ground, unmoving, and I look at Quinn with terrified eyes, but he just shakes his head, pulling me past the incident.

We're now even with the second float because we're getting closer to where my other boys should be set up. Surprisingly, this whole thing has flown by. Although, it's probably because I'm absolutely dreading what has to be done.

Dreading it, I say.

I gulp down air filled with the smell of cotton candy as the King works his way from one side of his float to the other, soaking it all in. He's a showman, that's for sure. It isn't just the parade that has me thinking that either. His whole demeanor is all about the effect, the presentation. It's very clear that he put a lot of thought into this day.

As he works the crowd, I take a second to check him out. He's tall, but a little heavier than your average Elf. Nothing like Thrill though. Not even close. In fact, I don't think any Elf is as big as Thrill.

We sidestep a group of kids, and I'm on my tiptoes trying to see. King Tobin is still working it, and his stark-white hair that hangs past his shoulder waves in the wind. His hair is so odd though. It has one thick green stripe directly down the center of his head, and I wonder if that's natural. I've never seen anything like it, but it doesn't look like a box dye either, so I don't know.

Moving on.

While King Tobin's hair is odd, his sharp facial features are representative of the Elves, and his ears are extra pointy. He's probably middle-aged, as far as fairies go, but he isn't unattractive. The opposite actually. Which, now that I think about it, pisses me off. I was really hoping he would be horrifying to look at.

Distracted, I trip, and Quinn catches me, as he asks, "Are you okay?"

I assure him I am, and we cross another intersection. Quinn pulls me right instead of forward though, and we cut down an alley. The parade is about to make two right turns so they can get headed back toward the palace, and instead of following them, we're going to cut across the alley and meet them on the way back. We thought it might throw anyone following us off our trail. Although, I really don't think anyone is.

"It'll take them about ten minutes to meet back up with us, and then another fifteen before we'll pass the others." Quinn presses me against the wall since we have a few minutes to spare. "Everything's going to be fine."

"I know," I agree, bobbing my head, "I can feel it." I search the area, and seeing no one is anywhere near us, I add in a whisper, "This isn't the part I'm worried about. If we succeed out here, today, that doesn't mean the UnSeelie will just let us waltz into the palace. I still don't understand how we're going to get Tab and Tika back."

Quinn leans forward, his lips whispering across mine. "We'll figure it out. One step at a time, remember?"

I nod, and with another kiss, it's time to get into position.

***

Blake

We've been standing here for nearly an hour, and as boring as that's been, now that I can see the parade moving toward us on Center Street, I'm wishing we had more time. In just a few minutes, there are so many things that could go wrong, and since we'll be several blocks away from Ell when this all goes down, if something bad happens, we won't be able to get to her.

"You look too paranoid to be at a parade," Luke mumbles under his breath, elbowing me.

I know, I do, but no matter how hard I try, I can't seem to relax. Months of horrible shit is culminating in this one moment, and it's just too much. I've had to talk myself out of finding Ell and running a dozen times today alone, but I know I can't. Or, at least, shouldn't. I do try to get my face right as the parade grows nearer though.

As tall as I am, I still have to strain to see over all the Elves and Trolls surrounding us. I spot Nyx and Ari, and we make eye contact, nodding. We all know it's nearly time, and from the look on Ari's face, he's as worried as I am.

This next part is the part we spent the least amount of time planning. We needed more time on it, but with the whole repulsion magic thing, there just wasn't enough. I would've felt better if we'd had at least a few more days, but that wasn't an option. This is our chance. If we don't take it, we might not get another one.

When the parade passes in just a few minutes, we'll wait until Tobin's float is almost to the King's Circle. When it is, I'm up first. Once I do my part, magic will come into play. Ari will throw a fireball at the float closest to him, and with Nyx's help, they'll make sure it makes a massive explosion. We're hoping that will cause enough panic that people will rush toward the circle, hoping to get away from the chaos. We hope. If that doesn't work though, then we have to make them go the direction we want them to. Which means, we'll probably get caught and won't be able to escape. In the end, I'm okay with that, as long as Ell succeeds in her assignment. Because if she does, I know she'll find a way to get us freed.

My stomach is in knots as the first float approaches, and I lay eyes on the King for the first time. He looks like the definition of an Elf, although he is a bit on the chubby side. He's surrounded by gorgeous fairies though, and the crowd oohs and ahhs.

I catch Lucas rolling his eyes about the same time I do, and now the float is past us. The second float is almost to us now, and on it, there are eight guards, and several tall Elves dressed in blue gossamer doing something akin to belly dancing. Music plays on the speaker in time with their moves, and the crowd watching can't get enough of it.

It's then that the speakers crackle, the music cutting off, and I'm freaking out when the parade comes to a standstill. I try to wash my concern away, but I doubt it's working. This was not part of the plan. Why the fuck is the parade stopped?

ONE STEP AT A TIME

Ell

Before Quinn and I stepped out of the alley, ready to rejoin the parade, I used a touch of magic and changed our glamour. It was seamless, and from what we could tell, no one noticed. Now, as we walk casually behind the King's float, Quinn and I are both dressed as King's guard. We've gone several blocks, and no one has questioned us or paid us any attention.

So far so good.

And, I spoke too soon.

Why in the actual fuck is the parade stopping?

I can see the King's Circle up ahead, we're so close, so now what? No one said anything about this, not even Thrill. I can't imagine why they would do this unless, oh my God. They know we're here.

We're currently one block ahead of where the others should be set up, so at least we're close to them if things pop off. Unfortunately, I'm not sure what happens if they do. There is zero chance we could fight our way out of here. There are hundreds of guards, plus the King, and we wouldn't just be fighting them. If the UnSeelie and supporters lining the streets knew there were Seelie in their midst, they'd be fighting too. There's no way we win.

The music pumping through the speakers cut off a second

ago, so I jump when they crackle to life. "People of Fay!" The voice is coming from all around me, but when I look ahead of us, I can clearly see King Tobin holding a microphone to his lips. "As our parade of celebration comes to an end, I wanted to address the coming weeks. The Seelie have long since oppressed our people, but I say, no more!" He bellows the last words, and the crowd roars. "No more! Their Queen is an imposter, a child. She is nothing!" Again the fairies surrounding us scream, pumping their fists in the air. "We will destroy her, and everything the Seelie stand for." He pauses, for effect, and then he continues, "In one week, we will enact our plan to destroy the Seelie in a series of coordinated attacks. Our numbers are so great they do not stand a chance. They *will* be defeated. They *will* fall. And in their place, the UnSeelie will finally rise up to rule all of Fay…And beyond!"

The crowd is out of control now, and I'm knocked back. On the plus side, we might not need our own diversion, King Tobin might have just handed it to us on a silver platter.

"Calm," he shouts, finally, and shockingly, most do. Of course, it probably doesn't hurt that the guards are now actively beating several fairies into submission. "If you have not enlisted, do so today. Join us, and I promise you, the rest of our days we will live as kings." Again, shouts ring out, so loud my body almost vibrates with the noise.

Proud of himself, the King hands the microphone off to a guard, and then he reclaims his seat on the throne. The crowd calms slightly now, although a few are causing issues a block back as Quinn and I move out of the way of a group of guards, trying to push our way forward.

No more than a minute later, the procession begins moving again, and Quinn and I are already en-route. He and I both carry batons as we push our way through the chaos. For effect, Quinn nudges a fairy out of the way as we pass. The fairy stumbles back, and a fight breaks out as we rush down the final block. Any minute now, my boys will do their part, and we can finally finish this.

I'm still moving but I'm watching when King Tobin looks back over his shoulder, seeing the crowds pushing back against the guards. The fairy wine has definitely gone to their heads. No matter, the more chaos, the better.

When I take the next step, a fairy bumps into me, and when I turn, ready to knock him back, I see he looks no older than fifteen. He's being jostled around by a dozen or more Trolls as they jump and pump their fists toward the sky, so thinking quick, I graze my hand against his arm, sending magic from me to him. When it takes hold, he slowly floats above the crowd, and I beg my magic to deposit him on top of a nearby building.

While Quinn and I don't stop moving, I can't look away from the young fairy until I see he's out of harm's way. When his feet touch down, even though he's far away, I can see relief wash over him.

"We need to get closer," Quinn whisper-shouts, shoving a fairy that got too close to me.

I nod in agreement, and we put our heads down, staying close to one another. Together, we barrel through the mass of bodies, gunning for the back of the King's float, but when we're within feet, I hear screams coming from behind us. They aren't the screams of drunken idiots though. No, those are the screams of terror.

I know I shouldn't, but I look back anyway. The problem is I don't see anything, and neither does Quinn, if the look on his face is any indication. With my head turned though, I bump into someone, and when I turn back, facing forward, I see that someone is a King's guard.

"You two," he growls, "protect the King." Before the words are even fully out of his mouth, he's already moved on to three guards beating back the masses near an alley opening on our right.

With the guard out of earshot, Quinn chuckles, "Well, that couldn't have worked out any better."

"Agreed."

We rush the last few feet, meeting a line of guards with

their backs to the float we need to be on. They're the only thing standing between us and the King's float, between us and the King. Just ten fairies in a line is all we need to get through. Sure there are at least eight guards on the float now, but one step at a time, people.

"Who *are* you?" the middle guard asks; a Leprechaun.

"Elder and Quib, sir," Quinn answers, "The Captain re-stationed us to guard the King."

It's a good thing Quinn is with me, because I didn't even notice that guard was a captain. As far as I was concerned, he was just another guard. I guess Quinn could've pulled it out of his ass, but I don't think so.

The Leprechaun eyes us both, but he doesn't have much of a choice but to believe us, so he nods his head to the end of the line, and Quinn and I turn. We don't make it to the end though, because a boom sounds from a few blocks down, and the blast knocks everyone back. As I soar through the air, it dawns on me that I'm in for a very rough landing.

***

Nyx

We thought the King had done us a solid, because his little speech incited some serious chaos. Unfortunately, almost as soon as it started, it basically stopped. I mean, I guess the guards beating people to death probably helped with that.

At the time though, we weren't ready to enact our plan anyway, because we'd run into a bit of trouble when a couple fights broke out too close to Ari. If we'd been ready, all that craziness would've made our diversion that much more successful. We lost our chance though, and now, as Ari and I prepare to fuck some shit up, I'm just praying to God Ell and Quinn are where they need to be.

As I send up my silent prayer, Blake stumbles out into the street, his arms flailing and his head rolling all over the place.

He may be stone-cold sober, but he looks wasted, and that's a good thing, because it's all part of the plan.

"Here we go," Ari mumbles, and as he does, Blake throws a punch.

Blake's fist connects with a fairy seated on the front of a float, and the fairy falls forward, knocked out, while two fairies jump down to aid him. The crowd is going wild though, rushing for the center of the street, ready to fight. Honestly, I've never seen some fairies so ready to fight. I thought our little group was bad, but we don't hold a candle to the UnSeelie.

I shake my head as the brawl grows in number, and I lose sight of Blake in the melee. I spot Lucas though, and since he's where he needs to be, Ari and I both give him a nod at the same time.

Here goes nothing.

There's so many fairies surrounding us, no one seems to notice when fire forms in the palm of Ari's hand. It's a small ball, as far as fireballs go, maybe the size of a softball. He tosses it up like we're about to play a game, and when it rises above everyone's heads, I use my magic to force it toward the now empty float in front of us.

All that tissue paper probably wasn't a good idea, because as soon as Ari's fire connects with the trailer, the entire thing goes up in flames. Fairies scream, and when a small Elf, no more than five or six, ends up under the stampede forming, I sprint, gripping her under the arms and depositing her across the street inside a shop.

When I turn back, fairies are rushing away from the still burning trailer, but unfortunately, they aren't going the right way. Nearly every single one rushes *away* from the King's circle, and my heart sinks.

This is not good.

As of right now, no one knows we started that fire. At least, no one important anyway. But now, with everyone running in the wrong direction, we have no choice but to do more, and it will most definitely result in our capture. It doesn't matter though, because I know I speak for everyone when I say we'll do anything to protect Ell, we'll do anything to end this.

As the chaos continues, I realize Ari is still on the opposite side of the street. He's trying to fight his way to me, but it's just no use, and I see it in his eyes when he gives up, stepping back and settling for setting a vendor's cart on fire. I try to be discreet when I cast my magic toward him, using it to fan the flames. It does almost nothing in our favor though. Not one person even pays attention to it.

We need something bigger.

I don't get to think on it though, because someone grips me from behind, yanking me in the wrong direction. I try to pull away, but as I do, I realize it's Lucas. "We need to get past the crowd…get down a few blocks and do something to push them back the other way!" he shouts, barely audible over the pandemonium that surrounds us.

He's right, so I don't argue, following him quickly. The problem is, quick isn't quick enough. We can only move as fast as the herd around us, which puts us behind most everyone. We have to find a way to get in front of them.

I'm just about to levitate Lucas and I both over the masses, but as I ready my magic, there's a massive boom. Luke is thrown back into me, and I'm thrown back into someone else. I can still feel the force of the explosion when I hit the ground, and something wet runs down my neck. I know it's blood, I just don't know if it's mine or someone else's.

After only a few seconds, I somehow manage to sit up, even though my head is throbbing and I can't hear a thing. Upright, I send my magic, asking it to heal whatever is wrong with my head, and while it takes a minute, I do feel slightly better, but not by much.

As I shake my head, most everyone around me is still on the ground, and everyone seems to be in shock. I still don't see Lucas though, or Ari, for that matter, although there is no telling where he is by now. I know I need to find them though, but as I roll to my knees, nausea washes over me. I push it back, and grit my teeth as I make it to my feet.

The area around us is filled with a white smoke, and looking down Center Street, maybe two blocks down, everything is blazing. The fire burns so hot I can feel it from here, and it's then that the screams register.

Dear God, the screams.

***

Luke

I was thrown down a side street when the explosion rocked the whole area. I'm pretty sure I was knocked clean out, because when I came to, every fairy I could see on Center Street and beyond was lying on the ground dead or unconscious.

Now, I stumble through the mess of bodies, searching for the others. Blake was in the middle of Center the last time I saw him, but Nyx, he was with me when the blast threw me back. I don't see him anywhere now though. I was thrown a pretty good distance, but I'm back at Center now, and he's nowhere to be seen.

That worry will have to wait though, because the bigger question is who the hell caused that explosion? Obviously it wasn't Blake. Nyx was with me, and I know it wasn't Ari either because I had eyes on him. Plus, there's no way he could have done something like that, especially from where he was. So, who?

Regardless, whoever it was, their actions did *not* help us. The explosion killed or severely injured almost everyone within eyesight, which means fairies aren't going to be rushing toward the King's Circle like we had planned. That means Ell and Quinn won't have the rush of bodies to cover them. They got a diversion, just not the one they were hoping for, or one that will even help, for that matter.

Worried, I step over a pile of bodies and trash, moving into the middle of the street. I look toward the raging fires, and that's when I spot Nyx, digging through the bodies, probably looking for Blake and Arion. I jog to catch up to him, and when I reach his back, I see he has a nasty gash on the back of his head. It doesn't look life-threatening, but it does need to be treated.

"Any luck funding the other two?" I ask, startling him as he spins, ready to fight. Seeing me, he lets out a relieved breath, his shoulders slumping as he shakes his head. "You keep looking on this side," I suggest, "I'll start over there."

Without waiting for him to respond, I take off, heading to the opposite side of the street where I last saw Arion. As I move over bodies of all sizes though, I cast a quick look at the King's Circle, and when I do, my throat closes and I'm pretty sure my heart stops.

Frozen in my tracks, I shout for Nyx. "Look!"

Nyx is squatted down, digging through another pile, and when he looks up, he's annoyed with the interruption. I point, and he follows my gaze. When his eyes land on what has me frozen, his face mirrors my own.

The King's float wasn't on a trailer. No, it's a fucking platform. And now, as we watch in horror, it rises above the bodies, preparing to take off, probably to deliver the King safely back to the palace. The problem is, I don't know if I hope Ell is on it, or if she didn't make it on in time. Either way, this is worst case scenario for us.

LAMBS TO THE SLAUGHTER

Ell

I do *not* think this was part of the plan. Sure we wanted a diversion, but this is not that. This is mass murder. Or, at least, mass injury. When the wave from the explosion hit us, everyone was thrown back. I landed in a heap against the wall of a shop, and luckily, Quinn landed not far from me. When we shook it off and got to our feet, we were the only ones. Every other fairy in the circle or near it was on the ground. Piles of fairies dead or dying surrounded us, even the guards tasked with protecting the King weren't in much better shape.

It's been maybe five-minutes since then, and we've finally made it over the fairy covered street and back to where we started. The line of guards is gone, but the float that housed the King is still intact. Although, I damn sure don't see him.

"Where the fuck did that little twat go?" I whisper-hiss, leaning into Quinn, but he shakes his head and shrugs.

The float has a back on it, and since the top stands at around twenty feet, we can't see over it to tell if the King is on the other side. So, without discussing it, we work our way to the side, stealthily, not that it matters, and when we make it to the front, the King lies on his side, two guards standing over him.

"Your Majesty...Your Majesty..." one of them says over and over, shaking the King.

"This is our chance," Quinn tells me, not bothering to whisper.

I agree. This might be our *only* chance. I have a clear shot and we only have to get past two guards to get to him. I hate the idea of kicking someone while they're down, but you know, he's a dick so I don't really care.

Not wanting to waste any time, Quinn hops over the side of the trailer, reaching down and giving me a hand up. When I get my footing though, he lets go, causing me to fall back over the side.

Well, that was completely rude, and as I finally get back on, opening my mouth to tell him off, I freeze at seeing his face. He too is frozen, staring at something I can't yet see.

"What is it?" I hiss, but he ignores me, pulling away and stumbling forward as if he's in a blind haze. He's really starting to freak me out too, and I wonder if someone used magic on him. I don't know who it would be though, because there isn't anyone. The two guards haven't even noticed us yet, and the King is just starting to come to.

I realize I may be about to lose my very small window of opportunity though, so I step over an Elf in blue gossamer, working my way to the King. Unfortunately, I'm only halfway there when a hand reaches out, stopping me.

"You there," the Captain from earlier barks, "guard the front of the float while I get us moving."

Well, shit. Now what? He's just one fairy, plus the two guards now helping the King to his feet, so do I try to fight them, or do I play along, for now?

Quinn is clearly going to be no help, because he's now knelt over something or someone on the far side of the float, so I guess I'm on my own in this, no matter what I decide.

The Captain shakes me. "Snap out of it. Get it together, and get to the front of the float. We need to get the King out of here, ASAP."

"Yes, sir," I mumble, deciding to play along for a minute until I can figure out what Quinn's problem is.

When the two guards finally get the King situated in his throne, I make it to the front of the float. I take up a fighting stance, and prepare to fight anyone off that tries to board. Or, at least, that's what I want everyone to think.

With my back rigid, it's in this moment, as I gaze out at the empty King's Circle, that a worry hits me deep in my heart. I know the repulsion magic made us think all kinds of horrible things about one another, but what if they were grounded is some small glimmer of truth?

As soon as we boarded, Quinn left me, racing for the other side and leaving me. Even still, he sits on the far side of the trailer, as if he's guarding the King. *Is* he guarding the King? He said he had no love for King Tobin, but what if that was all a lie so he could lead us like lambs to the slaughter? But if that's the case, then you'd think he would've already revealed me to the King and his guards.

No, stop that. What are you doing? Quinn is one of your five, Ell. He would never do that. He loves you. There has to be a good explanation as to why he spaced out and abandoned the plan like that. There just has to be.

***

Ell

Two more guards come to and join us on the float over the next five-minutes or so, and Quinn is still out of it, lost in his own head. The King has a nasty gash over his eye, and he too seems spaced out. The Captain has been at the back wall of the trailer, working on something, but what, I don't know. And as for me, I'm just keeping my eyes on it all.

Another guard approaches, boarding next to me, and I realize I can't wait any longer. The long game isn't going to work. The longer I wait, the more guards are going to come to and move to protect the King. Not to mention, at any moment the float could move back inside the gates of the palace, with me and Quinn on it, and then we'd be royally screwed. I mean, they'd have to run over a bunch of bodies, but I doubt King Tobin gives a shit about that.

Turning my head, I see the King has his head down, his hand rubbing a spot on the back of his neck. He shakes his head twice, as if he's trying to clear the fog, and the two guards from before still stand over him, protective. No one is paying any attention to me though, so I know this is my chance.

I rest my hand on the guard next to me, my magic seeping from me to him instantly. I wish for him to sleep, and the magic takes hold before he can make a sound. Gently, I guide him over the front of the trailer, allowing him to slump against the front, and then I stand back upright, checking to make sure no one saw. When I'm sure they didn't, I search out Quinn one last time. I can see him clearly now, and while he sits with his legs over the side as if he's just chillin', I now know he's not. There's a body across his lap, a body that is scary still, and while I don't know who it is, it's clearly someone he knows.

There's no time for it though, so gathering all the magic I can, I let go of any chance of getting Quinn's help, and reaching inside the back of my waistband, I retrieve the dagger Helga gave me. All I need to do is kill the King with this, and all our problems are solved. Sure we'll have to get inside the palace and defeat the UnSeelie in general, but King Tobin being out of the picture will make that so much easier. So, here goes nothing.

One step for Ell, one giant leap for fairy-kind.

***

Quinn

When I stepped on the float, I saw her, and everything else flew away from me. I could focus on nothing but getting to her. I left Ell behind, and not caring about looking suspicious or out of place, I stumbled to Tika. She laid on her side, covered in blood, and I wasn't even sure why. No matter where I looked, I couldn't find the source of her injury. That was, until I turned her over. Tika had a massive gash in her back, most likely obtained when she was thrown by the blast, and the sight made me wretch.

I have no idea how long I've been sitting here, holding her. I'm clueless as to what's going on around me, even though I know I should be helping Ell. This was our one and only shot to take down King Tobin, and at the first sign of trouble, I bailed. She'll probably never forgive me for this, but I can't bring myself to get up.

Tika's breathing slows even further, and I can feel her heart rate dropping. She needs a healer, but with all the devastation around me, I doubt I'd find one in time. Nyx might be able to help, but this injury is so bad that I highly doubt he could save her.

"Tika," I whisper, and I'm shocked when her eyes flutter open, "Tika, oh my Devil, Tika!"

Her body shakes slightly, and her eyes close again. She isn't dead though, and she was with it enough that she opened her eyes on command, which means there's still hope. Hope or not though, until Ell does what we came here to do, there's no way for me to get Tika the help she needs. We need to finish this.

I don't move Tika yet, but I do look over my shoulder, seeking Ell out. She stands at the front of the float, and she turns as my eyes fall on her, facing the King. He's keeled over in his throne, and two guards stand over him, worried.

Looking back to Ell, I start to move my sister, but my eyes land on something horrible. A fairy, brown magic seeping from his hands, walks stealthily behind Ell. Her hand is behind her back, and I have no doubt she's going for the dagger Helga gave her, which means that's probably why the fairy looks down at her hand every other step she takes.

She's halfway there, and in one move I set Tika to the side and shout for Ell, "Behind you!"

I'm running before Ell can get turned around, and I sweep past her, barely blocking a killing strike from the fairy behind her. She shrieks my name, and still engaged with the fairy, I tell her, "Go! Finish this!" I don't know if she listens, my back is to her, but it doesn't matter because I'm kind of in the middle of something.

The fairy, an Elf, lunges for me, catching me under the eye with a knife he pulled out of nowhere. Seriously, I'm not sure where that came from or how I missed it. I guess I had an Ell moment and need to pay more attention.

I can feel the tiniest trickle of blood running down my cheek as I sweep to the right, my fist connecting with the Elf's kidney. Spinning to the other side, I get him in the other one, and he doubles over, his arms wrapped around his middle. He groans in pain as I send my magic out in every direction, searching for a major source of water. I finally get a hit, and I pull, my magic rushing back toward me just as the Elf straightens his back. He slits his eyes and growls, ready to lunge for me once again, but it's too late. Water in the shape of a spear slams into his back, throwing him into me and we both go flying.

Really should've thought that one through.

I'm pissed at myself as the Elf and I hit the ground together, but the force spins us in opposite directions. Pain reverberates through my body, and I roll end over end until I'm falling over the front of the float. It's only about four-feet off the ground, but the hard stone connecting with my back hurts as if I just fell from ten stories. The wind is knocked out of me and I gasp, rolling over on my stomach and trying to catch my breath.

With one last shake of my head, I climb to my feet. The first thing I see is the Elf, unconscious and lying in a heap a good twenty-feet away. The second thing I see is Tika, still lying semi-unconscious where I left her. The last thing my eyes land on is my worst nightmare. It's instantly clear Ell lost the element of surprise, because as I clamber, trying to get back on the float, she fights four fairies by herself, and the King is now standing, ready to make her pay.

***

Ell

The heads up Quinn gave me was much appreciated. However, it screwed me out of the element of surprise. As soon as he shouted for me and sprinted across the float, every other fairy near us trained their eyes on me. The Captain, who had been working to get the float moving, turned away from what he was doing, and it was then I realized behind the panel he was blocking, sat a set of controls. As he moved, the two fairies caring for the King had also stepped in my direction, and before the fight even started, two more fairies stepped into view.

Now, Quinn fights the Elf behind me, while the other five ready their magic and I do the same. Carefully, I secure the dagger back in my waistband because I cannot take a chance on losing that thing. The whole plan would be fucked, and we might as well surrender.

With my dagger returned, the two fairies nearest the King stand shoulder to shoulder facing me, and they're the only thing between me and King Tobin. The other three fairies, including the Captain, are further to the left, so if I can rush these two assholes, I might be able to do this. The other three might kill me in the end, but at least we killed the King, at least we put a stop to him creating a new realm, and as much as I don't want to die, I think it would be worth it.

I take one step in the King's direction, and water sprays all over me, slicking the trailer floor beneath my feet. I feel a whoosh over my head, my hair flipping over my shoulders, and from the corner of my eye, I see Quinn fly past. I hope he's okay, because I don't really have time to help him right now.

Sending up a mental prayer for Quinn, I slide closer to the King and toss out some magic in my path. As I do, I'm pretty sure I hear Blake in the back of my mind. You know, like I used to. I can't be one-hundred percent sure, but the back of my mind is tickling, and I think Blake is groaning. That probably isn't a good thing, and I just pray he's okay.

I have to ignore that though, so I thrust some more magic forward, and the guard on the left takes a direct hit and ends up in King Tobin's lap. The King doesn't look happy about it either, and he dumps the fairy on the floor, growling and trying to stand, but whatever injuries he sustained in the blast have him falling back in his seat.

Looking away from him, I realize the other guard doesn't seem fazed by my magic, and he's still coming for me. We slam together, slipping on the wet floor, and slide nearly to the far edge, each of us gripping the other for support.

My heels are over the edge when we finally stop, and the guard grunts, trying to make me lose my balance and send me over the edge. I'm just barely hanging on when something slams into me from the side. The guard and I fall, our clothes soaked, and now there's a third fairy on me. We grapple back and forth, and I pull the water from the floor, using it to help my cause. It isn't doing much though, and I'm pretty sure there's now an extra body on me.

Through the chaos of the fighting, I hear Quinn shout my name, but there's too much going on to figure out where he is or if he's okay. I'm pressed front to front with one fairy, with two more on top of us, and another one to my left. As I wiggle around though, I manage to get my hand on a guard's stomach. His eyes go wide as my magic seeps into his body, and to be honest, I'm not even sure what will happen to him. There was so much running through my mind, I don't know what I intended.

I don't have time to worry about it though, because I'm yanked back by the hair and slung across the trailer. My back hits something hard, knocking the air out of my lungs, and when I finally get a breath, I'm pressed to the throne and the King isn't sitting in it.

Where the fuck did you go, you sneaky little bastard?

Scrambling, I'm back on my feet just in time to block a stream of deep-green magic. It hits my shield hard, forcing me back, and I have to shield my eyes. It's so bright that I'm fairly certain I'm now blinded for life. This is *so* not the time.

Still barely able to see, I square up, pushing back, probably looking like I'm trying to walk through gale-force winds. The force is so great I can't do anything but fight it though. It's strong enough that I don't think it's coming from an average fairy either, which means it's probably coming from the King himself. And that, my dear Watson, is *so* not good.

The force is too much, so I can't seek him out. I just have to focus on blocking instead. Being on the defense is not a good place for me, and I still don't know where Quinn is or what's going on with him.

And that's when I stumble. But not because of the magic, because we're fucking moving. Not forward or back. No, we are definitely moving up. What in the actual fuck?

ONE-TIME USE KIND OF DAGGER

Ell

Abort mission. There's no time to do what needs to be done. No, now it's time to bail, because the trailer we thought was a trailer is *not* a trailer. That fucking Captain is flying us higher in the sky, and it's now a reality that we are, in fact, on a platform. If we don't get off this thing and soon, we'll be inside the palace walls with no chance of escape.

Already we're a good twenty-feet off the ground, and rising quickly. Quinn fights an Elf, and it seems like he has the upper hand, but I'm still fending off this massive line of green magic, and I really need it to stop.

I close my eyes, digging in deep, and when I'm sure I've pulled everything I've got, I thrust it out in front of me and hope it's enough. The magic escapes my body, and the force is so massive that everything goes silent. My ears pop as I watch a guard tumble over the side. That just leaves one more, other than the one Quinn is still fighting.

I search the space, and the guard I'm looking for is kneeling over the King. Whatever my magic just did, it was a lot, because the King is flat on his back, gasping for air, so I trudge forward despite the effect his magic still has on me. As I move only inches, I'm keenly aware of how high we are already, and I know I shouldn't, but I take two seconds to check where we are.

When I lean over the side, I see we're directly over the King's statue in the center of the Circle, but as I push forward, I feel us turning. We're headed directly for the palace gates now, which means I'm out of time.

Unfortunately, I don't make it another step because Quinn slides up to my side, gripping me by the forearm and tugging me away from where I need to go. "Come on. We need to grab my sister and get the hell out of here."

"Quinn, no." I try to pull away but his grip is too tight, and also what does he mean; his sister? "Is your sister *here*? Where?" He nods in the direction he's still tugging me, but again, I pull back. "If we leave now we won't get another chance, Quinn. Get your sister and get the hell out of here."

He freezes in his tracks, his eyes wide with indecision. "I…"

"Just go, please. I've got this."

I rip my arm from his grasp, slipping past him and seeking out the King again. He's now sitting up, and the guard is trying desperately to help him to his feet. I only have seconds left before he gets it together though, because when he does, I won't stand a fucking chance. I'm too worn down at this point. And, the scariest thing of all, I just realized I can't feel my boys. None of them, except Quinn. It's like their tethers are just gone. I don't even want to think about why that is.

Worried, I reach my hand behind my back, and retrieve the dagger for the second time today. Seeing me, the King's guard steps in-between us, and the act causes the King to stumble back. The guard swipes his baton at me, and I take a hard hit to the forearm, the pain snaking up my arm and into my shoulder. That might be broken, but it doesn't matter. I need to finish this.

"Get out of my way," I growl, pushing with all my might.

I know I can't risk using the dagger on the guard. What if it's a one-time use kind of dagger? I can't take that chance. So instead, I juke left, spinning and popping my elbow into the back of his head. He falls forward, and I reach around, funneling a burst of magic into his back and wishing for him to fly away. Instantly, as if all the gravity around him was sucked out, his limbs flail out and he floats upward. I hope he comes back down eventually, but that isn't my problem right now.

As the guard disappears above me, my eyes connect with King Tobin's for the first time since this fight started. I slit mine, and he does the same. We both square off, ready to charge, and then we just stand there, like neither one of us wants to be the one to make the first move.

I'll be your huckleberry. God, I love that movie. Best movie of all time. Change my mind.

Getting my head back in the game, I go in for the kill, not even bothering to use magic because I'd rather feel my fist connect with his stupid face. And it does, twice, before he finally decides to participate. He punches back, hitting me once in the stomach as I swipe wildly with the dagger, but he blocks me every time, and I can feel him gathering his magic.

We reset, and once again, the King lunges for me. As he does, the air around us feels charged, most likely due to the blueish-green orb surrounding his fist. He thrusts the orb at me more than once, but I side step each time, until finally he shakes away the magic, and instead, throws two bare punches. I block them both, but then I slip, and no matter how hard I try, I can't keep myself upright. I face-plant, my body skidding across the wet surface, and before I can get turned over, the King is on my back.

"Ell!" Quinn shouts for me, and I can hear the terror in his voice.

Yeah, I get it. I think I just lost this fight, but I'm not quite ready to give up, so I shoot a pulse of magic out of my back. Unfortunately, I don't feel the King's weight leave me. What I do feel is his hands gripping my hair. He pulls my head back, and then slams it against the floor. Instantly, my head throbs, and I think I might puke. When he does it a second time, I'm not sure how I'm still conscious.

I'm so dizzy now that when I crane my neck, trying to find a way out of this, I can barely see anything in front of me. My stomach is churning, and it's almost like I can feel a knot forming from where my head connected with the platform's floor. I'm trying to shake it off, but I'm not sure how much more I can give.

Sucking in a deep breath, my vision blurs in and out as I feel the King's weight leave my body, and I don't know how, but I manage to roll to my back. As soon as I do though, the King is back on me, and I growl.

"Did you honestly think a glamour would work on me? I'm stronger than you, little fairy. The sooner you realize that, the better," he spits in my face, his words a growl, "You've been a real fucking problem for me, Queen of the Seelie." His tone is gruff, malice dripping from his lips. "I'm going to enjoy this."

His hands charge, and the energy feels dark and dirty as I resign myself to death, turning my head to the side and not wanting to see this coming. When I look down though, my eyes connect with my hand, and I feel like a dumbass as I realize the dagger is still gripped tightly in my fingers. That's how fucked up I am right now, because I can't even feel it. I can feel my arm though, and it feels like a lead weight. Despite that, I beg my appendage to move, and it shudders as if it wants to but just doesn't have anything left.

Trying once more, the King puts his clammy hands on my face, grossing me out, but that fact gives me a small burst of energy, and my hand jerks up, limply wielding the dagger. It's barely hanging on by a thread though, so when it connects with the King's side it doesn't even go in. Sadly, it leaves nothing more than a scratch on the skin I can see through a tear in his shirt, and my heart sinks. Once again, I have to push back the bile rising up in my throat, and I can barely see because my head is throbbing.

My tank is empty and I go limp, knowing that was my one and only shot. I look at the King, a fucking grin on his face, and I'd give anything to wipe it off, but as I watch him, ready to finish me off, his smirk slowly changes. His eyes get bigger and bigger, to the point I'm worried they might pop out, and then he's scuttling back.

"Wha…what…did you…do to me?" He scrambles as he tries to make sense of something I don't understand.

With his head shaking in disbelief, he crab-walks away from me, and I feel arms grip my underarms. Looking up, Quinn stands over me, a body thrown over his shoulder. He doesn't speak as he attempts to throw me over his shoulder too, but I can't imagine him being able to carry two bodies. Plus, I'm not sure he realizes this, but we have to be inside the palace walls by now.

Despite the two bodies, Quinn does manage to get a grip on us both, and moving to the edge, he looks down. "Ell, I don't know if you have anything left, but levitation isn't my forte."

"Or mine," I groan, my head swimming. Being upside down is only making it worse.

"You gotta try, baby, you gotta try. There's dozens of guards underneath us just waiting for us to land."

I mentally curse because I don't have the strength to do it out loud, and that's when I see the King. He's convulsing, as if he's having a seizure. His eyes are rolled back in his head, his tongue hangs out of his mouth, and there's a white foam starting to form. What the hell did I do to him? Is he dying?

"Ell, I need you to focus," Quinn tries again, as I feel the platform lowering closer to the ground.

Closing my eyes, I nod my head, hoping he can feel it as I beg my magic to encase us, to deliver us somewhere else and not into the clutches of the guards beneath us.

I don't know if it works until I feel Quinn jump. And it's *definitely* not working because we are *definitely* falling.

***

Ari

I have no idea how long I was unconscious after the explosion on the parade route. When I came to, I realized I'd been thrown through the front windows of a storefront. Tiny shards of glass covered nearly every inch of my body, and a massive piece protruded from my left calf.

It took me at least five-minutes to sit up, and another ten to make it back out on Center Street. The sight before me made me stumble back though, and when I looked to my right, I found Nyx, Blake, and Lucas fighting a small contingent of guards, but it was in the middle of that fight that I realized the King's float was gone. While he continued to fight, Nyx had filled me in.

That float isn't a float, but a platform, and now, it's completely gone from our sight as we finish off the last of the guards. With that done, no one has to say a word, and we're all running toward the King's Circle. Lucas saw the platform head toward the palace gates, which means if Ell was on it, she is now completely cut off from any help from us. If she isn't on it, then she's out here somewhere in the sea of bodies. Honestly, I don't know which is worse.

Stumbling over a dead fairy, I slow, stopping everyone else. "We need to play this smart. We can't just charge the gate."

"What do you suggest then?" Lucas asks, although it isn't said with annoyance, but more of a genuine question.

Rubbing my temples, I try to think, but nothing reasonable comes to mind. I'm supposed to be our leader, and I can't even lead. Ell and Quinn are missing, and probably inside the palace by now. How the fuck do we get them back?

Lucas interrupts my thoughts, as he suggests, "Let's take that alley around the block. We'll come in on the front side of the circle, and we'll have a straight view of the gates."

Not able to think of anything better than that, I nod, and we're all jogging again. As we move, we do our best not to step on any bodies, but it's next to impossible. You can barely see the stone street for all the fairies piled up. I've seen a few starting to wake up, but I think most of these fairies are dead. We didn't do this, and I just can't imagine who did. Whoever it was didn't give a shit about loss of life. There were innocent fairies out here. There were *fucking* children.

That thought makes rage bubble up inside me as we make it to the main street, now able to see straight to the palace. The statue of King Tobin makes it a little difficult, but craning my neck, I can just make out hundreds of guards lining up around something. I can't tell what it is, but when I turn to Nyx, I breathe out a dozen cuss words in a row.

"What?" Nyx asks, freaking out.

"Your glamour...it's gone," I stumble on the words, not wanting to think of why that is. I know, but I refuse to admit it or say it out loud.

"*What*?" Nyx repeats, as he turns his head in a circle, looking at each of the others. "How do you know that..." He curses, slamming his fist into the wall. His knuckles split, but he doesn't seem to care.

"How do you know?" Blake asks. "I mean, you all looked like yourselves to me before too, so how can you tell?"

"The magic is gone," Luke chimes in, running his hand through his hair, "It's...gone."

He's right. It is gone. And now that I'm thinking about it, I can't feel Ell's magic on me. Before, I could feel it constantly grazing across my skin, but now, it's just gone.

"What the fuck does this mean?" Blake asks, panicked. He turns his hands over and back, not wanting to believe what we're all seeing.

"She's..." Lucas trails off, looking back to the gates, "No... she...she could just be unconscious. Right?"

"Yes," I agree, "But..."

Lucas' head shoots up, his eyes skyward as he points. "Look. Is that...?"

I don't see what he's talking about at first, but when I scan a second time, I spot something floating high above us. It's too far away, but as we watch, whatever it is disappears behind the clouds.

"Could that be..." Nyx mumbles, almost to himself, as he shakes his head.

"Leave me here," Blake barks, "I'll be fine. Just get up there. See if it's her."

I agree with the idea, but if we fly up from right here, everyone will be able to see us. I just don't think that's a good idea. Sure most everyone is still knocked out, but there were some guards waking up, and that's not even thinking about the ones we saw behind the gate.

As I think that, a shout comes from behind us, and we all spin, turning and preparing to fight off whoever it is, but as I ready my magic, I stop as my eyes land on Thrill running toward us. Honestly, I've never been so relieved to see an UnSeelie in my entire life.

"They're coming!" he shouts the words, running and waving his arms for us to go. "Go! Go! Go!"

We start running before he reaches us, even though none of us is sure what we're running from. I don't want to look back either, because that's the worst thing we could do right now. Fortunately, I don't have to, because Thrill catches us, and for a big guy, he's fast as hell, passing us easily.

"We can't leave Ell!" Nyx shouts at him, and then he turns over his shoulder, his eyes bugging out. I don't even want to know what that's about.

"We aren't leaving her, or Quinn," Thrill calls back, "They already got out. I saw it with my own eyes. Now, come on!"

We each put on a burst of speed, turning two corners in a matter of seconds. We may be running for our lives right now, but I've never been so relieved. Ell and Quinn are both out, and if we can get away, this might all be over. Well, assuming Ell did what she was supposed to do.

God, let it be over.

ORGASMS IT IS

Ari

It's not over. Ell didn't kill the King. She said she barely even scratched him. Sure he had some sort of seizure, but as Ell and Quinn floated away after nearly falling to their deaths, Ell saw King Tobin get back up as if nothing happened.

After that, Ell, Quinn, and Quinn's sister barely escaped with their lives, and when Thrill led us back to the pub, we found them in our room. Ell and Quinn were both worn thin and sleeping, but when we all piled on the bed, minus Thrill who stood in the kitchen, Ell and Quinn filled us in.

That's when we found out the pub owner had helped Quinn get his sister to a healer. That's where she is now, and she isn't doing great. Quinn said she could need weeks to fully recover, but the important thing is she's no longer in the King's clutches.

That was all last night, and this morning, none of us are feeling much better. Not physically, and not about the fact that we failed. Whatever Helga saw us achieving didn't happen. Ell was supposed to kill the King, and she didn't. Don't get me wrong, I'm just glad she's alive. Unfortunately, it's probably a temporary reprieve because when the King creates his new realm, we're all dead anyway.

Thrill left last night, saying he had a friend he was going to hide out with, so right now, it's just us. Blake is in the shower, but the rest of us are piled on the bed, resting. My back is pressed to the wall, and Ell's head rests against my stomach. The strap of her black tank falls loose, bearing her to me, and despite the situation, I'm now only thinking about fucking her.

It seems Nyx has the same idea, because he rolls over, grabbing the strap in his teeth and pulling it down further. She sighs, a contented sound, and it's music to my ears.

My hand slides under her tank, ready to take this to the next level, but Lucas stops us. "Wait..." He doesn't finish his thought at first, as we all stare at him waiting. So long passes that I'm just about to brush him off and get back to fucking Ell, when he starts again, "Helga didn't say Ell had to kill him. She said the magic was in the blade, and Ell had to use the blade to break the Dryad magic. *She* didn't say Ell had to kill him, *we* said that." His words are so low it's almost as if he's talking to himself, trying to figure things out. "I don't think she failed."

In that moment, Blake steps out of the bathroom, a towel covering his waist. "What do you mean?"

"Actually...you could be right," I turn to Lucas, not bothering to fill Blake in, "Ell did say he had a seizure. What if that was the magic breaking? What if it wasn't a seizure at all?"

"Yeah," Nyx agrees, still trying to pull Ell's tank down, "I don't know a lot of seizures where you can just pop up and go about your business when it's over."

"I guess I didn't think about that," Ell mumbles, considering what Nyx said but not bothering to push him off of her, "But if that's the case, now what do we do? I mean, just because the magic is broken, or...*might* be broken, doesn't mean he can't go through with the next two sacrifices. It doesn't stop him from creating a new realm."

She's right. It doesn't. We thought King Tobin would die today, and that would stop all of this.

"If we're right," I muse, now up and pacing the room, "and if the Dryad's magic is broken, then that means...Well, that means we still have to do something else to stop him from moving forward with his plan. Either kill him, or something else."

"Like what?" Nyx asks, removing Ell's top and plopping a nipple in his mouth.

Ell's head falls back, and she runs her fingers through his hair. "I have to kill him. If I broke the magic, he's now killable. I don't need the dagger...Ohhh, yeah, right there..." She stops mid-thought, clearly enjoying whatever Nyx is doing. "If I don't have to use the dagger, I can kill him with magic."

"She's right," Lucas agrees, watching Ell and rubbing his hand across his crotch, "We just need to get Ell close enough to him." He pauses, immersed in Ell and Nyx's foreplay. "And we need to do it fast, because the third sacrifice is coming quick."

"Right," Ell mumbles, groaning in the back of her throat, "but I think we have time for a few orgasms, right?"

Nyx pops off her tit. "Right."

When he pulls her jeans down to her ankles, baring her to us, I'm not sure how I can argue with their logic. Orgasms it is.

***

Ell

When the fate of the realm rests in your hands, and your boyfriends fully support a timeout for orgasms, you know you've found the right ones. They are perfect in every way. Sure I know I'm difficult to deal with sometimes, and I can be downright selfish in others, but no matter what, I know they always have my back. We're end game.

I've known it all along, but it really hit me today, especially after what happened yesterday. And now, as Nyx shimmies down my body, ready to tongue-fuck me, I'm even more certain of it.

"You get five orgasms," Ari tells me, watching from the foot of the bed, "one from each of us, and then after that, we need to figure out what to do next." His arms are crossed, and he looks so sexy with a single strip of hair slipped across his eye.

"Twelve," I negotiate, arching my back and moaning when Nyx's tongue slips inside me.

"Six, and not a single one more," Ari bites back, serious.

His tone leaves no room for argument, so I don't bother. I'll get what I need and want before today is through, and I'm already so close to finishing the first one.

Wiggling to the left, I run my hand down my belly as the others watch. "Nyx," I groan, "to the left."

Being the dear that he is, he moves his tongue to the left, hitting the spot I like, and goosebumps break out on my skin. The pressure building feels so intense, and I hold my breath, lifting my butt off the bed to get closer to his mouth.

"More," I call, begging the rest to join us. In fact, I'm not sure why they haven't. That isn't like them, unless we're playing Ari is the boss again, but I know we aren't because he hasn't said a word since he negotiated for six orgasms.

I search Ari out, and he's still at the foot of the bed. His arms are crossed tightly against his chest, and he stares at me, his eyes filled with yearning. He doesn't rub his dick though, or anything else. He just watches. It's kind of hot, and I'm panting, about to come when someone else finally joins the party. Blake kneels beside the bed, and his paw of a hand kneads one of my breasts. Each time he loosens his grip, he flicks his thumb across my nipple. It feels fucking magical, and with his help, I feel my core clench. I call out, although I don't think those were English words.

Nyx chuckles as he lifts his head from between my legs. "Were those actual words?"

I pant, "I...don't...know..."

"My turn," Luke insists, pushing Nyx aside.

I guess we're taking turns, and I'm totally okay with that. More orgasms for me, and it means I can drag this out most of the day if I want to. Yes, I know I'm stalling. We need to make a plan, but...

"Fuck me," I growl, as Luke's dick splits me near in two.

I guess he gave up on the no sex because of the baby thing, and I couldn't be happier about it, as I yell out.

Hearing my scream, Ari can't hold back anymore, and he climbs up the bed, pushing Nyx to the side as he goes. He grips my jaw, wrenching my head to the side, and as fast as lightning, he undoes his pants, whips his dick out, and shoves it down my throat.

I like it rough, but damn.

"Take it," he growls, his voice raspy with desire, "Take all of it." And I do, my pussy growing wetter with his demands.

Ari leans over me, and since I'm on my back and can't really move, he fucks my mouth while Luke fucks my pussy. Blake is still toying with my nipple, and given Nyx and I already finished, Quinn is the only one unaccounted for. With Ari over me though, I can't seek him out.

Giving up, Ari hits the back of my throat, and I gag around him, but he doesn't stop. He does move though, in-between the next stroke, and now he's straddling me, his back to Luke.

In this new position, I feel like I have a little more range of motion, so I flick my tongue across the underside of his head, and when I open my eyes, I spot Quinn. He stands in the middle of the room, and just like our first sexual encounter, his pants are around his ankles as he pleases himself. With his next stroke, our eyes lock, and he winks, causing me to melt.

I wish I had more holes. I really do. Just once, I want every one of them inside me at the same time. Is that too much to ask for? Anatomy says it is.

I don't have time to dwell on it though, because Ari grumbles under his breath in one second, and in the next, his cum coats the back of my throat, warm. He stays seated in me long enough that I start to panic though, but then finally, he pulls back, and with a brief kiss, he steps away to make room.

With Ari gone, Luke enters me over and over while I watch Quinn. I don't want him to just watch though, so I call, "Quinn, come here."

As he removes the pants around his ankles so he can do as I asked, Luke picks me up, and one-handed, he turns me around and sets me on my knees. Blake follows without argument, content with having access to my tits.

Luke barely misses a stroke, and now he's back to pounding

into me. He has one hand around my throat, while his other guides my hips back and forth, and when he enters me again, the bed dips and Quinn is finally in front of me. He rests his forehead against mine, and then he's kissing me. It isn't easy, what with the pounding I'm taking, but we somehow make it work.

When I'm pulled back again with another one of Luke's hard thrusts, I reach down, gripping Quinn in my hand and giving him a light squeeze as I slide down the length. His lips pull away from my lips, and his hand wraps around mine. Together we work his dick harder, but when it starts to feel dry, I pull away. He watches lustfully as I lick from one end of my palm to the other, getting it nice and wet, and then I slip my hand under his again, back to stroking.

When he swells, calling out my name and slumping forward, he bumps into Luke who's also slumped against me. Neither one of them seems to be bothered by it, and I'm surprised by how much their proximity turns me on. Sure it turns me on that they're on me, but for some strange reason, it's also sexy that they aren't turned off by each other. Honestly, I think they ag each other on.

I've only had one orgasm so far, but the thought of them touching each other is the last thing I needed to make it number two. My body quivers from one end to the other, and my insides clench, my core throbbing.

No sooner do I finish than I feel Luke get his too, and something about that has me coming again. Or, maybe the last one wasn't over. I don't know, but it feels so good. It feels good to be near them, to have them inside me, and when I reach for Blake so he gets his chance, I convince myself that nothing else is going on in all the realms except this right here.

A UNIQUE TURN OF EVENTS

Ell

The only things we did yesterday was fuck and eat. Oh, and I took a shower. Wait, no, actually, I fucked in the shower too so it doesn't count. We needed yesterday though, because today, we can't keep ignoring reality. Today we have to find a way to get to the King and finish what we started.

We've planned to do a walk of the city after breakfast, see what we can find out. Quinn went down earlier, and his old boss told him over one-thousand fairies were killed in the parade explosion. Another eight-hundred were badly injured, and the King has ordered an eight block lockdown surrounding the palace. He's issued a reward for information surrounding the explosion itself, and doubled the bounty on my head. He might not know I'm still here, but he at least knows I was, and so he's also had patrols out searching houses for me. Apparently, they've started on the opposite side of the city, so we should be okay for now.

"Ready, Ell?" Ari motions for me to join the others as they leave the room.

I join him, letting him slip my hand around his elbow, and guiding me, we follow behind the others. I check our glamour one more time as we descend the stairs, and feeling like it looks good, there's nothing stopping us from heading out to scout the city. We wavered about whether we should all go, but we agreed, with the guards searching for me, it was better for us to all be together.

We're nearly to the pub's front door when we stop short. An unusual amount of shouting is coming from out front, and we aren't stupid. That can't be good. The UnSeelie are an unruly bunch of fairies, but not the last two days, not after what happened at the parade. Everyone lost someone in the explosion; brothers and sisters, parents, aunts and uncles, or even just friends. This city has had a black cloud hovering over it, and I feel their loss. It wasn't supposed to go down like that. Those people didn't deserve to die.

My heart clenches with that thought as the pub owner rushes past us, swinging the door open, but whatever he sees on the other side has him stumbling back. When he turns to face us, he doesn't fill us in, instead he sprints for the stairs, calling for his family that lives in one of the apartments down the hall from ours.

"What the hell is going on?" Ari grumbles, letting go of me and pushing past Luke. He grabs the door roughly, pulling it open just enough to stick his head out, and then he too stumbles back.

Okay, that's about enough of this.

"Step aside, boys," I taunt, pushing my way past them.

"Ellie, no."

But it's too late, because I'm already out the door, and the sight before me is beyond anything I imagined. Fairies of all kinds run for their lives, screaming and begging. Magic zips everywhere, and there's so much of it, I'm not even sure where it's coming from or who's causing it.

Is the King attacking his own people? Surely not. That doesn't make any sense.

As I contemplate that, Ari wrenches me back inside, and then he's filling the others in. As he does that, I pace, trying to process what's happening. It's like there's a war going on outside that door. But if that's what it is, then who started it?

"We need to get the hell out of the city," Ari worries, his hands pressed to his mouth as if in prayer, "We weren't safe before, but we damn sure aren't safe now. King Tobin must be attacking his own citizens to get to us."

"But why?" I ask, joining their circle. "I mean; does he think I'll expose myself to save them? Yes, I agree, they don't deserve to die, but I'm not about to turn myself in, because if I do, a lot more fairies will die when King Tobin opens a new realm. So if he thinks I will, his logic is shitty at best."

"Assuming the logic is right," Luke chimes in, "We don't know it's him."

"But then who?" Blake shakes his head, as confused as the rest of us.

"Who else could it be?" Nyx speaks up, the color drained from his face.

Ari rubs the back of his neck, his head down. "It doesn't matter." He looks at the rest of us, one at a time, and then he adds, "We need to get out of the city. Right. Now."

"But...we didn't stop the King. We don't...even know if we broke the Dryad magic," I stammer, not willing to just give up and run. If we do that, everyone else will suffer because of it.

Ari turns to me before running his hands up and down my arms. "Ellie, we need to get out of the city and regroup. If the guards find us, we have no hope of stopping the King."

"Yeah," Nyx agrees, and I look at him, "It's okay to admit defeat, bail, and live to fight another day. This isn't over, but we can't win today, Ellie Mae."

Looking around the group, it's evident that everyone agrees except for me. I just can't imagine leaving though. I get that shit is crazy out there, and everyone is looking for us, but when did leaving and giving up become an option?

Apparently, right now, because Ari is trying to nudge me toward the back door that opens into the alley. At first, I struggle, still not wanting to give in, but the closer we get to the door the less of a fight I put up, but when we reach the door and Ari grips the knob, I stop him. "Promise me. Promise me we'll get out of the city and regroup, that we'll come back. Not in weeks or months, but days at most." Ari sighs, shaking his head, so I add, "No, promise it or I'm not leaving."

He doesn't respond right away, as he looks to each of the others, but finally, he turns back to me. "I promise."

***

Ari

Ell spent five-minutes making sure we looked like regular fairies before we all stepped out into the alley. There wasn't anyone back there, and since there was no magic flying around, we easily made it to the end. Now, when we got to the cross street, that was another thing. It was total pandemonium, still is, actually. We haven't even crossed yet because every time I poke my head past the wall, I have to jerk back to avoid being pummeled by an array of magic.

Pulling my head back again, I motion for the others to pull back. "I don't know how we're supposed to cross," I worry, and then looking up, I add, "Or up for that matter."

Everyone else looks skyward, seeing what I see. There's just as much magic zipping across the sky as there is at street-level. It's just too dangerous. There's almost no chance we could fly out of here without at least one of us getting hit by something, or worse, spotted. Unfortunately, the same can be said for the street.

"Then what?" Luke asks, scratching his chin.

I don't know how to answer that, and it doesn't matter anyway, because as I turn toward him, opening my mouth to speak, a swarm of fairies zip past the opening of the alley, forcing us to seek cover behind a dumpster.

When we get squatted, I nearly gag. It smells worse than death back here. We are each having to cover our noses to keep from losing our breakfast, and from the look on Ell's face, she might not make it.

We have no choice but to stay where we are though, and we wait five minutes just to be safe. Then, pushing down a gag, I peek my head around the edge of the metal bin. There's fighting on the street directly in front of us now, and there's so much magic it's creating a haze around everything. The area past the alley has a brownish-black aura, and there's no way in hell I'm taking Ell out in that.

I reposition, ready to turn back to the group, when something catches my eye. "What the fuck?" I curse out loud, stumbling out from our hiding place. "Nyx, is that…" I don't finish my sentence, because I'm just too dumbfounded.

Nyx stands, bumping into me, and now we both wear matching looks of shock. I don't know how long we stand like that, but eventually I realize our whole group is standing, exposed.

"Ellie, get back. It isn't safe." I reach for her, gripping her elbow, but per usual, she pulls away.

"Is that Jack?" she asks no one in particular, as she takes another step closer to the mouth of the alley. "Wait, is that *Rykus*?" She starts a slow jog, and then despite the raging battle in front of us, she shouts, "Rykus!"

Rykus issues a killing blow to a Leprechaun, and then he's searching for the fairy that called his name. He spots Ell, and grins, leaving the chaos behind to join us. When he makes it to Ell, she throws her arms around him, giving him a hug, and then he chuckles.

"Well, aren't you a sight for sore eyes," he laughs. "Your Majesty, I'm so glad to see you're okay. Helga said you would be, but…"

"Helga's here?" I ask, stepping closer.

Rykus chuckles, crossing his arms against his chest, but before he answers, he casts a quick glance over his shoulder to make sure we're still good. "Everyone's here. Helga, the Pixies, the Celestials. *Everyone.*"

"Why?" Ell wonders, shaking her head.

"We're at war, don't ya know?" Again he laughs, his chest

shaking. "Helga said we had to come. She said it was the final act."

"I didn't kill the King though," she tells him, her eyes dropping.

"We know," he admits, reaching to pat her on the arm, but he stops himself at the last second. I assume he realized it wouldn't be proper for him to touch her first, and she seems to realize that too, reaching and grabbing his hand instead.

"Tell me what I need to do. Or, tell me where Helga is." Ell's tone sounds desperate, and I can't blame her. This is a lot to process.

With a bob of his head, Rykus tugs us back in the alley. He tries two doors before finding the pub door unlocked, and pulling us inside, he shuts the door quickly and lays out everything he knows.

"Helga pulled together a small group of what she called leaders. Myself, Bree, Layla, and King Oberon were in the bunch. She said you broke the magic the Dryad's had over the King, and that meant all you needed to do now was kill him. But the only way for that to happen was for us to attack with everything we had."

"So we're supposed to fight with all of you until we breach the palace gates?" Nyx asks exactly what I was thinking.

"She didn't say that," he shrugs, reaching behind the bar and pouring himself a shot, "You know how seers are. It was vague. I think you have to do what you have to do, and that doesn't have anything to do with the rest of us."

"You're starting to sound like Helga," Ell jokes.

"Ha, I'll take that as a compliment. That 'ole girl is starting to grow on me." Rykus throws the shot back, slamming the glass on the bar when he's done.

Ell's eyes practically have hearts in them as she squeals," Eeek, I'm totally setting you up with Helga when this is over."

"Whoa, whoa," he stops her, "Don't embarrass this old fairy." I'm pretty sure he's blushing.

"Yeah, yeah," Ell brushes him off, "I won't say anything at

all. Scouts honor." Behind her back, she has her fingers crossed, and I'm not surprised.

"Don't go mixin' in," he tells her one last time, before moving back to the door. "Anyway, I better get back out there." But before he leaves, he turns back to face Ell with a fatherly look in his eyes. "You stay safe, Your Majesty."

"You too, Rykus."

When the door closes, no one has to tell us to huddle up. We all know we have to regroup. Our army being here changes everything. We can no longer leave the city. No, now we have to figure out how to get to the King.

"Well, this is a unique turn of events," Ell tries to make light, but I can tell her nerves are thin. "So I don't know why, but I have this feeling we need to fight our way through this mess to the palace."

"Seems kind of obvious," Nyx kids, giving her a wink.

"Hardy, har, har," she mocks, shoving him in the arm. "Moving on…my feeling doesn't say the army will be with us when I get to the King though. Anyone else having any feelings? Other than Nyx. He doesn't count."

"Hey," he jabs, "not nice."

"Focus," I order, pulling them back to the issue at hand, and then I admit, "I feel pulled to fight, but that's about it."

I look at Lucas, standing next to me, as he says, "I don't know what I feel. Maybe a small tug toward Ell, but honestly, that could be me wanting a quickie."

"There's time," she says, deadpan.

"There isn't," I insist, pulling her back when she tries to throw herself at Lucas, and once I have her secured against my front, I turn to Blake and Quinn. "Either of you? Anything?"

Quinn shakes his head, but Blake bobs his. "Honestly, I kinda feel a pull to Ell too. So, maybe that's a thing?"

Ell turns back over her shoulder, grinning. "See, *Arion*, there *is* time. Everyone says so."

My jaw ticks at her antics, and I hand her off to Nyx. "Okay, I say we head toward the palace as discreetly as we possibly can."

No one argues or comes up with a better plan, so as a group, we hurry through the pub. I open the door a crack, and there's been no change in the last twenty minutes. It's still utter chaos, so my whole discretely comment probably isn't going to be a reality. It doesn't matter though, because here goes nothing.

MY ARM'S TIRED

Ell

Discreet, *my* ass.

Once we stepped out of the pub, it was obvious there was no way we were just going to be able to sneak our way through the city and to the palace gates. We still had our glamours on, so we didn't draw attention for that reason, but it didn't matter, both sides were attacking us right out the gate. Because of the glamour, the UnSeelie thought we were Seelie, and the Seelie thought we were UnSeelie. We were taking hits from both sides, and it became pretty clear really quickly that we needed to pick a side.

Seelie for the win.

I removed just enough of our glamours to let our marks show, except for Quinn. In his case, I changed his Devil-mark to a God-mark, and almost instantly we found ourselves in much better circumstances. Sure we were still getting attacked by the UnSeelie, but at least *our* team realized we weren't a threat.

As of now, we've been fighting our way to the palace for almost an hour, and if I was to guess, I'd say we've barely made it two blocks. We stumbled upon Bree a few minutes ago though, and that's been the only highlight of this battle. Now, she and a horde of her people fight alongside me and my boys. There's been no sign of Helga though, but she does have a way of disappearing when the fighting starts, so I'm not too worried.

"We're not getting anywhere!" Ari shouts, thrusting the palm of his hand into a Troll's nose. I hear a crack, and have to force back a gag.

"What do you suggest?" Luke yells over the fighting, "Not much we can do but keep at it."

"At this rate we'll either be dead or totally out of energy by the time we make it. It could be days," Ari hollers back.

They're both right. They *are* going to run out of energy if this keeps up. I, on the other hand, might wear down my body, but if I do, I should be able to pull from the others. I still don't know why their tethers disappeared the other day, but they're back now, and I'm definitely going to need them. My gut tells me so.

My gut also tells me to leave. Right now. Not the city, but as in, leave the group. Head out on my own. I know Ari would have a fit though. Hell, they all would, but deep down inside, I know it's the right decision. As a group we're never going to get there, but if it's just me, I might stand a chance.

As that reality sinks in, a Troll bumbles toward me, swinging his arms wildly, and I step to the side, letting him fall past me. I touch my finger to his nose as he goes by, and wish for him to sleep. His eyes grow heavy, and he looks around with a dopey grin on his face, but I don't have time to see this through because a worthier opponent has decided to try his luck against me.

An Elf with cloud-white hair pulled up in a man-bun glides toward me, his eyes trained on me and me alone. He motions for me to join him, and I shrug, because why not.

I'm game.

"Let's do this," I tell him, and he tilts his head like he can't hear me. It's almost funny that he actually cares what I said. "You know what," I shout, louder, "never mind!"

The Elf wields a sword of metal, and around it's edges there's a green hue. He flicks it back and forth expertly, and I prepare my own sword. *My* sword is solid magic, and it shimmers in my favorite color.

If you don't know my favorite color by now, we can't be friends.

The Elf strikes first, and I wasn't ready. His blade arcs toward my head, but luckily, at the last second, I sweep right, spinning and bumping into one of my own. The Celestial guard helps me reset, and I take time to thank him.

As I've said before, there's always time to be polite.

For some reason, the Elf waits, making sure I'm ready, and I guess he must be old-school. He's seeking an honorable kill, which means he must be very, *very* old.

I really hate to kill him, but I swing my sword toward his torso anyway. He blocks, and I pull back. The next swing, *he* makes, and *I* block. It's sort of beautiful as we go back and forth with one another, but I can tell with each of his swings, he's skilled in the art of swordsmanship, and given that I am not, it's only a matter of time before he gets a hit in on me. Also, my arm's tired.

One-handed, I swing again, and with my other hand, I let loose a stream of magic. He easily blocks my sword, but my magic singes his shirt, a hole spreading quickly and forcing him to step back as he tries to pat out any residual flames.

"Well played," he commends me, and I almost feel like he's my teacher. "Again."

He swings first, and while I'm ready, it isn't *my* sword that blocks him. Luke's wielding two short knives, and he crosses them, blocking the Elf's blow. He pushes the Elf back, and over his shoulder, he shouts, "Go!"

What is that supposed to mean? Go? Go where?

Unsure, I stumble away from their fighting, and almost in a haze, I walk down the street. When the haze begins to fade, and I look back, Luke and the Elf are small, and I realize I've made it two blocks without even knowing it.

As I turn back toward the palace, I wonder if Luke meant for me to go, go. Like, leave them. That's what I was feeling, and I think he must have been too. I probably should've let the others weigh in, but they would've tried to stop me, especially Ari. No, this is my mission, and the universe says I have to do it alone.

***

Ell

I had to fight a few fairies along the way, but for the most part it was pretty easy making my way through the city, all things considered. I'm sure my boys have realized I'm gone by now though, and they are no doubt freaking the hell out, but there's not much I can do about that now.

When I made it to the King's Circle, there were hundreds of Seelie and UnSeelie fighting, and I knew there was no way I was getting in that way, so instead, I circled around, going slightly out of the way and ending up near the back of the palace. I noticed a staff entrance, and for the last ten minutes, I've been trying to come up with the best way to get inside. I don't want to make a scene. I need to get in and to the King unnoticed. Or, at least, unnoticed for as long as possible.

As I think, I hear humming, and I'm startled back to reality when a Brownie skips around the corner in a maid's uniform. She's wearing brown from head to toe, her hair color matching her outfit, and she seems completely oblivious to the fact that we're kind of in the middle of a war here.

I can just hear Ari saying, 'Remind you of anyone, hmm?'
Whatevs.

The Brownie is almost on top of my hiding spot in the bushes when she pulls a badge from her pocket, twirling it around her finger. She still hasn't seen me, and that's good. I need the element of surprise to pull this off.

We're far enough away from the guard shack that if I pop out now, I don't think they'd see me, but if she screams, I'm screwed. So, I release just a touch of magic, silencing her, and then I jump out, snatching her and yanking her into the bushes. She wiggles and squirms, and I can barely maintain my hold on her. I try to get her twisted around so I can calm her, but she pulls free, crawling out of the bushes. I yank her back, and she claws the dirt as I pull, like in a horror film. I'm probably not doing a great job of not scaring her. Probably should have come up with a different plan.

Regrouping, I push more magic into her, and seconds later she slumps, sleeping against my chest. Not having to fight her, I have time to look her over from head to toe, taking in every inch of her, and when I'm sure I've got it, I glamour myself in her image. I doubt the King recognizes every single staff member, but just in case, it's better if I imitate someone known by others. Plus, this way, I can use her badge.

I don't see the plastic card now though, so I move her over trying to search it out. It's nowhere to be seen, and that's bad. My plan is contingent on that badge. I can't just magic one, because I have no idea what they look like, other than the fact that they're rectangular in shape.

Worried about that but knowing I'll just have to figure it out, I give her another dose of sleep-magic to make sure she remains in slumber, and then I crawl from my spot.

Ha. There it is. Come here, ya rectangle bastard.

Snatching the badge, I straighten my clothes, wishing I had a mirror to make sure it's right. I feel like it is, but with glamours you never can tell. I'll just have to hope this one is good, because it's time to go.

Hearing someone coming, I casually make my way to the guard shack, but at the last second, I decide to skip. I need to act just like…Miriam. *Awe*, that's a cute name. She kinda looks like a Miriam too. Well, yeah, because she is. Yes, I know I ramble when I'm nervous.

Anyway, as I approach the shack near the gate, an Ogre steps out from the small building, demanding my badge, with his hand thrust out. I give it to him willingly, and he looks it over twice, while eying me carefully. When he hands it back, he says, "Gotta be extra careful today, Mir. You know, war and all."

I giggle, hoping that's something *Mir* would do, and when

he nods and lets me pass, I let out a sigh of relief.

I hurry along, across the back lawn and through a small service door. It looks very similar to the service door on my own palace, and I'm just hoping this is where Miriam would need to enter. Regardless, as soon as I step inside, I'm snatched, a clammy hand gripping my forearm tightly. I try to pull back, but an older than dirt Elf has me gripped tightly. Every once in a while, she looks over her shoulder, giving me a dirty look. I'm not sure what I ever did to her, but damn. Two seconds inside the UnSeelie palace, and I'm already in trouble.

***

Nyx

"Where the fuck is she?" Ari barks, gripping Lucas' shirt, and I'm suffering from a serious case of déjà vu.

"Back off," Lucas bites back, his teeth gritting, "I told her to go. Like, get out of the way, get to safety, not run off and leave us. How the fuck was I supposed to know she was going to take it literally?"

Ari growls, his jaw ticking, and he lets loose of Lucas' shirt, throwing his hands in the air. He looks in the direction of the palace, indecision warring in his eyes. We're several blocks away from the gate, and the battle is raging. It could take us hours to make it there, which has me wondering how Ell slipped away so easily.

Before I can voice that question out loud, Blake beats me to it. "It's been two hours and we've barely made it a block. How the hell did she slip away? Not only did we not notice, but what? She had no resistance? How is that even possible?"

"My point exactly," Ari grumbles, as Lucas muses, "Maybe it was meant to be."

Everyone looks at him, even Ari, who stops his grumbling and pacing. With all eyes on him, Lucas shrugs. "I'm just saying, when I told her to go, I didn't even think about it. I was near the alley, fighting two Ogres, and when I finished them off, I spotted Ell. She was fighting an Elf but she was holding her own. It's not like she needed my help. Despite that, I felt drawn to her. So I went. Telling her to go just came out. I didn't even think about it. So…maybe this is what was supposed to happen."

Wiping a bead of sweat from my brow, I agree, "He could be right, Ari. Most things haven't made sense these last few months. We've all been driven to something at one point or another since this whole thing started."

Ari relaxes just a bit, although his jaw still ticks and his shoulders are nearly to his ears. "Maybe…" he mumbles, looking to us for our input.

Everyone agrees, so the next question is, now what? Do we stay here? Or, do we go after her? There's a really good chance she's going to need help. It won't be easy getting close to King Tobin, much less killing him. My worry is she'll need us and we won't be there. But, it's not like getting there is going to be easy.

When no one speaks up for quite some time, I ask, "Does anyone feel pulled toward her?"

"No," Blake and Quinn say in sync, and I look to Luke as he agrees. Ari is the last one, and with a sigh, he admits, "No. Well, I *want* to be with her. I want to know she's okay, but as far as a tug, no, I don't."

"Me either," I confirm, noticing a Mer inching his way toward us, magic at the ready, so without a word, I flick a magic infused blade his direction, and it connects with his thigh. He yelps, causing the others to finally notice his presence, and I skirt past Quinn, ready to finish this fairy off. I don't get the chance though, because before I can make it two feet, he turns tail and runs. And, to be honest, I really don't have the energy to chase him. So instead, I shrug it off, and let this one go.

"That was a good shot," Lucas compliments me.

I appreciate it, and thank him, but we still need to figure out our next move. Just because we don't feel pulled toward Ell, doesn't mean we don't need a plan of action.

"Okay," Ari starts, drawing everyone back in, "We don't feel pulled to Ell, so there's no rush to get to her, but that doesn't mean there won't be. So, I think we should at least start working our way toward the palace."

"I thought that's what we were doing," I chuckle.

"We need to try harder," he growls, my sarcasm going right over his head.

Without any further direction, he motions us to leave the alley, but as soon as I take a single step out of the safety, I'm plowed down by an Ogre. We tumble and roll, and as we do, all I can think is that I really don't want to die by squishing. That would *not* be a good way to go.

THE UNIVERSE SUCKS

Ell

The pissed-off old Elf dragging me through the halls of the Un-Seelie palace is apparently the head of housekeeping. I mean, what are the odds, man? She was waiting on me when I stepped in the staff entrance, and there was no doubt whether I was in trouble or not. Well, not me, but the Brownie I'm currently impersonating. Also, it's pretty clear this Brownie is a real fuck up. I swear, I have the worst damn luck.

The fairy's grip on my wrist is leaving a bruise, and I try to wiggle free as she tugs me around another corner. She growls her contempt for me, and casts evil eyes in my direction every few feet. "You're going to be the death of me, Miriam," she grumbles with a huff. "You're thirty-minutes late again today. And with everything going on too." She turns over her shoulder as we barrel into a room. "You are aware there's a battle raging outside, right?" I open my mouth to speak, but apparently it was a rhetorical question, because she cuts me off, "The King is in a foul mood today, and you being late only makes things worse. Get your cart and get your ass up to the royal wing."

She points out the cart in the corner, already loaded down with cleaning supplies, and I hesitate only slightly before tromping over. The cart has everything a maid could possibly need, and then some, so I grip the handle, shimmying it out of the tight space and moving it across the laundry room.

A death glare is still fixed to the head of housekeeping's face as I approach, and she taps her toe impatiently as I move. When I pass her, she demands, "No lollygagging, no skipping, and *absolutely* no singing." She points to the hall, and adds, "Hurry up!"

Well, she seems like a real bitch. I don't argue though, knowing I don't have time for it and don't need to draw attention to myself. I feel bad for Miriam though. She sounds like my kind of fairy. Lollygagging? Check. Skipping? Definitely. Singing? One-hundred. I'm pretty sure she and I would be besties, and she doesn't sound like your typical UnSeelie either. She doesn't fit in here, which makes me feel bad that I left her asleep in the bushes. At least I didn't kill her, so that's a plus.

Knowing I'll go back and check on her when my mission is complete, I hurry down the hall, but when I hit what looks like a sitting room, I realize I have no idea where the royal wing is. Probably should've thought that one through, Ell. No matter. I'll let the universe guide me.

***

Ell

The universe sucks. I've been wandering around this damn palace for at least twenty minutes. If the head of housekeeping finds out or stumbles across me where I'm not supposed to be, I'm going to be in real trouble, but I don't know what else to do. I could ask a guard, but I'm pretty sure that's going to be very *sus.* i.e. my favorite video game reference. Look it up.

Anyway, when I turn the next corner, there's a small enclosed set of stairs, and I decide to see where it leads me. The cart is on wheels, which tells me either Miriam would use magic to get it up there, there's a better way, or this is not the way to the royal wing. It doesn't matter though, because I don't know what else to do.

Spitting a ring of magic around my cart, it hovers a few inches above the bottom step, and with a quick glance around, I hurry up. At the first landing, the hall is long and dark, and I don't see anyone, not even a guard. At the second landing, I see a Brownie step out of a room a few doors down, and she's pushing a cart similar to mine. She spots me, but she doesn't speak, which makes me think she doesn't know Miriam.

"Hey," I call to her, waiting for her to turn back toward me, "so it's my first day."

The petite Brownie grimaces as she leaves her cart behind and joins me near the top of the stairs. "That sucks," she replies. "So, does that mean you have no idea where you're supposed to be?"

"Ding, ding, ding." I tap my nose with each ding.

"Where did Ester tell you to be?" she asks, a kind smile on her face as she tightens her messy bun.

"Um…is Ester the super aggressive head of housekeeping?" My eyes dart around the room, and I sheepishly grin.

She giggles, "Yeah, that's the one." She leans in after searching our surroundings, and seeming satisfied, she whispers, "She's the worst. Do not, I repeat, do not get on her bad side."

We both share a laugh, and I promise not to, even though I know it's too late for the real Miriam.

"I'm Kit, by the way." She thrusts her hand out, and I take it as I introduce myself as Miriam after almost saying Ell. That would've been no bueno.

I drop her hand, stepping back. "She said I was in the royal wing today."

Kit's eyes go wide, and I'd dare say they are filled with terror. "Whoa. Seriously?" I nod my head, and she curses, "Shit. Okay. I'm ahead of schedule today, so I have time to sneak you over there. We'll take the back stairs."

I thank her, and leaving behind her cart, we push mine back down to the first floor. At the bottom of the stairs, we turn right, but she has to hurry us into an alcove to avoid being seen by two guards making their rounds. Once they're past, we sneak to the opposite side of the palace, and Kit opens a service door, motioning for me to follow her through. We ascend quickly up three flights, exiting the door and closing it behind us without a sound. This hall is fairly dark too, but it's far more opulent than the one Kit was cleaning.

As my eyes adjust, Kit points to the first door on the right. "This room is reserved for the King's favorite. He grew tired of the last one and doesn't have one right now, so it doesn't need to be cleaned today. You'll dust it on Fridays when it isn't occupied." I nod, and she points across the hall. "That's a supply closet," and moving further down, she adds, "That's the first door of the King's chambers. This one enters into his study. The next door goes into his sitting room, and the next his smoking room. You have to go into the sitting room and down the hall on the right, that's where you'll find his bedroom."

That's a lot to take in, and I know my face shows my overwhelmed feelings.

Kit pats me on the back, giving me an understanding smile. "Did she happen to tell you what was on the schedule for today? Like, are you supposed to clean *his* room?" When she says his, it's nearly a whisper.

"No, nothing." I shrug.

"Well, you'll just have to play it by ear." She shakes her head, her face telling me she's baffled. "It's rare for a newbie to clean up here. I can't believe she did that."

You and me both, honey.

Although, it couldn't have worked out any better. This way, I'm supposed to be here. It'll be less suspicious than if I was supposed to be somewhere else and got caught in the wrong place. Now, I just have to hope I don't screw things up once I get in there.

Kit and I say our goodbyes, and I try to slow my heart rate.

There's no way around going in there, but I'm terrified because I have no idea what I'm walking into. And as I turn the knob, pushing my cart inside, I have this horrible feeling I'm walking into a trap.

***

Ell

When I walked into King Tobin's study, I kept my head down until I got to the far side of the room. I pressed my cart against the wall, and started dusting a long credenza, hoping I looked like I knew what I was doing. I worked my way around to the end, because I could feel others in the room with me, but hadn't laid eyes on them yet. At the time, I'd been hoping it wasn't King Tobin. I wasn't ready. Well, too fucking bad. Because when my eyes cast up, they landed on the fairy himself, seated at a luxurious mahogany desk. His head was down as he read over some papers gripped in his hands, and now, five-minutes later, he hasn't looked up once.

I've pretend-cleaned the credenza, two side tables, and I thought about cleaning a window before thinking better of it. Now, I'm standing next to the couch, leaning over and picking up a piece of lint from the floor. This place is immaculate. Whoever normally cleans this room, Miriam, I guess, does a fantastic fucking job. Unfortunately, that overachieving Brownie has done her job so well it doesn't leave me much to do.

Picking up a stack of magazines from the coffee table, I walk them over to a side table so I can look like I'm actually doing something. When I turn to go back though, I freeze, my eyes landing on my worst nightmare.

Tab.

I mean, no, she isn't my worst nightmare, but her being in here right now is. When I make my move, she could end up in the crosshairs, and that's the last thing I want. Not to mention, I assumed she was a prisoner, but she looks nothing like a prisoner as I stare her down.

Her iridescent blue hair is done up in curls on top of her head, as if she had a hairdresser do it. She's wearing a long, flowing greenish-blue dress, with one strap slipped off her shoulder, and she sits in a pile of pillows, comfortable, as she flips through a book, oblivious to her surroundings, oblivious to me.

If I didn't know any better, I'd say she's enjoying being in here, that she hasn't had a hard time as King Tobin's leverage over me. That realization worries me. What if she likes him? Or worse, what if she *likes*, likes him? Like, they are fucking. Oh God, what if they are doing the nasty? Then what? Will she fight me when I try to kill him, or try to stop me?

There are so many questions running through my mind right now that I can't even keep up. But you know what; it doesn't matter. If I was to guess, she did what she had to do to survive, and I can't blame her for that.

With that in mind, I slowly make my way to the cart, getting some spray and a small cleaning cloth. With the supplies in hand, I check to make sure King Tobin is still engrossed in his work, and seeing he is, I cross the room, stopping at a short table just feet from my bestest bestie.

I'm not sure how I'm going to get Tab's attention without drawing the King's though, and as I stress about that, I spray way too much cleaning solution on the table. Yeah, that's probably ruined, but oh well. Serves the King right for being a total dick.

I pretend to wipe the surface clean, trying to be discreet when I kick Tab's foot lightly. At first she doesn't look up, so engrossed in her book, but when I do it two more times, she finally lets the book flop down on her lap.

She looks at me, annoyed, her brow quirked. "*What*?"

I look over my shoulder at the King, because that was loud, and then turning back to Tab, I whisper, "Look closely."

"Look closely," she repeats, even more annoyed than before, and if she doesn't lower her damn voice she's going to get us both caught.

I drop the rag, bending down to grab it. "*Closely*."

She sighs, staring straight through me, but she just isn't getting it. I'll have to try something else.

"Dude," I hiss, "you're the Glaze to my donut."

Tab jerks back, her eyes going wide and her cheeks turning white. Her lips are nearly blue with the lack of oxygen as she holds her breath, looking from me to Tobin three times fast. When our eyes connect again, I can feel her magic grazing mine, like two old friends that haven't seen each other in forever.

"Balls," she curses under her breath. "Are you alone? Dear God, you're alone. Leave right now. I mean it, you can't win this by yourself." Terror laces her words, as she begs me, "Please, go. You shouldn't be here."

"Don't worry," I assure her, keeping an eye on the King, "I've got this, just stay back."

Tab grabs my wrist, yanking me closer. "No, E..." she stumbles, stopping just short of saying my name out loud, "I mean it. Go. Right. Now. He knows..."

A manly laugh filled with malice assaults my ears, and I pull back, my head shooting in the King's direction. He is leaned back in his seat, and his laughter shakes his whole body. He throws his hands in the air, as if he's praising God. Or, I guess, the Devil.

I don't know what's so funny though, and I'm still not certain he knows I'm me. So, trying not to blow my cover, I grab my rag and stand back up. I move straight to the cart, never once looking at the King. When I try to push my cart to the door though, his laughter stops and he stands, slamming his hands down on the desk, the wood cracking.

"Did you honestly think I didn't know it was you?" He laughs again, his chin quivering with excitement.

Well, I'm glad you think this is funny, ya big ass-turd.

I can't help but look annoyed, even though I try to tamp it down. And, I'm still moving toward the door, in case you were wondering. My cover is blown, so I need to bail and regroup. *Shit*. Or not. *Fuck*. I don't know. I think Tab said it right earlier; *balls*.

Finally, I can't hold back any longer, and I turn my head in his direction, our eyes connecting, our mutual hatred evident. His laughter has stopped though, and now he just looks pissed.

Samesies.

"I've known since the second you stepped foot inside the palace," he mocks me, a grimace marring his somewhat attractive face.

"Then why not stop me?" I ask, irritated, "Why not come after me then?"

"Well because," he chuckles, grinning, "now I have you right where I want you thanks to Tabatha."

Again I say; *balls.*

HOME FIELD ADVANTAGE

Blake

It's taken us nearly three hours, but we finally made it to the King's Circle not long ago. Just behind it stands the palace gates, and while the streets have been filled with UnSeelie guards, they don't even come close to comparing to the numbers near the gate. I tried to count, but with all the chaos, it was just too hard to get an even remotely accurate number. I counted two-hundred and fifty on this side of the gate before giving up, and that's just the UnSeelie lined up blocking us from entry. That doesn't even count the ones engaged in the fighting on this block and the surrounding ones.

Behind the gate is even more overwhelming though. There's no way to know for sure, but when I look over the heads of those fighting around me, and strain to see past the gate, I see no lush, green law. I see no dirt, no road leading to the palace doors. No, I see only guards. Hundreds of them, lined up in formation, just waiting for us to step one foot across the threshold.

I doubt they have anything to worry about though. Our numbers are big, but I'm pretty sure the UnSeelie outnumber us. Plus, they have the home field advantage. They know this city inside and out. *We* don't.

On top of that, it isn't just guards we're up against. It was clear to me on day one the UnSeelie like to fight, and today is no exception. Regular fairies, those not associated with the guard, have joined the fight against us. It's a wonder there aren't more of them, and it's a good thing too. If there were, we never would've made it this far.

Ari has me looking for a way in since I don't have magic to fight with, but I'm not sure there is one. I've been at it for a good ten minutes, and I don't see any way past unless we overtake the gate. That's unlikely, but I'm guessing Ell made it inside or we would've seen her by now, so if she got in, then surely we can too. But how?

I push past two Ogres fighting one of the Celestial guards, and circle around the block, nearly running into King Oberon and Layla. They're tag-teaming an Elf, and from the looks of it, they're winning.

The Elf is pushed back, falling into my arms, and I give him a hard knock on the head, the force vibrating up my arm. It was hard enough to knock him out cold, and I drop him on the ground, not caring when his head cracks on the concrete.

King Oberon looks impressed, and he slaps me on the back. "Blake, how's everything going at the Circle?"

"Same as before," I tell him, disappointed that I can't report better news. His face falls as I look around, gaging the fighting on this block, and looking back to the two of them, I add, "Looks like you two have this block under control."

"Yeah," Layla giggles, "except for the line four deep of fairies guarding the wall. We tried to breach the line not long ago, and we lost a lot of good fairies in the process, so we had no choice but to pull back."

"Shit," I curse, wishing there was some way for us to prevent any more loss of life. "Listen, Ari sent me to try to find a better way in. Any ideas?"

They both think on that, Layla now absentmindedly fighting a stack of Gnomes. She kicks her foot out, and their stack topples to the ground, each of them rolling like Weebles. I have an Ell moment when the Weebles song pops into my head, but

I shake it off as King Oberon tells me, "I heard the Pixies were around back. The King has the skies guarded pretty well, so they circled around. We know Ell's inside, so she had to have gotten in somewhere. You just have to find that weak point."

I nod my head, thanking him, and then I'm jogging off. I make a wide circle, having to stop twice to fend off guards, but finally I make it to the far side of the palace. When I round the corner, I can see dozens of UnSeelie guards fighting, and above them is a swarm of Pixies, *our* Pixies.

There's still a line of guards, four deep, between us and the wall, plus the ones fighting further out. There's no way Ell got in over here. Unless, I mean, I guess it's possible they didn't have their defenses up when she came through here. That is, assuming she came through here.

I'm jogging closer to what looks like a guard shack, but I stop short when Bree appears inches from my face. Ell's right, they really are going to have to work on boundaries if they truly want to integrate into Fay society.

"Sup?" Bree tinkles in her tiny voice.

"Looking for a way in," I tell her, taking a step back to get some space. "Any ideas?"

"Na here," she chirps, shaking her miniature head, causing her rainbow colored hair to flip back and forth.

"There's no way Ell just walked in the front gate, even if she *was* wearing a glamour," I muse, "So it's more likely she got in back here. I bet this is a staff entrance or something."

She shrugs, her wings fluttering rapidly against her back. "Na know..." She turns her head, looking up and pointing. "Na up."

"Yeah, I heard they've got heavy security up top."

I'm scanning the area, searching for any possible solutions to our problem, when I hear a groan coming from the bushes behind me. I spin, and Bree flits over, her face set in a scowl, ready to destroy whoever it is.

With all the trees back here, there isn't a lot of light to see by, but I can just make out a shoe. It's brown and the sole is nearly worn through. I squat down, grabbing hold of the person's ankle and tugging. Another groan, and now I can see the person on the other end of this leg is a fairy. And, without a doubt, I know Ell's been here. Not just because I found a fairy half-unconscious in a bush, but because she's wearing the clothes Ell had on earlier today, which means Ell is probably wearing hers.

"Brownie," Bree says, curt, "Blugh."

She acts as if she's gagging, and I roll my eyes, helping the Brownie sit up. "Do you actually like anyone other than Pixies?" I ask Bree, as we wait for the Brownie to come around.

"Like Ell." Her hands are resting against her hips with an attitude, and with her words, she jerks her head back and forth, and then snaps her fingers in a wave.

"Wha…" The Brownie's still pretty groggy, as she tries to make sense of her current situation. "What's…"

Her eyes go wide, and she tries to scramble back, but I stop her. "Nope, you aren't going anywhere. I need you to tell me what happened."

She stutters, "Please, just…let…me go. I didn't do anything wrong. I promise."

She looks young, and she's clearly terrified, so I try to calm her. "Listen, we're not gonna hurt you…"

"Speak self," Bree huffs.

"Not helping…" I grimace, giving her a look, and then turning back to the Brownie, I try again, "No one is gonna hurt you. We just need to know how you ended up in the bushes."

She's visibly shaking, tears forming in her eyes, as she cries, "I'm gonna be in so much trouble." Now she's openly sobbing, a hiccup forcing its way past her lips. "Some fairy grabbed me. I was just trying to go to work. She used magic on me, and I guess I fell asleep. I don't remember anything else. I swear."

I believe her, but Bree doesn't. "Tell truth."

"I am, I promise. Why would I lie?"

Bree bares her pointy teeth at the young thing, and I hold her back, my fingers lightly pinching her tiny arm. "Hole back, hole back," she shouts loudly for a Pixie, swinging her arms in an arc as she tries to get to the Brownie. Honestly, it might be the funniest thing I've seen in a while.

"Bree," I chastise through a chuckle, "settle down. I believe her. Ell loves nothing more than her sleepy-time magic. You know that."

Bree's flailing slows slightly, and she seems to think about that. Eventually, she realizes I'm right, and even though she tosses the finger at the girl, she does back off. I can't help but laugh as she flies over a few feet, leaving me with the girl.

"We think she used your clothes to get inside the palace. How would she have gotten in?" I ask, giving the girl time to speak.

"Um," she mumbles, looking down, and then the fear is back and her head shoots up. "She stole my badge."

"Of course she did," I say under my breath, and then turning my head over my shoulder, I tell Bree, "She's in there right now impersonating a maid."

Bree giggles, puffing out her chest. "Tha ma friend."

This doesn't surprise me at all, but I need to verify where she went in, so turning back to the Brownie, I ask, "Would she have gone in there?" I point toward the guard shack. "At the guard shack?"

The Brownie bobs her head erratically, her tears finally drying, and with a sigh, I help her to her feet. Once steady, she dusts herself off, the color returning to her cheeks, and in an instant, her whole demeanor changes. She starts to hum a tune, seeming almost oblivious to what just went down. No wonder Ell picked her. And, no wonder she didn't kill her but only forced her to take a nap.

"Listen," I get the Brownie's attention, "you need to run as far away from here as you can. The fighting is all over that side of the city, but if you go that way," I point north, "I think you can get away."

She stares at me as if I have two heads. "But I'm late for work. Ester is gonna kill me."

I grip her shoulders, giving her a gentle shake. "Your job isn't worth your life. Go! Go on, get out of here!"

I spin her in the opposite direction, giving her a shove, and without another word, she skips off. She doesn't even look back, and I'm left shaking my head in disbelief. I've met a lot of odd fairies since I got to Fay, but that might have been the oddest.

I watch the Brownie for longer than I should, but before I can turn back around, Bree is back in my face. "We go in."

"Yeah, but I gotta get everyone else. Security is tight back here, but not as bad as the front gate. I'll get Ari and the others, and be back as fast as I can. You put the pressure on until we get here."

Bree gives me one quick nod, and then she buzzes off.

Knowing I have to hurry, I take off at a gallop, doing everything I can to avoid anything that might slow me down. As I round the side of the palace, I send up a silent prayer. Hopefully nothing has changed since I've been gone, but that's probably asking a lot.

***

Tab

The last few weeks could've been worse. I mean, I *am* a prisoner, after all. But the thing is, I haven't really been treated like a prisoner. The King gave me my own suite one floor down from his, and I've basically been given anything I want. I've been fed like a Queen, had my own stylist, and he even had an entire wardrobe purchased for me, among other things. So yeah, things definitely could've been worse.

The first few days after I arrived were probably the sketchiest, but then I realized if I did whatever he wanted, and acted like I would help him take down Ell, he suddenly wasn't so bad. He's like most kings. Give him what he wants, and he'll give you the world. Cross him, and you'll end up with your head on a spike. So, I did what I had to do. I convinced him that I would help him lure Ell out, even if that only meant me sitting here and waiting for her to come. I knew she would too, and so did he. That's why I wasn't surprised when she plopped down at my side a few minutes ago, but even though I wasn't surprised, that didn't mean I wasn't terrified.

I didn't realize he knew she was there, but I knew he knew she was coming. He's known for days when she would arrive, foretold by his very own seer. The seer was very graphic too, describing how the King would defeat her. Graphic, as in, cutting off her head. I mean, that's not really something you want to imagine happening to your best friend.

Over the last few days, the King hasn't even spoken of Ell though. It's like he was a totally different fairy. We laughed, we joked, we drank. Honestly, it was a good time, and I almost forgot that he was the harbinger of death, the one who wished to destroy our lives as we know it. Well, Ell and the rest of the Seelie, because honestly, I don't think he will hurt me. I think I've grown on him, and frankly, he's grown on me too. I know that's crazy, and I can't even believe I let it happen, but it's true.

Sure he can be a dick. Obvi, he wants to kill my BFF and destroy Earth and probably Fay too, but surprisingly, he's actually not that bad to be around. I'd even go so far as to say that we've become friends. Like real friends, not just fake friends because we're using one another.

I know all that ends right now though, as Ell tries to casually work her way to the door, and the King laughs maniacally. He won't let her step one foot out of this room though, and we all know it.

I don't know what I'm supposed to do though. Should I try to convince him not to hurt her? I don't know. No, I *do* know. Of course I have to try to talk him out of this. But the question is; will he listen? Probably not, but I have to try.

RULE NUMBER EIGHTEEN

Ell

"I knew you'd come for her," King Tobin laughs, "You are nothing if not predictable."

I purse my lips, annoyed with this fucker already. "I'm so glad I amuse you, King Turd."

He growls at my name calling, his whole demeanor changing. "I knew you couldn't just fight out there with your snotty friends. I knew you would come for her, and I knew you would be alone. *So* fucking predictable."

Okay, maybe I am predictable, but the universe told me to do it. It's not like I can just say, 'fuck you, universe'. That's a good way to get smited. And I am *not* trying to get smited today, thank you very much.

King Tobin skirts around his desk, his hands resting against his belt as he rocks back on his heels, so casual, like this is just another day at the office. "Do you honestly think you can beat me? You have a seer, yes?" He doesn't wait for me to respond, as he chuckles, "Then you should know I win in the end. Or, did she forget to tell you that part?"

I try to remain unaffected by his words, but I know it isn't working. Not only is he suggesting he's going to win this fight, but that Helga knew and didn't tell us. I was fully prepared to die for this cause, I knew the minute I left the boys I might never see them again, but this is bigger than us. I *had* to do this. But, if Helga knew and didn't tell me, well, that hurts.

"She didn't, did she?" He laughs at my expense.

"You know," I grumble, "you're really starting to grate on my nerves."

My words only make him laugh harder, and his belly shakes with the force. "Well," he brushes a fake tear away from his eye, getting it together, "no matter."

He's trying to act so casual right now, and I'm sure he thinks I don't know, but I can feel him gathering his magic. So as he does, I move away from my cart, taking up a position in the center of the room and making sure I'm between him and Tab. I don't want to take any chances on him using her to get me to surrender. Or worse, her getting killed by accident.

"You're just a child," King Tobin mocks me. "If you fight me today, you *will* die."

Wait, the way he said that makes me think it's an option not to fight. I'll take door number two, please.

"Because I like your friend," he starts, his head nodding in Tab's direction, "I'll let you surrender. Allow me to bind you, and you can live out your days in the dungeon. And, if you're a good fairy, I might let Tabatha come visit you every once in a while."

What in the hell is happening right now? He *likes* Tab? The way he's talking it's like they're friendly. Maybe not *friendly*, friendly, but friendly. Surely to God not though. Tab would never, ever be friends with the likes of this piece of shit. Right?

But instead of questioning all that, or voicing my worries, I rephrase, "You want me to surrender? You're serious?"

"Very."

I don't even know how to respond to that, and before I can think of something, Tab speaks up for the first time. "Ell, please, listen to him. This is your only chance at survival. Just surrender. We'll figure everything else out later."

I move so I can put my back against the wall, allowing me to see them both without having my back to anyone, and when I look at Tab, I know she can see the shock I'm wearing. Apparently, it's the newest trend.

"What the fuck, Tab?" I bark the question, and she flinches. "So what, you're with him now? You've turned your back on your own people, on your family…on me?" That last part comes out almost as a whisper, and I wish it hadn't. It made me look too vulnerable in front of the King.

"Ell, it isn't like that," she implores, "Please, I'm begging you. You *are* going to die."

So clearly she's heard what the seer told King Tobin, and whatever he said, it must've been convincing for her to be begging me like this. She really must believe I'm going to die if I fight him today, but it still pisses me off.

"You know, Tab, your lack of faith in me is disappointing."

Tab sighs, and seeing she won't have any luck with me, she turns to the King. "Tobi, *please*. Don't kill her. She's my best friend."

Tobi?

The fuck?

Tobi's eyes almost look like they have a tiny bit of compassion in them, but he shakes it off quickly. "I promised you I would give her a chance to surrender. I did that. That's all I can do." He pauses, looking down at the floor before adding, "I'm sorry."

Tab cries out, and I take a step forward, ready to get this party started, but I'm stopped when Tab rushes me. She throws her arms around my neck, and I'm taken back, but I keep my eyes on Tobin. He eyes us, but not suspiciously. In fact, he doesn't seem at all worried that Tab would turn on him.

"I'll help you," she whispers, "but please, don't kill him if you don't have to. *Please*."

I pull back from her, my mind not wanting to process what she's saying. Or, maybe it's my heart that's struggling, because if I didn't know any better, I'd say Tab hasn't just tolerated King Tobin these last few weeks, I'd say she's developed feelings for him. *Real* feelings.

I'm reeling when Tab stumbles back, still sobbing, and I'm not sure if she's putting on a show for the King's benefit, or if those are real tears. If I'm right about her feelings for him, then they're probably real because she realizes that one of us, King Tobin or I have to die today.

When Tab makes it back to the center of the room, King Tobin goes to her. "You should go. You don't have to watch this." He wraps his arms around her, pulling her to him, and she doesn't push him away.

What am I watching right now? This is like a bad reality show. You know, where the sweet girl falls for the bad boy. Okay fine, Tab isn't all that sweet, but you know what I mean. This is like the fucking Twilight Zone, and I want out.

***

Tab

Tobi pulls me in for a hug, and I let him. I really have grown fond of him. Those feelings haven't gone past friendly, but there's something deep down inside of me screaming that if things were different, my feelings would be different. *More.*

Knowing that, I relish his hug, because I know it might be the last one, just like I relished the hug Ell and I shared moments ago. I told her I'd help her, and I meant that. At the end of the day, she's been my number one since day one, and I can't turn my back on her. But more than that, what Tobi wants to do is wrong. Thousands will die if he succeeds, and I just can't be a part of that. I wish things were different though.

"Tobi, please," I whisper against his neck, begging, "I... please don't kill her. I can't lose her, and..." My words trail off, and I'm unable to finish.

"And..." he encourages me to try again, but I don't know if I can, know if I should.

"And..." I stumble, sniffing and wiping my snot on his shoulder as I stretch on my tiptoes, "I don't want to lose either of you." That was a hard thing to admit out loud, and it seems Tobi is just as surprised as me that I said it.

He pulls back, his eyes filled with shock. "Tabatha, I can't. You...you know how I feel about you, but I have to do this. I can't let anything get in the way of that."

Tears pour down my face, soaking my dress. "Promise me, that if you don't have to, you won't kill her. Promise me, Tobi."

He leans forward, kissing me on the forehead. "I'll try."

Those two little words break me in two. The fact that he would try for me, well, it destroys me. It destroys me that after that, I have to do this...

I gather up every ounce of magic I have while we're still close, and before he pulls back, I let everything inside of me rush into his chest. I'm not strong like Ell, but he does stumble back. Unfortunately, it wasn't enough. Yeah, basically, I just pissed him off.

***

Ell

Excuse me, can someone explain what just happened for the kids in the back?

Hi, I'm the kids in the back.

I mean, holy hell. She really had me going. All of that must've been an act, because as soon as he kissed her on the forehead, and something else was whispered between them, she hit him with everything she had. Sure it wasn't much, but I still think everyone in the room is in shock. Okay fine, I'm the only one in shock. No, scratch that, Tobin is definitely in shock too, and pissed. Oh, he is *so* pissed.

I snap myself out of whatever stupor Tab just put me in, and rush to press the advantage, but before I can make it across the wide room, Tobin is on his feet, and he's enraged, screaming obscenities in Tab's direction.

"So what? Was all of this just an act?" I can tell she's affected by his words, but he doesn't wait for her to respond, instead he thrusts his hands out, a ball of magic forming, and it swirls straight for Tab.

I'm not going to make it in time, and I know it. Tab knows it too, her face set in a resigned look as the ball hits her in the stomach, and she careens backward, slamming violently into the couch. She tumbles over the back, and I don't see where she lands.

"Nobody messes with my bestie!" I scream, letting out a war cry as I sprint the last few feet.

I let loose a torrent of magic, and I'm pleased when some of it hits the King. He jerks to the side, his shirt singed, but somehow, he shakes it off. Almost instantly, he's coming for me, and we clash with both fists and magic. Remembering my training, I throw an impressive roundhouse kick, clocking him in the cheek.

Rule number eighteen in Zombieland; limber up.

And thank God I did, because the King tilts to the side, and his eyes roll back. I must have gotten him good, because I think he might pass out. Nope, never mind. He's back, shaking his head and coming at me again.

With one hand, he pushes magic at me while I push back with my own. His other hand reaches for a knife at his belt, and I can feel instantly that it's made of iron. That's not good. Any cuts I take from it will be ten times worse than a knife made of any other metal. The iron will seep into my bloodstream, weakening me, so I know I have to avoid that thing at all cost.

He swings the knife, trying to get me across the cheek, but I manage to roll out of the way at the last second, tumbling across the room and willing my magic into the shape of a blade, mimicking his own. Once it's formed, I lunge forward again, and my blade cuts him from elbow to shoulder, but it isn't deep. The magic runs under his skin though, burning, and he lets out a scream.

"Fucking bitch," he hisses, spit flying from his lips.

"There's no need for name calling," I scold him, trying to get under his skin. Maybe if I can irritate him enough it will throw him off his game. I'm willing to try anything at this point, because I wasn't prepared for him to be this strong.

As we come at each other again, there's a tickle in the back of my mind that I haven't truly felt in months. I guess there hasn't been a reason for it since Blake and I have been together most of that time, but as Tobin and I exchange blows, I know for sure it's the magic Blake and I share. I don't know why it's kicking in now though.

Ignoring it, for now, I suck in a gasp when Tobin nicks me with the tip of his blade. Almost instantly, I feel the poison hit my bloodstream, and I weaken just a bit. It's a sluggish feeling, maybe a little nausea, and as I feel my energy declining even more, I know that's how he's going to win this fight. He doesn't have to kill me. He can keep his promise to Tab even though he probably hates her now. All he has to do is get another few nicks in with that knife, and I won't have enough energy to lift my arm, much less fight him.

As I grow weaker, Tab grumbles from somewhere behind me, and I ask my magic to help me out, pushing it to my injured arm. I can feel it trying to heal the wound, but I don't know if it's capable of ridding my blood of the poison. I just have to hope my magic can heal me enough to keep me in this fight until I can figure out a way to win.

Focused on my healing magic, I'm not paying attention and trip over something on the floor, falling over a side table and ending up face first on the floor. I'm up quickly though, but when I spin around, Tobin is right on top of me, and by the time I see the back of his hand whizzing through the air, it's already too late. His hand connects with my cheek with a crack, and once again I'm falling back. When I crash into the same table, I curse the stupid wood, wishing it would just disappear.

Really should've thought that one through.

My magic can be such a bitch sometimes, because she took my wish literally, and since I was lying across the table when it disappeared, I found myself back on the floor. It stuns me enough that I don't get back up right away, and I realize the kind of shit I'm in right now since I can't see where the King is or what he's doing. And when I hear Tab shout, "No," I know it's bad.

The King grips my hair, yanking me to my feet and slamming me into the back of the couch. I can now clearly see Tab, tears pouring down her face as she tries to climb up from the floor. She's babbling incoherently, but I'm pretty sure she's begging *Tobi* not to kill me because I caught a word here and there.

As she begs again, I'm wrenched back, and Tobin slides one hand around my throat, while the other still grips my hair. My scalp is throbbing, as he growls in my ear, "You're going to die today, and I'm going to enjoy it." And then I'm flying.

BESTIE ESP

Ell

I hate to admit this, but I'm losing badly. I've been chunked across the room more than once, and I have two more cuts on my arm courtesy of the King's knife. Plus, I'm pretty sure he's ripped out half my hair, and what's worse, my right eye is nearly swollen shut which is making it very difficult to see.

I'm in a heap in the corner after being chunked from the opposite side of the room, and I track his movements. He doesn't make his way to me yet, no, this fucker is enjoying this, savoring every little moment. I, on the other hand, am doing everything I can to keep from puking, because I can almost feel the iron coursing through my veins. I really wish I knew a way to get it out, to heal myself of it, but I just can't think of anything.

As I beg my magic anyway, Tab startles me when she crawls toward me, coming up on my right side. She tucks her legs under her body, and begins checking me for injury, her hands roving all over me.

I can tell by the look on Tab's face I look bad. Hell, I can *feel* that I look bad. Is that a thing? Well, it is now.

"Move!" the King shouts at Tab, but he stays on the other side of the room, not willing to attack me with Tab in the way. Or, at least, that's what I'm assuming. I think he really does have feelings for her. That reality still blows my mind. I don't know why, but I guess I didn't think he was capable of love, compassion, or empathy.

"Tabatha, move right now," he orders, "I don't want to hurt you, despite you hurting me, but I will if you don't get out of my way."

Tab twists, giving me her back, but she remains squatted in front of me, and I don't need to see her face to know she's giving Tobin an evil death-glare. "She's done. You promised. You don't have to kill her. She can't fight anymore, so just bind her and get it over with. Or, hell, *I'll* bind her."

"You can't be trusted anymore, Tabatha," he nearly whispers, his tone more sad than angry, "And my promise was null and void the minute you stabbed me in the back."

"You know I had to do that," she insists in a begging tone, "She's my best friend. I couldn't let you kill her. I had to give her a chance. It's not like I actually hurt you, so stop being such a freaking baby. You always have to be so dramatic." Tab huffs, turning over her shoulder to check on me.

I'm doing better, actually. Their little convo has bought me time. Maybe that's why Tab is doing it, maybe not, but either way, it's working in my favor. If she could just stall for another five minutes that would be great, thanks.

Tab continues to engage the King in conversation, and as she does, I press my back to the wall, using it for leverage to shimmy to my feet. Tab notices, and she too stands, still positioned between me and the King.

With both of us on our feet now, Tab's words from earlier come back to me. She offered to bind me herself, and her offer has given me an idea. But, if I want this to work, not only am I going to have to sell it, Tab is going to have to realize what I'm doing. I sure hope our bestie ESP is working today.

"I…" my voice cracks on purpose, "Tobin, I…you win. I… can't…"

He tries to hide his shock at my words, but it's no use, I see it. He doesn't respond right away though, and I'm worried he's not buying it fully, so I double down.

"Just bind me, Tab…I've got nothin' left." I cough, acting as if I'm hacking up a lung, and she turns her back on him, eying me. She doesn't look suspicious though, more curious. "Just do it," I grumble, trying to sound disappointed in myself

Either Tab has caught on, or she truly believes the shit I'm selling, because she picks up my hands, holding them between us. "I'm so, so sorry, Ell." Her eyes cast upward. "God, please forgive me."

Shit. I think she really thinks I want her to bind me. She isn't stronger than me, so under normal circumstances I could break her binding, but as worn down as my body is right now, I'm not sure I could.

Why is our ESP not working?

There's no time to answer that question though, because we both jump when Tobin shouts, "Stop! What are you doing?" He stomps a few feet closer to us, but Tab stops him, "Back off. You know, you're being a real dick today. She surrendered. Give her a little fucking dignity."

With that, I watch in horror as magic seeps from her hands, coating mine. She isn't putting a literal binding on me though. No, this is more like what I did to Jim, binding his magic to mine so he couldn't use it, couldn't get away. Unfortunately, if she goes through with this, the fight really is over.

Tab's head lowers as she pushes more magic into me. "I'm so sorry. I promise I'll make this right…someday."

Her magic is now inside me, I can feel it. It coats all of me, but I don't try to push it back. It's no use, because I already know I'm too tired to fight it. I guess I'll just have to regroup and find another way. Maybe the boys will stage a rescue attempt, and better that I'm alive when they do.

I don't struggle as Tab turns and grips me by the elbow, ready to escort me away. She tilts her head, resting her temple against mine, and then she mumbles, "In three, two, one…"

She lets go of me, and we charge, our hands in the air as we shout, "Bestie power!"

Okay yes, that was cheesy, but whatever, because we're on

top of the King before he knows what's happening, and he stumbles back, going over a chair and landing in a heap. While he's down, I push all the magic I can into him, and will it to stop his heart temporarily. I think Tab would be devastated if I killed him, so I'm going to do everything in my power not to do that.

My lavender mist hits Tobin hard, but he must've been ready, because most of it bounces off. A tiny amount seeps into his chest, probably only enough to cause his heart to skip a beat and nothing more. Certainly not enough to stop it, which means I'm pretty sure we're right back to square one.

Tobin's face turns red with rage as he realizes Tab double crossed him for the second time today. He screams out her name, and she flinches. I know it hurt her to do this, but it's not like there was any other choice. Tobin is a bad person, Tab is not.

"I'll have both your heads," he screams, spittle flying from his mouth.

Tab tries to ignore his words, as he pushes back while she circles around. Now he's pinned in-between us, and he has to turn sideways to keep an eye on us both. He has one hand out facing me, and the other facing Tab. With a shuddering breath, his magic forms into the shape of an ax, flying toward us both. The one coming for me misses, but the other grazes Tab's thigh, and she stumbles back, nearly falling over the credenza.

I guess he assumes she's taken care of, at least for now, so he turns his back on her, and jerks toward me. At the same time, we both fire everything we've got. The magic meets in the middle, and the force pushes us both back. My ears pop, and everything sounds like I'm in a tunnel. I try to dig my toes in, but I can't get any traction. That is, until Tab smashes a vase over Tobin's head. Shock sweeps over his face, and he lets his magic go for just a second. It's enough for me to get my footing again, but not enough to do much more. Tab's action only bought me a matter of seconds, and now mine and the King's magic is locked up once again.

As I search for a crack in his magic, a greenish ball forms

around the King, and I assume it's some sort of shield. I can't believe how much magic he has that he can waste it on a shield while he's pouring so much into me though. I'm supposed to be the strongest fairy in all of Fay, so how is he holding his own right now? I wonder if he's pulling from the sacrifices he's already made.

I know there isn't time to answer that though, because the magic around the King pulses out as Tab tries to reach for me. The force blows her back, and I'm pretty sure she's unconscious again because she doesn't get back up. That's okay. In fact, it might be better. This fight was supposed to just be me and Tobin. This is how it was always meant to end.

***

Ari

Blake filled us in on his theory, and we all agreed it sounded like Ell. She overpowered a Brownie, and she's in there right now, alone, impersonating a maid. That leaves us out here, trying to figure out a way in.

Our whole group, including Bree, Layla, and King Oberon, now fight near the back wall of the palace. I even spotted Firo and his son Cody a few minutes ago, and I was honestly surprised they chose to come. They didn't have to, and I'll make sure Ell knows when this is all over.

In front of us is a line of no less than four hundred guards, their backs to the wall. In front of them is at least another two hundred engaged in fighting, and above us, *our* Pixies fight *their* Sprites. This has been the status quo for the last hour, no side besting the other. This could legitimately last for days or even weeks, but while that might be true, I know Ell's fight inside won't last near that long.

That realization has my stomach in knots as I lead a group of Celestial guards, once again attempting to break through the UnSeelie line. We clash with the front, and I'm swept back with the force of the magic. Despite my bad luck though, the others seem to be doing well. Nyx has pushed past the front line, and is engaged with three Elves in the second line. If we can keep pushing, we just might break through.

Three Gnomes fly over my head, courtesy of Blake, as I force my way forward again. I ready fire in each of my hands, and careful with my aim, I lob them against the wall itself. Stone rains down on the fairies beneath, and they scramble back, creating a hole.

"Push!" I shout, "Push!"

Our group surges forward, and I'm bumped sideways by Luke as he wizzes past, his shoulder slamming into mine. I'm pushed back the other way when a group of Celestial guards move forward, their swords ready in front of them. They're deadly with those things, and more than one UnSeelie in front of them loses a limb, or two.

"Over here!" Quinn shouts, "Ari!"

Searching him out, I spot him not far off, and he, along with about a dozen of our own, have managed to push past the guard shack, so I call for others to follow me. Not waiting to see if they do, I sprint, and have to stop twice to fend off attackers.

Finally, I make it to Quinn's side, but as I do, he falls, his head thrust back and his eyes on the sky. I'm not sure what's happening though, and from the look on the Elf's face he was just fighting, he doesn't know either.

The Elf shrugs, thrusting his hands toward Quinn, but I step in the way, erecting a wall of fire in front of me, effectively creating a barrier. The Elf lets out a scream of pain, and through the flames, I watch him fall, his hands still engulfed.

"Protect Quinn," I call, turning to face him and seeing he's still on his knees as if he's in a trance.

Our guards don't waste any time following my order, and within seconds, there's a perfect circle around us. That's good, because I need more time to assess the situation. There's no logical reason for Quinn to be in the position he's in, and I'm not sure what to do.

I grip his shoulders, shaking him. "Quinn!" He doesn't respond, not even a flinch, so I shake harder. "Quinn, what's wrong with you?"

No matter how hard I try, he doesn't answer. It's like he isn't even there, so I spin around, looking for our only Elf in the group. When I spot Nyx, he's back where we started the charge, and I know there's no use in yelling for him. He's just too far away.

When I turn back, Blake skids to a stop next to me. "What's going on?" he asks, looking between me and Quinn.

"No clue," I admit, trying to keep an eye on our surroundings. "He just fell like that. He was fighting an Elf, but *he* looked as surprised to see him go down as I did."

Blake looks concerned. "Should I get him out of here?"

"Yeah," I agree, "that's probably the best thing. Carry him to the back of our line. Order a couple guards to keep watch on him."

Blake nods, leaning down and scooping Quinn up with very little effort, his biceps bulging out of his shirt. He carries him through our guards, headed toward the wooded area behind us, but just as I'm about to turn back to the fight, Blake falls, Quinn going down with him.

I have to fight my way to them, and while they lie on their side, their eyes are still wide open, staring off into space. It really is like they're in a trance, but the question; why? Someone has to be doing this.

I know I need to get the others, because there's obviously a pattern here. If Blake and Quinn went down, are Nyx, Lucas, and I next? If we are, then we don't need to be in the middle of the fight when it happens.

With that realization, I scan the area and spot both Nyx and Lucas fighting alongside one another, which is good. At least I can get them both at the same time. But knowing I have to hurry, I grab two guards, telling them to watch Blake and Quinn, and then I'm rushing in the direction I last saw the other two. I'm halfway there when my stomach bottoms out though. My head swims, and my ears ring as I drop to my knees. Everything around me seems so far away, and as I slip away, the last thing that runs through my mind is Ell's face.

***

Ell

Oh how the tables have turned. Moments ago, I was ahead, pushing Tobin back and filling him with my magic. Sure, he blocked most of it, but it held him in place, and that was better than nothing. Then it was like someone flipped the script, and all of a sudden, *I* was pushed back. The difference in me and him is I didn't have enough left to push him off. I have all the magic in Fay, but every ounce I use drains my body. I'm only fairy, so when my body is drained of energy, there isn't a damn thing I can do about it until I recharge.

And I really needed to do just that, because my stream of purple magic turned grey as it waned and cracked under the pressure. Then that stream rushed back inside me, almost as if it was scared of what was about to happen. And I just remember thinking; same, girl, same.

Tobin saw that my magic was retreating, and he pushed the advantage, his body touching mine. He snarled, letting out a witch-like cackle. "This is it, Ell of Fay, this is where you die."

At the time, I could hear Tab scrounging around on the other side of the room, but I knew she wouldn't be able to offer me a reprieve like she did earlier. That was a one hit wonder, never to be repeated. At least not today, because I knew she was injured badly, and I knew she needed to get to a healer pronto.

Knowing I needed to speed this up for her sake, I sucked in a breath, retrieving every last ounce of strength I had, and with it, my knee rose. It connected with the King's balls, and I felt them squish, giving me an immense amount of satisfaction. With the force, he fell back, but since he had me in his clutches, I went down with him, and when he stopped our roll, he was on top. He leaned over me, a crazed look in his eyes, and with my defenses down, I couldn't stop him when his magic slowly began to seep into my body. It enveloped me, and my body temperature dropped to a dangerous level. I felt my heart rate slow, and my blood pressure drop, my head pounding. I tried to fight back, but my body had given out.

That's when my mind wondered. The first face I saw was Quinn. I don't know why he was first, but he was. He waved at me, a smile on his face, and I pulled. I was terrified when he dropped to his knees, his eyes going vacant, but something inside me said he was fine.

Blake was next. He appeared to me in a field, the one where we did recon together at Peg's house all those months ago. He and I were running, side by side, and then I pulled from him too.

When I saw Blake drop to the ground, well, that was when my mind was jerked back to reality. Tobin's hands had been gripped tightly around my throat, and I could barely breathe. I clawed, digging my nails into his skin, but he was unfazed.

Probably due to the lack of oxygen, I slipped away again, seeing Ari's face next. He was barking orders to some of my guards, and I felt a sense of urgency, so I wasted no time pulling him to me. Ari fell just like the others, and then I was once again thrust back to the present.

Now, I know I'm fading. I didn't have time to see them all, and that breaks my heart more than anything. If I just had another minute, I would have time to see their faces one last time.

My head lolls to the side as my oxygen supply is almost completely cut off. I'm keenly aware when my eyes roll back in my head, and I pass out. Or, maybe I didn't pass out, because there's Nyx.

I wave, and he practically skips toward me, his arms going out as if he wants a hug. I want to return it, but no matter how hard I try, my body won't budge, and for whatever reason, it seems like he can't come any closer.

Realizing our dilemma, I internally wish him to me, taking

his essence and tucking it behind my heart for safe keeping. Then, Nyx blinks out of existence, which worries me, because the others didn't do that.

I don't have long to stress over it though, because Luke pops up, his magic raining a thin mist down on his head. His arms are crossed, and he looks slightly irritated, but when he sees me, he winks. Like always, I melt, and once again, I'm pulling.

They're all inside me now, and I plan on taking them with me. I doubt this will be like last time though. I don't think they'll be able to bring me back from the other side. This is most likely where my story ends, but if it is, I think I'm okay with that. I have a little piece of each of them, tucked away in a safe place, and I'll hold on to it tight in the afterlife, until they join me.

I'm going to miss them so much though. I hope they go on, getting over me quickly and finding another great love of their life. I doubt they'll all stay together, but I do hope they remain friends, especially Luke and Ari. I hope they find a way to connect.

Of course I'll haunt them, if that's a possibility. If ghosts are real, I'm totally gonna be one.

A FREAKING VEGETABLE

Ell

I have no idea how long I stayed in that dream-like state, but when my eyes popped open, I could hear Tab and King Tobin arguing. Someone else was in the room too, whispering softly to Tab, but I wasn't sure who it was.

That was at least five-minutes ago, and no one has noticed that I'm awake. I don't dare move though. I don't want to risk the King realizing he didn't quite finish me off. That fact has my mind reeling though. I was so certain I was a goner. But, I guess not.

"I did what you asked," Tobin growls, "I didn't fucking kill her. Are you happy now?"

"No," Tab bites back, "she's probably gonna have brain damage now. What good is she to me if she's a freaking vegetable for the rest of her life?"

Tobin huffs, "Ugh, you're unpleasable. I cannot make you happy. I did what you asked, and you're still not happy. Do you have any idea how much restraint it took to not finish her off? I did that for *you*, despite what you did to *me*."

Tab lightens her tone, and whispers, "I know that." There's a long silence between them, and I think the conversation is through, but then Tab adds, "But now what?"

Without even thinking, Tobin answers, "Now, I finish binding her, and she spends the rest of her life in the dungeon. Now, I finish what I started."

"You know this is wrong," Tab tells him, "I know you know it is. I know there's good in you, Tobi. If you open a new realm, you'll kill millions of people in the Earth realm, and God only knows how many in Fay."

"You don't know that," he argues, sounding like a pouty child, "No one knows what will happen. My seer has assured me Fay will remain intact."

"Your seer is a fucking idiot," she barks, "And to be honest, I'm pretty sure he's lied about a lot of stuff. I have this feeling that he isn't who he says he is, and he's going to do something bad."

Their arguing continues, but while they've been hashing things out, I've been ever so slowly inching my head around. Tobin stands near his desk, while Tab sits on the edge. The other voice I heard in the room earlier is a healer. He doesn't work on Tobin, like I would've thought, but instead, he heals Tab.

Once again I realize the true depths of Tobin's feelings for her, and to be honest, her feelings for him are pretty fucking clear too, even if she hasn't admitted them yet. Sadly, that makes what I'm about to do so much harder.

I know now why I saw each of my boys while I thought I was dying. I pulled everything from them. Their tethers now send a steady stream of magic to me. Well, except for Blake. In his case, I'm getting energy, and my body is already starting to feel better. So much better that I'm able to slowly rise to my knees. Tobin's back is to me, and he's totally oblivious to what's coming for him.

It's me. I'm coming for him.

I don't want to waste any energy though, so I don't bother standing, but I know the moment Tab sees me in her periphery, because tears begin to slip from her eyes. Tobin jerks toward her, wanting to offer comfort, and she lets him, keeping him distracted.

With one final tug, I open myself up to the boys, letting all of them flow through me. It mixes with my magic, making this shimmering rainbow of a color as it flows from my wrists. It builds and builds, and the force is so great, I don't know how much longer I can hold on to it.

It grows even stronger, and Tab throws her arms around the King. He nuzzles against her neck, and she lets him, but while they're connected, I speak to my magic, whispering in my mind and hoping to God she listens.

The magic has formed a massive ball of energy in front of me, and now I know I can't keep it any longer, so mentally preparing myself, mine and Tab's eyes connect as she looks at me over Tobin's shoulder. Ever so slightly, she nods her head, but her eyes, they are begging me.

Without warning, she shoves him back as hard as she can, shouting, "Now, Ell!"

I scream as the energy bursts forth, gunning straight for the King. It hits him so hard he's slammed into the wall, the plaster cracking with the force. He's frozen in place, his back against the wall, and he's unable to move as my magic, infused with my boys, pummels him, causing blood to drip from his eyes and nose.

I feel Tab move away from him, and I can't help but look at her. Those tears that were fake earlier are very much real now. Her cheeks are flushed, her eyes swollen already, and she chokes, her hand moving to cover her mouth.

Unfortunately, the magic is out of my hands now. I'm not sure if I could stop it even if I wanted to. The weird part; I kind of want to. Tobin is a terrible fairy in my eyes, but clearly Tab sees something in him, something redeemable. Maybe under different circumstances he could've been better, but under these, he cannot be allowed to continue with his plan. He has to be stopped, and my magic knows that better than anyone.

Determined, I turn back, seeing Tobin is still pressed flat against the wall, his arms and legs splayed out. His eyes have turned this endless black color, you can't even see the whites anymore, and it makes me shiver.

I can actually feel my magic ripping him apart at the seams, and I go to Tab, putting my arm around her and pulling her close. "I'm so sorry," I tell her, and I mean it.

My words only make her sob harder, and her whole body shakes against me. This was clearly more than a friendship, there's no doubt of that now, even if neither of them had acted on it yet. They would have, if they'd had more time together.

That realization makes me sick to my stomach on a whole *lotta* levels, as Tab chokes my name, and I feel my magic waning, which has me jerking back to face Tobin. Slowly, my magic leaves him, finding its way back to me, and without it holding him up, Tobin slides down the wall, hitting the stone floor with a crunch. His body lies in a ball, his right leg twisted at an odd angle, and seeing it has me searching for the healer. Not for that, but I know he was here before all this started.

Scanning the room, I don't find him, and I figure, like a weasel, he probably ran for his life. You can't really blame him though. He probably knew his King was about to lose, and thought he would be next. If I was to guess, he probably alerted every guard on his way out too.

When I turn back, Tab rushes to Tobin, throwing her body over his, the tears still falling. Her head rests against his shoulder, and her legs are tucked against his side as she grips him tightly.

My heart breaks for her. Whether he was alive or not, a relationship between them would be impossible, and I think she knows that. I *hope* she knows that.

Seeing Tab with him has me wanting my own boys though, but I can't imagine it will be easy getting to them. Just because I defeated the King doesn't mean the UnSeelie will just lay down their weapons and give us control of their capital. No doubt someone is lying in the wings just waiting to pick up the King's crusade. I don't care though, because I know no matter what, we'll defeat them too.

Tab sucks in a gasp, and I jerk toward her. Her eyes connect with mine, and she whispers, "He's still breathing."

I pop my hip out, wagging my head. "You're welcome."

***

Ell

Just call me an 'ole softy. I can't help it. I love that Selkie. She's mine, and there was no way I could stand to see her heart break. So before I let my magic loose, I begged it to bring him to the brink of death and no more. And for once, she listened.

Come to find out, she also stripped him of nearly every ounce of magic he possessed. I didn't even know that was possible, but when Tab revealed he was still breathing, and I pushed her back to bind the King's magic to mine, there wasn't any. Well, I found a tiny speck, but it wouldn't even be enough to warm your morning coffee.

When Tab realized what I'd done though, she rushed me, throwing her arms around me, and all out refusing to let me go. I swear it was the longest hug of all time, but after an eternity, she finally let me go, only to rush back a few minutes later for another one.

Now, she hovers over him, trying to wake him. I doubt he will for some time though, at least not without a healing and a few weeks of rest.

Even without his magic, I have no intention of setting him loose in Fay. I'm not sure what I'll do with him, but I'll figure it out. Maybe I'll have the staff build him a cushy room in the dungeon so Tab can visit him if she wants, and she will want, a lot. Yeah, we should probably soundproof that room.

I squat down next to Tab, knowing I need to hurry this along. "Tab, I want you to have your moment, but the fighting is still going on out there, and it's only a matter of time before the guards learn of the King's defeat. They'll come for us. We can't fight them off. Not with just the two of us."

Tab scrubs her hand across each cheek, clearing the tears.

She sniffles, nodding her head in agreement. "I know, but how do we get out of here. If it was just the two of us, maybe, but not having to carry him too."

That's a good point, and I don't know the answer, so I stand, leaving Tab and making my way through the now messy room. I peek out the large picture window along one wall, and look out over the lawn that leads to the back gate.

"Holy shit," I mumble.

"What?" Tab squeaks, and I hear her rushing to me. She looks out the window now too, and repeats my sentiment, "Holy shit."

Every inch of the lawn below us, and stretching all the way to the wall, is covered in a massive battle. Fairies of all kinds fight, and even from here I recognize a few. Our people breached the wall, and I'm filled with pride at the realization.

"There has to be a way to stop the fighting, to prevent even more loss of life," I breathe.

"Yeah," Tab smarts off, "good luck with that. The UnSeelie love a good fight. I don't even think they will care when they find out their King lost to you. They'll just keep fighting. Honestly, they'll keep on until everyone is dead."

Sure, that's what we've always been taught. We were brought up knowing the Seelie are good and the UnSeelie are bad. But what if that's all about environment, or what if the UnSeelie are bad because everyone assumes they are. Just look at Quinn, he's one of the most amazing fairies I've ever met, and yet, according to what I was taught, he should be evil.

With that thought, I turn my wrist over, eyeing my mark. Such a simple little thing to cause so much trouble. It's the thing that separates us all, but why do we have to be separated? Why can't we rule together? Why can't that be good enough?

"But what if we could stop this?" I wonder out loud, "I mean, we should at least give them the benefit of the doubt, right?"

A 'humph' bubbles up from Tab, but I ignore her. Instead, I grip her wrist, and forgetting about the King lying in a feeble state, I rush us out of his room. We stumble along in the near dark, the sun almost set outside, and Tab asks three times where we're going, but I brush her off, knowing exactly what I want to do.

At the end of the hall, I swing open the door, and know we're headed in the right direction when I see a spiral set of stairs leading up. We take them two at a time, and Tab has given up on her incessant questioning once we reach the top, busting out the small wooden door and finding ourselves exactly where I wanted us to be; on the roof.

There's a small recess wall around the edge, and the two of us move quickly, looking out over the veracious battle. There are hundreds dead already, and when I look to the right, there's fighting over there too. I'm not going to waste time checking the other sides, because I know it's the same all the way around, so instead, I grab Tab's shoulder for support, carefully climbing onto the half-wall.

It's then I realize I'm still holding on to my boys, and I wish I'd realized that earlier. I hope my magic didn't affect them too badly. I hope they aren't hurt because of it.

With that worry, I let them go, and I feel their essence rushing back to them, hurrying across their tethers. It only takes a second, and then I feel their magic snap back into place. Almost instantly, I'm relieved. I wish they were here with me right now, but I can at least take solace in knowing they're okay. I can feel it.

Now that that's taken care of, I gather my magic again, and will it to project my voice for miles. I have no idea what to say though. I mean, it's not like I wrote a script or anything. I could really use some note cards right about now.

No matter, in true Ell fashion, I'm totally about to wing it.

"Fairies and humans of Fay," I speak at a normal level, but my magic causes the sound to travel, booming out across the raging battle, "All of Fay kind, hear me now! I stand before you not as a Queen, but as one of you, a fairy, a friend, a sister, a daughter." Slowly, the fighting lulls, although more than half ignore me, but I continue anyway. "I am not here to conquer you. I am here to liberate you."

With those words, more fairies stop what they're doing to search me out. Someone points, shouting my location, and hundreds of heads turn toward me. I give them an almost goofy wave, waiting another minute to gather more attention.

"I could have killed your king," I tell them, and a roar of anger sweeps through the crowd, so I hurry on, "But I didn't. I spared him, just like I'll spare you. There's no reason for anyone else to die." I pause, allowing that to sink in. "Your King, he had lofty ambitions. He planned to create a new realm. His actions would've destroyed Earth, and Fay would've been not far behind."

Now the angry shouts have settled, and hearing the King's plan, fairies whisper and discuss the bombshell I just laid at their feet. It's obvious to me that most of them had no idea what King Tobin was planning, and that's good. It'll make things a lot easier.

Holding my hand out, I call for silence, and I'm more than a little shocked when most listen. "What he wanted to do would have destroyed us all. He had to be stopped. But…our fight isn't with you. Seelie and UnSeelie, there's no reason for us to hate one another." This causes a few mumbles, but most are hanging onto my every word. "Why would we? Hate each other, I mean? Why? Because our mothers and fathers told us to? Because history says we should? Well," I shout the word, and it echoes back to me, "I say; no more!"

There's a few cheers, hands pumping in the air, but I notice most of them are Seelie and Celestial. That's okay, at least the UnSeelie have stopped fighting. It's a start, we just have to convince them there's no reason to go back to fighting, at least not today.

"I want to go back to my family," I continue, "Do you? Why should we die for a cause that has nothing to do with us? I have zero desire to fight you. I have no desire to see you bleed. I want you to go home. I want you to lead a good life. You are my people too."

More cheers go up, and this time, a few UnSeelie join in.

That's when I spot Ari. He's making his way through the crowd, stopping beneath the shadow of the very wall I stand on, and just behind him are the rest of my boys. I doubt they can see my face right now, but I'm grinning, giving them a wink and sending them all my love.

As my heart flutters, I look back to the crowd, and the shouts die down, so I know I need to wrap this up. "Let's end this. Right here, today. Let's decide that Seelie and UnSeelie are no longer enemies. From this day forward, we are friends."

The crowd roars, and it's so loud I think fairies will be able to hear it on the other side of Fay. I watch as the fairies beneath me pump their fists, jump up and down, and one rotund Ogre even walks around giving everyone high-fives. It's kinda cute.

Sure, there are a few UnSeelie in the mix refusing to accept my words. A few even stomp off, leaving the battle and the promise of friendship behind. I knew I couldn't win them all over, but if I even win over half, the others will know they can't stand against us.

And with that, I finish, "You're tired. Go home. Rest. Hug your loved ones. And tomorrow, we start a new day."

IT'S 5 O'CLOCK SOMEWHERE

Ell

So, who thought that was gonna work? No? Same.

Honestly, I thought I could win over a few, but I still thought there would be a decent number that would put up a fight, but no. A few dozen fairies, and no more, refused to leave peacefully, but they were easily taken into custody. After my speech though, not another fairy or human lost their life. I did good, if I do say so myself.

After everyone dispersed, Tab and I rushed back downstairs. She went to King Tobin, and I fumbled my way through the labyrinth of halls and out the back door. I found my boys first, and I spent the next hour letting them hold me. I just couldn't get enough, and neither could they. In fact, it's a wonder things didn't turn dirty, if you get what I'm saying.

After that, there was some minor cleanup, and then our army started setting up encampments around the UnSeelie palace, making a place for everyone to sleep. We were able to give rooms to some inside the palace, but there was only so much available space.

My group and I have claimed one of the rooms on the royal hall. Not King Tobin's room, but the one across from it. The one reserved for, and I quote, 'his lovers'. I just couldn't see myself staying in his chambers. It just felt too weird. Although, I'm sure there's been a lot of sex in the room we chose too. It didn't really matter though, because we were all so exhausted when we first got inside, that after a round of showers, we pretty much collapsed. I was completely content to just feel them around me. I didn't need anything more. But, that was before and this is now.

It's 3:00 a.m., and I need some dick. Is that too much to ask? I let them rest, and I took a little catnap to rebuild my energy, but now I'm ready to go. Actually, I'm ready to come, like a dozen times.

Normally, I would wiggle, huff and puff to get what I want, but this time, I decide to be a little more direct. "Boys, wake up!"

Ari grumbles first, the lightest sleeper, but he rolls back over and ignores me. Nyx has his head on my lap already, and he nuzzles his face against my panties. I wiggle, and he bites me, playfully.

But, he's the only one paying me any attention, and I need more. Plus, it isn't just that I need more, I also want to give more. I can be a giver too. I can. And I wanna give right now. Who needs sleep when you could be coming? Am I right?

I giggle, a thought popping in my head. "Who wants a blow job?" Five hands shoot straight up, and I laugh, but also, yes, now we're getting somewhere. "Nyx gets to go first because he was the first one to pay attention to me."

Ari and Luke groan against their pillows, and Nyx pops up on his knees, naked in a flash. *Damn Elf magic.* He winks at me playfully, and I don't make him wait. I crawl forward, my hands gripping his hips, and in one motion, I take him all the way in, his head hitting the back of my throat. Nyx isn't the only one that groans, and my stomach clenches.

Bobbing, I slide my hands across his hips, and move around to his backside. I squeeze as I swallow him, and when I slide down the next time, I hum, causing Nyx to let out a slew of curses.

"Damn," he moans, as I feel someone grip my hips.

Ari.

My oversized t-shirt is pulled up, and my panties are wrenched to the side. I'm being fucked before I know it, and it doesn't take long for us to get a steady rhythm going. When I pop off the end of Ari's dick, he slaps my ass, the burn feeling so good. I'm so drenched, it's easy for him to slide back in, pushing me down Nyx's shaft as he goes.

My pussy is on fire as a hand slides under my shirt, and it's so cold I shiver. Pulling back, I let Nyx's dick slide out so I can say, "Warm those puppies up, man."

Blake chuckles, and then his hand leaves me. I hear him making friction, and then he says, "Nyx, can you magic her shirt away or something? It's really screwing up my easy access."

As I let Nyx fill my mouth, he snaps his fingers and my shirt is gone. Hopefully it's not gone, gone, because I really liked it. I'm gonna need that back. I don't mention it though, since my mouth is kind of full at the moment. Literally.

My tongue laps along Nyx's shaft, and my lips slide across his head. In that instant though, he comes, the warm, sticky substance running down my lips and hitting my tits. I don't know if Blake realizes it, but he's now smearing it around like he's working on a science experiment. I don't mind though, because it feels great.

With Nyx done now, he leaves me and is replaced by Luke, and he doesn't waste anytime grabbing my hand and sliding it down his length. We work together, building him up to release, and he comes faster than I was expecting, spilling his seed in my hand. He leans down, kissing me long and hard before moving aside for the next person in line. Only, no one appears in the empty spot. Ari is still pounding away, and Blake seems to be content with my tit in his mouth. I'm content too, but where's Quinn?

I don't get a chance to look for him because Ari picks up the pace, slamming into me so hard I grunt with each thrust. And then, he blows my mind. His thumb trusts inside my other hole with zero warning. I would complain but good, God it feels amazing. The double penetration inches me so close to the edge, and when Ari groans my name, his dick swelling inside me, I come.

"Fuck," I drag out the word, followed by a slew of very foul language.

That was totally unladylike.

Not caring, I sink to the mattress, Ari on top of me, and we both pant for air. Ari doesn't stay on me long though, and when I feel him move, the cold night air hitting my bare back, I see Quinn. He's standing in the dark corner, just finishing. This seems to be his thing, and honestly, I'm okay with it. It's fucking hot. Well, I'm okay with it as long as every once in a while he puts his dick inside me.

My body lifts, two warm, beefy paws securing me to an equally beefy chest, and I breathe Blake in as he carries me across the dark room. Seeing the clock, it's nearly five, so I know we might as well get up, but I was hoping we'd get to cuddle for a little while. I guess Blake has other plans though.

I'm carried into the bathroom, the door shutting behind us when Blake bumps it with his butt. He sets me on the counter, removing his clothes quickly before starting the shower. When he turns back to me, my eyebrow is quirked, questioning him without words.

"What?" he asks. "You're dirty."

I can't help but snort, and I don't argue when he picks me up, the two of us huddling close under the spray. It reminds me of when we first started dating, that day at Meemaw and Peepaw's. It was just the two of us then, and it's just the two of us now.

The memory makes me sigh, and I rest my head on his chest as his arms wrap around me. We stand like that, neither of us saying a word, and it's exactly how I wanted to start my day.

***

Ell

We've gathered everyone up for a meeting. It's time to hash out everything that happened, and everything that needs to happen next. Sure we stopped the King from opening a new realm, but was it enough? My biggest concern is that someone else will step in to replace him, leading the charge in the same direction he was, and I know we can't let that happen.

Almost everyone is here now, seated around a large oak table, lined with goblets of fairy wine. All the boys questioned my choice to serve wine at this meeting, but I said, 'It's five o'clock somewhere, right?' We all deserve this. We've been through a lot. And with that in my mind, I down the contents of my goblet before retrieving another as we wait.

The only person not here is Helga, and she's the most important. I was told she would be here, and it's odd that she isn't on time. She isn't one to be late, which has me worried a bit, my knee bouncing, and Blake reaches over, pressing his hand to my thigh. We exchange a smile just as the door to the room swings open.

"Well," Helga croaks, clearing her throat, "aren't y'all sweet, you waited on me."

"You are kind of the reason the meeting was called," I joke, playfully.

With my smart-ass attitude, I half expect her to give me a swat, but she shares in the joke, laughing jovially as she takes a seat at the opposite end from me. She wiggles her bottom until she gets comfortable, and then she motions for me to start.

"Now that we're all here, I want to use this opportunity to thank all of you for everything you've done. This was a long, and hard fought battle, spanning months. We couldn't have done it without each and every one of you." I take the time to make eye contact with every person around the room. My boys first, then Bree, and then Tab, followed by Layla. King Oberon and I exchange a regal head nod, and then I spot Thrill who gives me a wink.

Oh, hell naw. There'll be no winking at me. I'm all winked out.

Shaking that off, the last person I look to is Helga, and something like respect passes between us, before I continue, "King Tobin isn't dead, but he has no magic left. He'll be returned to the Seelie palace where he will live out his days in my custody."

At my declaration, a few murmurs circle the table. I know this is news to King Oberon. From the look on his face, I think he disagrees with my decision, but it is just that, *my* decision. Maybe I'll come to regret it, but I don't think so.

"With that said, we'll need to leave a contingent of Seelie guards here to ensure the UnSeelie remain peaceful. We need to help them form a new government, of sorts, and then when the time is right, we can pull back." When I finish, I see nothing but agreement from my friends around the table.

As I think about what I want to say next, King Oberon clears his throat, drawing my eyes to him. "The Celestials would like to volunteer for that posting."

Layla's eyes go wide, making it clear he didn't discuss this with her first. That surprises me. I assumed they were a team, even a couple, although no one has ever come right out and told me that.

"What about your home?" I ask, keeping my eyes on Layla.

"We still have a good number of guards back home," he explains, "but I think we need to be here right now, myself included. We need to make friends, and this is a good way for us to do that."

"Very well," I agree, loving that he volunteered to do this, "We would greatly appreciate your help."

We exchange a nod, and then I move on to the next topic up for discussion. This is the part I've been dreading. I'm terrified that when I bring it up, Helga is going to know something. What if she reveals our fight isn't over? I'm pretty sure I have nothing left to give.

Sending up a silent prayer, I start, "We may have stopped

King Tobin, and the UnSeelie may have walked away from the battle yesterday, but I think we need to consider the very real possibility that someone else will step in and pick up the torch."

"Someone already has," Helga says, point blank.

All my worst fears are realized with her words, and my heart nearly beats out of my chest. "Who?" My question comes out as a squeak, and Ari reaches over, holding my hand.

"An imposter," she answers, firm, "It's the so-called seer that King Tobin was employing."

"So does that mean he isn't a seer at all?" Tab asks, concern in her tone, and I know why. She put a lot of faith in the things the seer said. In fact, she may very well have been privy to other things he saw that she just hasn't told me yet.

"He is not," Helga confirms, giving Tab an understanding look, and then looking back to me, she asks, "Do you want the good news or the bad news first? No, you know what; I'm gonna lead with the bad." She scoots forward in her chair, her arms resting on the tabletop. "The bad news is he's taken up the cause. The worse news is…"

"Whoa," Nyx stops her, his hand going up in a stop motion, "You didn't say anything about worse news. You said bad and good. Not worse."

She rolls her eyes at him, irritated with the interruption. "As I was saying, the worse news is he isn't a fairy either."

"A human?" I ask, because I can't think of anything else, unless he's from the Heaven or Hell realms, but that doesn't make any sense. They rarely intervene.

"Nope," she pops the p, "He is a witch."

Shocked whispers circle the table, and I'm pretty sure my heart stops. A witch? Didn't I just have this discussion? Witches aren't real. They just aren't. Sure there are some fairies that live on earth and try to pass themselves off as witches, mostly in Louisiana, but that's just it, they're posers.

As I try to process this revelation, the room quiets down, and I ask for clarification. "Hold on. I didn't think witches were real. I mean, are we talking about one of those voodoo people on Earth? A fairy trying to portray themselves as a witch, right?"

"Did I or did I not say it was not a fairy?" Helga grumbles, "I swear, it's as if no one listens to me." She scratches her head, and then she adds, "He is a witch. W.I.T.C.H. Witch. And yes, they are very much real, and he is one. He was posing as a seer the whole time so he could kill King Tobin after the two of them created a new realm. This Seer…I believe he goes by Puck. So, his goal was to open a new realm so the witches would no longer have to pose as humans."

"Shit," I curse, "So what, this isn't over? We now have a whole new fight on our hands?"

"No," she answers, not elaborating.

"No?" Ari asks, waving his hand and trying to get her to explain.

She shakes her head in annoyance. "No. It isn't your story."

"So…" I trail off, processing, "Someone else is supposed to stop him, not me?"

"Correct," she confirms with a wave of her hand, "Your path is complete. Well…as far as this is concerned. Now you can go home, and spend your days rebuilding a better Fay."

Honestly, that's the best thing she's ever said to me. But despite that, I can't help but worry about this Puck guy, and my mind is still reeling at the realization that witches exist. I get that it isn't my concern, but what if whoever's concern it is, well, what if they fail? Then what? My worry is it will affect Fay and Earth, that makes it very much my concern. I don't think I can just sit back and let someone else handle it, but from the sound of it, I might not have a choice. Not that I'm not satisfied with the work I will be doing as I rebuild Fay, and not that I won't be enjoying a heap of orgasms without having to worry about when the next battle is, but still.

I suck in a deep breath, processing everything we just learned. "Okay, I guess that settles it. It's time to go home."

***

Ell

After that, the meeting ended, and my boys and I went back to our temporary room. We lounged around for a bit, and then we had dinner brought up. Everything we learned was a lot to process, and that's on top of everything we've been through. We were all exhausted, and we didn't feel like company.

Now that dinner is done, and we're all relaxing in the small sitting room, I try to push away all my worries about what Helga said, and just focus on the time I have with my boys. Ari sits next to me, his thumb circling my wrist, while Blake sits on my other side. Nyx is in the floor at my feet as usual, and Luke and Quinn sit side by side on the loveseat across from us. The two of them talk in low murmurs, and I make out a few words, realizing they're talking about what will happen next, with us all living at the Seelie palace.

"You know," Nyx speaks up, causing Quinn and Luke to cease their talking, "I hate to even say this out loud, but…this is weird, right?"

"Yes," I answer quickly, as Quinn asks, "What do you mean?"

Nyx wraps his arm around my calf, resting his head against my knee. That can't be comfortable, but he seems content. "I just mean we aren't running from anyone. There's no battle looming in the near future. I don't know…I guess I just keep waiting for the other shoe to drop."

"Me too," Blake agrees. "When Helga dropped that bombshell on us today, I really thought that was gonna be the other shoe." He chuckles, and I giggle.

Everyone agrees, and then after a few minutes of silence, Ari says, "Helga hasn't really been wrong about anything. Sure there've been times she's omitted things, or didn't explain them well, but everything happened the way she said it would. And now we're done. I for one am grateful for that."

"Samesies," I agree, snuggling against his side. "Tomorrow we go home, and then all that's left to do is live our life."

"That sounds really great," Luke admits, and I wink in his direction.

As I turn back though, I realize that Quinn hasn't spoken up much since the conversation started, and I can't help but notice an odd look on his face. Concern? Or, I don't know, self-consciousness, maybe?

"Whatcha thinkin', Quinnie boo," I ask, trying out a new nickname. I'll work on it. It was pretty bad.

And it seems Quinn thought so too because he cringes. "I… Nothing…I just…"

"Out with it," I encourage, "This is a safe space, a no judgment zone."

He nods his head, sucking in a breath. "Yeah, okay. I guess I was just thinking now that everything is over, and we aren't fighting for our lives, you don't need your five."

"What?" I gasp, my hand going to my chest as I sit straight.

Ari's body goes tense too, and Luke's jaw is dropped. I can't even believe Quinn just said that. Never in a million years did I imagine he would want to leave me. It makes me feel like he was only with me because he had to be, not because he wanted to be.

That breaks my heart, and I feel the tears start to fall. "You… don't want…me?"

"What?" Quinn squeaks, "Ell, oh God." He stands from his seat, stepping over the coffee table and pushing Blake to the side. "God no, that's not what I meant." He wraps his arms around me, and I grip his shirt tightly, not wanting to let him go. "I just…Well, I'm an UnSeelie, so now that everything is over, I didn't know if you would want me in the group. I don't want you being with me to make you look bad in front of your people. The Seelie won't like it, and I get it. I'm an outsider."

I pull back, pushing him. "You shut your dirty mouth." I glare at him for even saying such a thing. "You are mine, UnSeelie or not, and I don't give a fuck who has a problem with it."

I sweep my hand around the sitting area. "All of you; I don't give a fuck if anyone has a problem with my choices. Because they are just that, *my* choices. You are mine and I am yours, period."

Apparently, I wasn't convincing enough, because Quinn whispers, "I don't want you to feel like you have to keep me."

A pillow flies across the room, slamming into Quinn's face. I turn, shocked at seeing that Luke was the one that chunked it. He doesn't look mad or annoyed though. No, I'd say his actions were playful, if anything.

"Dude, stop trying to leave the band," Luke jokes, grinning, "You're not allowed to break up with us, and we aren't breaking up with you."

"Yeah," Nyx agrees, "Ell is sort of a lifetime commitment."

Quinn chuckles, and just to make sure he truly gets it, I climb on his lap. "You're mine," I tell him, firmly. I kiss him, letting my tongue explore his, and when I rub against his crotch, we both moan.

When I pull back, I nod my head. "Now, we'll never speak of this again."

Quinn laughs, "Got it."

I slide off his lap, and move to steal his original spot. The topic of conversation has moved on to other things now, like the trip back home, and integrating the Pixies, but I'm not participating. I just watch them, taking it all in.

The last few months were an absolute nightmare, but they were also the happiest months of my life. I went to Earth, met Blake, and fell in love for the first time. I came back to find Ari back from his posting at the Summer Court, and despite our constant bickering, I knew I couldn't live without him, even though for a while, twice, I thought I might have to. Then Nyx came out of nowhere. I didn't even know he had a thing for me, but I'm so glad he threw his hat in the ring, because our group wouldn't be the same without him. And then there's Luke. Oh, Luke. We may not have had the best start, and there was a time when he was willing to do anything to have me all to himself, but now, he's one of us, part of the group. Even Ari is starting to warm up to him, and that makes my heart happy. As for Quinn, he might've been the last edition to my harem, but he definitely isn't the least. Sure we've had less time together, but he completes our Star. He's right for us, and we're right for him.

My heart swells as the boys laugh at something Luke just said, and I realize how far we've all come. I fully admit I'm a selfish brat a lot of the time, but these boys, they make me better. I still have a lot of growing up to do, I know that, but with these boys at my side, I feel like I can do anything.

That thought causes my chest to puff out as my hands rake across my stomach, and Luke notices. We exchange a smile as he scoots over, his arm wrapping around my middle. Now we both caress my tummy, neither of us saying a word, and I realize everyone else has gone quiet.

"Is it weird that I almost forgot there's a baby inside her?" Nyx asks, awkwardly.

"Sounds like someone is in denial," Ari jokes, causing us each to laugh.

"There's a baby in me," I breathe, because up until this moment, I couldn't even think about that fact. There's just been too much going on.

When I first found out, I was terrified, and maybe a little angry. This shouldn't be happening, not without me wanting it to, but it is, and there isn't anything I can do about it. But oddly, now that things should be settling down, I don't want to do anything about it. We're having a baby, and I'm weirdly happy about it.

The topic of conversation changes again, and I let my hand slide down my belly and into Luke's palm. I relax into him, and one by one I search out each of my boy's faces. Once again, they're laughing and joking, immersed in some story Nyx is telling about the battle yesterday, and I feel content. We may not have any more literal battles to fight, but I'm sure there will be plenty to keep us busy. I'm looking forward to just spending time with them, us getting to know one another better and as a group. And as I look at each of their handsome faces, I know without a doubt, the best is yet to come.

THE FAIRY END

EPILOGUE

10 Years Later...

Ell

You know, I seem to recall a certain someone telling me that if I was crowned, all hell would *not* break loose. That was a damn lie. Having five husbands, three kids, and a sixteen-year-old little sister seems like the definition of all hell breaking loose. I mean sure, it could be worse. We're no longer running for our lives on the daily, no one is trying to destroy our home, and I haven't been kidnapped in years. So yeah, things could definitely be worse.

Of course, that doesn't mean things are perfect. The odds have been stacked against us more times than I can count, but the worst of it all has been dealing with my sister, Blue. Who knew teenagers were such a pain in the ass? Someone should've prepared me for this moment. Actually, you know what; I'm pretty sure my dad tried. Unfortunately, he isn't here anymore. I mean, it's not like he's dead, but I did make a few changes in the last decade. One of which; making my dad the Ambassador to Earth. No, that doesn't mean humans know we exist, but it does mean that I have him preparing for that inevitable day, and trying to find fairies causing trouble in the Earth Realm. But, because of that, he isn't here to deal with my bratty sister.

Now that task falls to me, and I'm pretty sure I'm failing at it. I've done a decent job with my own kids, if I do say so myself, and we even have one on the way, but as for my sister, it's like she thinks I'm the Devil or something. The sad part is I remember a time when she thought I hung the moon, and vice versa, but not now. Oh Lord, not now.

And that fact is what has me hiding in my closet behind the winter coats. I've been in here for at least an hour, praying no one finds me, but I know it's only a matter of time. You'd think I would be hiding from my ten, seven, and five year olds, but no, it's the sixteen-year-old that terrifies me.

I shiver just thinking about her as I hear my bedroom door groan and Ari whispering, "Ellie?"

I'm just gonna ignore that because I cannot deal. Not right now.

"Ellie, I know you're in the closet. You have to come out eventually. It's almost time for Blue to leave."

Shit. Is that today? Damn it.

I grumble and groan as I climb to my feet, pushing the coats back and making eye contact with Ari. "Do I have to?"

He chuckles, "Yes, now come on." He reaches his hand out, helping me up and pulling me snug against his chest. "This will be good for her. The Academy is the perfect place for Blue right now."

I bury my head in his warm chest, grumbling, "I know. But… is it bad that I'm terrified of her?"

He laughs, tugging me out of the closet and through my room without answering my question, which means it *is* bad. Oh well. I didn't sign up for this. He is right though, the Academy *will* be good for her, but that doesn't change the fact that she hates me for sending her there. She acts like it's a punishment. It isn't, for the record.

Fay Arts Academy is run by one of my dad's childhood friends, and in the last decade since the academy was built, he's done an amazing job of creating the realm's best schooling for up and coming fairies. And my sister is definitely that, so I just don't understand why she can't see that. Or, at least, that's how she was acting last night when she stormed into my room and demanded I get my deposit back from the headmaster. After I told her no, she stomped out, and I haven't seen her since, so maybe she's seen the error of her ways. *Maybe.*

Nope. Nu-uh. She hasn't. Every fairy for herself. I'm making a break for it.

And I try, but Ari and Blake both yank me back, forcing me to face Blue as she pouts at the bottom of the steps. I growl at them, demanding they let me make a run for it, but they refuse, and I have no choice but to make direct, very hateful eye contact with my pissed-off little sister.

Her normally bright-blue eyes are more of a grey today, and her irises swirl as she glares in my direction, her hands perched on her tiny hips. A slew of hate-filled words spill from her lips as Blake and Ari drag me down the front steps. I couldn't even understand half of what she just said, but in case you wanted the gist of us; I'm awful, I must hate her, and she's never going to forgive for this.

Teenagers, am I right?

Sucking in a deep breath, I try to be the adult here, and thinking of what my dad would say, I tell her, "You'll thank me for this one day."

"Okay, *Dad*." She rolls her eyes with a huff.

Well, I *was* trying to pull from my inner dad, so at least there's that. Unfortunately, that's about the only thing I can think to say right now to make this better. She clearly isn't going to change her mind and see the error of her ways, so I'm not sure what else I can do.

My thoughts are cut off when I hear squeals behind me from all three of my little fairies as they tromp down the stairs, diving for their Aunt Blue. As they pounce on her, her whole demeanor changes, and she squats down, letting them throw their little arms around her.

What the hell, man? Why can't I get treatment like that from her? This is some bullshit.

I look at Ari and Blake with annoyance, and they both chuckle as Luke and Nyx finish loading the carriage before joining us. Quinn pops up next, giving me a peck on the cheek before loading one final trunk he just brought out.

"Alright, girls, it's time for Aunty Blue to leave, come on," Nyx coos at them, throwing the two youngest over his shoulder while Blake grabs our oldest.

As soon as the girls are out of the picture, Blue's attitude is back, and she tries to turn without another word, but I know I can't let her get away with that. "Nu-uh," I call, "Stop right there. You can't get away from me that easily."

I hop down the last two steps, and snatch her back, forcing her into a hug that I know she doesn't want right now. Her body goes limp, thinking I might let her go, but there is zero chance of that. I *will* stand right here hugging her until she returns the gesture.

And it seems Luke knows that to be true, because he says, "Blue, you know she's going to hold you in a vice grip until you hug her back. The faster you give in, the faster she'll let you go."

She must realize he's right, because as flippant as she can muster, she slaps my back, as if that constitutes as a hug. It does not, so I refuse to let her go, and finally, she loosely hangs her arms around my middle, but her shoulders are still slumped. I don't care though, I'll take what I can get.

Without letting her go, I whisper, "I know you can't see it right now, because of teen angst, but I *do* love you. And I promise, someday you'll realize the Academy is the best place for you right now. You're going to make so many new friends, and learn tons of shit."

She snorts, because she knows I'm not the best at adulting, as she flippantly brushes off my words of encouragement. "Whatever. I had friends here."

I sigh. "I know, but they'll still be here when you get back if they're your real friends."

When she doesn't respond, I pull back, forcing her to make eye contact. "You really will thank me some day." She rolls her eyes, so I add, "We'll come see you soon, I promise."

She shrugs, acting as if she doesn't care, so I step back and away from her. There's a round of hugs with Blue and each of my boy-toys, along with another round of hugs and kisses from the kids, and then Blake helps Blue into the waiting carriage.

Once she's settled, the coachmen boards, preparing to take off as we watch, and the whole time Blue never looks at us. I kind of assumed that once it was a reality she would realize how much she was going to miss us, but I guess I was wrong.

Seconds later, the guards call out for forward march, and we watch as the carriage disappears, and as it does, I pray I'm doing the right thing.

"You are," Ari assures me, proving I still haven't mastered the art of thinking to myself, "And you're right, someday she'll see it."

I nod, because deep down I know he's right, and I let him and Luke guide me up the stairs and into the sitting room, my movements more of a waddle since I'm eight months pregnant. I'm helped onto the couch, and it takes me several minutes to get comfortable. Blake and Nyx don't join us, instead taking the kids to the playroom, but Quinn plops down across from me and removes my shoes, starting a magnificent foot rub. I moan, stretching out and enjoying the tingles his ministrations are causing.

Enough time passes that I start to doze, but I'm pulled back when Blake and Nyx enter the room, with Nyx sitting in the floor, and Blake joining Quinn across from me. The room stays quiet though, and I'm still content with Quinn's epic foot rub.

Unfortunately, Ari is not okay with the silence, because he prompts, "So..."

"You just had to ruin it," I quip, giving him a good eye roll.

"What?" he barks as if he has no idea what I'm talking about.

"Silence is golden. Silence says there are no crying kids, and my sister isn't telling me she hates me."

"She doesn't hate you, Ellie Mae," Nyx assures me, rubbing my calf, adding to Quinn's foot rub, "She's a teenager, and I'm pretty sure, if you think hard enough, you'll realize she reminds you of someone we all know."

"My dad. I know," I admit, sighing.

"Yeah," Luke chimes in, "I don't think that's who he was talking about."

I peek one eye open, and realize they're all staring at me. I jerk my head back, pointing to my chest. "Me? Nu-uh. I was nothing like that."

They all bust out in full belly laughter, with Nyx keeling over and acting as if he can't breathe. This goes on for some time, and my annoyance increases with every passing minute. When the laughter begins to die out, Blake is the first one to speak on it, "Yeah, you were exactly like that, and I didn't meet you until you were nineteen."

"Trust me," Nyx chimes in, "it's like they are identical twins in the personality department."

"Rude," I comment, huffing.

"Regardless," Ari starts, "she'll grow up, just like you did. Trust me."

"Yeah," Luke agrees, "This is *her* story now."

They're right, and I know it. It was in my teenage years that I changed the most. Of course, there were a lot of factors that changed me. My mom's death started things off, and then my uncle's early abdication, followed by two kidnappings and a ton of epic battles. I had to change, and even though all those things were awful, they still helped shape and mold me into the fairy awesome Queen that I am now.

Obviously, I hope my sister doesn't go through anything near what I went through, but I have no doubt she'll have her own trials. They'll shape her into the person the universe wants her to be, and all of that begins at the academy. And while she's gone, I can continue to build the Fay I always dreamed of.

Together, my boys and the team we've put together have already accomplished so much. Within two years of us defeating King Tobin, the Pixies had integrated into Fay society. They still aren't comfortable with everyone knowing they can grow to full size, but they've still come leaps and bounds from where they were, and I know that's partly due to mine and Bree's friendship. I still see her a lot, actually, and next month she's even getting married. She's been dating Ty and Jasper for five years, and I can't wait to see where life takes them.

On top of the Pixie's integration, things also changed for the better with the Celestial kingdom. King Oberon and Layla finally got married, proving I was right about them, and while they still rule over their own kingdom, one year after everything settled down, the Seelie and the Celestial King signed a peace treaty. It was unprecedented, and there were a lot of old-school fairies that had a problem with it, given the whole fairy, human thing, but I made it very clear; fairies can love whoever they want, and yes, that includes humans. I think it helped that I claimed a human of my own, and Blake was made the official Human/Fae relations ambassador. He's done some amazing work, and the humans living in Fay are treated much better now than they were a decade ago.

So yeah, we've accomplished a lot, but there's still so much more that I want to do. Years ago, I said I wanted to leave my children with a better, more tolerant Fay, and I still intend to do that. We're closer now than we were then, but I won't stop making our realm better until my last breath. And the best part is, I'll have my boys with me every step of the way.

AFTERWORD

Thank you for reading The Fairy End, the sixth and final book in A Fairy Awesome Series. I hope you enjoyed reading it as much as I loved writing it. While this series is complete, for now, I have several other books in the works that I hope you'll add to your TBR. For more information, follow me on Instagram.

Don't forget, as a self-published author, your reviews are even more important, so please take the time to leave me your feedback on Amazon and Goodreads. Thank you so much for your support!

ABOUT THE AUTHOR

Ellie Aiden

I'm a wife and mother of three very ornery boys, and yes, my husband is ornery too. I'm from the great state of Texas, currently residing in Dallas.

I may be an author, but I'm a reader first, and I'm sure to keep that in mind when creating books I think my readers will like. I've been writing most of my life, including being a columnist for several local newspapers, but it wasn't until 2020 that I decided to take the plunge and commit to writing full time.